BOOKS BY PATRICK SAMPHIRE

The Mennik Thorn Novels

Shadow of a Dead God

Nectar for the God

The Casebook of Harriet George Series

The Dinosaur Hunters

A Spy in the Deep

The Secrets of the Dragon Tomb Series

(for children)

Secrets of the Dragon Tomb

The Emperor of Mars

Short Story Collection

At the Gates and Other Stories

AT THE GATES AND OTHER STORIES

PATRICK SAMPHIRE

FIVE FATHOMS PRESS

For all the editors who have published my short stories over the years and the readers who have loved them. Loved the stories, not the editors. I have no opinions on readers who love editors. I mean, obviously readers should love editors, but it's private, not my business.

CONTENTS

FOREWORD

I didn't set out to write short stories.

I always thought I would write novels (and I do, of course), but short stories came upon me almost by accident. There's no denying that there can be a type of perfection in a well-crafted short story that just isn't present in the same way in a longer work, a single idea flawlessly expressed, the one exquisite flower rather than a complete garden. When I read *Flowers for Algernon* or *Light of Other Days* or *The Ones Who Walk Away from Omelas*, I am experiencing something that is astonishing and perfect in its form and size. (And, yes, I am saying that *Flowers for Algernon* should never have been expanded into a novel; fight me.)

Some ideas just *are* short stories, and there is a great deal of satisfaction in crafting them. While I'm not claiming to have written anything to match the stories I've just mentioned here, I genuinely do not think that *Uncle Vernon's*

Lie or *Finisterre* or *Camelot* or *Dragonfly Summer* in this collection would have worked a fraction as well if I had tried to stretch them into novels or even novellas.

I've included sixteen of my short stories in this collection, ranging from from some of the first stories I ever wrote, like *A Veil, a Meal, and Dust* and *Dawn, by the Light of a Barrow Fire* all the way through to *Slipper of Glass,* which I wrote in 2020. Most of the stories, though, were written in a period between 2002 and 2010, and reading back through them for this collection, it's fairly easy to see the themes that I was interested in exploring at the time.

Although most of these stories have been published before, this is the first time they've been collected in a single edition. I hope you enjoy them.

And, yes, there are a few stories that I published that haven't made it to the collection for whatever reason, but you can read all of them for free on my website.

Finally, if you want to keep up-to-date with my new stories and novels, subscribe to my newsletter, and you'll be the first to find out about them.

– Patrick Samphire, December 2020.

AT THE GATES

ABOUT THE STORY

I've always liked the idea of magic hidden in the mundanity of everyday existence, the potential for something extraordinary that is almost within reach, no matter where we are, who we are, or what our situation. Although I hadn't realised it until now, a lot of my short stories are about this, and this is one of my favourites.

This story was written when people still had iPods, which does kind of date it.

AT THE GATES

1. Monday

Grace heard the whimpering before she saw the dog.

She was on her way home from school, hands shoved deep into her jacket pockets, head hunched down, watching the pavement. Her iPod buds were in her ears – it made people leave her alone – but the music wasn't playing. She'd forgotten to charge the iPod last night, and it was out of power. It had cut out half-way through 'Welcome to the Black Parade', leaving her ears ringing with the silence.

If it hadn't been out of power, she would never have heard the dog. And if she hadn't heard the dog, everything would have been different.

The whimpering was coming from the alley. High, close walls of Victorian brick enclosed the alley in deep shadow. Most people would have hurried past, but Grace had never been able to turn away from an animal in distress.

Her mum would kill her if she brought another dog home. But what else could she do? It wasn't like she could leave it there.

There had been a time when her mum wouldn't have minded, when her mum would have even come out and helped Grace carry the dog in. Found a blanket, warm milk. Would have sat up half the night. *Before*. That was how Grace thought of that time. Just, 'Before.'

Taking a quick look around, Grace stepped into the mouth of the alley. The shadows closed in, like black cobwebs drifting down. She shivered.

Jeez, Grace. Still afraid of the dark?

You bet.

She dropped down into a crouch and held out the back of her hand for the dog to sniff. If it was hurt or frightened, it might snap to protect itself.

The dog was huddled against a bin, wrapped up like an old, balled blanket. If it hadn't been for the whimpering, Grace wouldn't have even recognised it as a dog.

"Come on, old thing. I won't hurt you."

The dog turned its head to look at her. The whites of its eyes were sharp in the darkness.

"You really are a poor old mutt, aren't you?" Grace said, keeping her voice soft.

Its coat was matted and dirty. In places, its skin was bare. If it had been clean, Grace reckoned it would have been white and brown, but at that moment, and in the poor light, it was a near-uniform grey. The dog whimpered again, then stretched out its muzzle towards her.

"Good girl."

No collar.

The dog licked Grace's hand with a dry tongue.

"So," she said, "will you follow me, or do I carry you?"

HER MUM WASN'T IN, AND NEITHER, THANK GOD, WAS Malcolm. But Sean was running wild with little Craig from across the street. She bumped the door closed behind her with her hip. Two eight-year-olds let loose and uncontrolled. Perfect.

The headache that had settled behind her eyes after she'd left the alley thumped once, like a giant heart.

"What the Hell are you two doing?" she snapped.

The two boys stopped in mid-shriek. Craig's eyes widened.

"You've got a dog."

Grace shifted the poor beast in her arms. "You don't say."

"You have," Craig said, excitement pitching up his voice.

"Mum's going to kill you," Sean said.

"No, she's not," Grace said. "Because you're not going to tell her. Okay?"

"She's going to kill you."

Grace pushed past the boys. They parted.

(*Like dry bones under iron wheels*).

She stumbled. Where the Hell had that come from? She didn't feel well.

She would put the dog in her bedroom with a bowl of

water and something to eat. Rice. She'd heard that was good for sick dogs, and this dog was really sick. She was shivering in Grace's arms, and her skin moved loosely over her bones.

"I'm going to call you Hope," Grace whispered in the dog's ear.

"You better go and see Mr. Uri," Sean called.

Grace closed her eyes. "Why?"

"Because he hasn't paid his rent. Again. Malcolm's getting mad."

"And he's making smells," Craig added.

She heard their footsteps slap on floorboards.

"Don't go outside," she shouted, to the sound of the slamming door.

CRAIG HAD BEEN RIGHT ABOUT THE SMELL. THE CORRIDOR stank of boiled vegetables, or worse, boiling laundry. Between the smell and the headache that was still swelling behind her eyes with every pace, Grace felt sick.

Mr. Uri was her mother's tenant. Somehow, they'd inherited him with the house when her mum had bought it. Grace didn't really understand how that had worked. She'd only been a kid when they'd moved here. But she did know it had made the house cheap enough for her mum when they couldn't afford anywhere else. That had been 'Before'. Before Malcolm and before his money. Grace was glad. Mr. Uri was the best thing about living here. Sometimes she thought he was the only good thing.

6

She stopped outside Mr. Uri's door. The smell here was atrocious. If Mr. Uri was cooking in his rooms again, Mum would have a fit.

She laid a palm on the hard wood of the door. She could feel the rough grain against her skin. Her nerve endings seemed hypersensitive. *Fever*, she thought, and hoped she was wrong.

There was a virus going around school. Half her friends had come down with it. She had almost hoped Dean would catch it so she could have an excuse to go around and nurse him, but no such luck. She'd been sure she hadn't got it, though. She *never* got the flu. And the last thing she needed right now was

(...*bodies choking on swollen tongues*...)

to be sick. God!

She let out a breath. She was *not* going to give in to this virus.

"Mr. Uri?" she called gently.

No answer. She hadn't really expected it.

She rapped on the door.

Still no answer. She smiled. *Here we go.*

She tried the handle, and of course it was open. He'd told her that he never worried about burglars. "What can they take that I haven't already lost?" he'd said. But she knew he really left the door unlocked so that she could come right on in.

She pushed the door open and stepped through.

The window was open. Bright late-afternoon sunlight slipped between the swaying curtains. Grace could hear birdsong from somewhere outside, but she didn't know where; there were no trees in this street, no parks nearby. Mr. Uri sat in his armchair, head resting on the wing. He was dozing, and snoring slightly. His thin white hair haloed his wrinkled scalp in the sunlight.

Funny. There was no smell in here. It must have been something else. Not the drains, she hoped. God, how she hoped. She'd be up to her shoulders in them before Malcolm would even consider calling a plumber. Good for her character, Malcolm would say, but Grace knew he was just tight.

She crouched in front of Mr. Uri and took his frail hand. "Mr. Uri?"

He let out one final, shivering snore and then blinked at her.

"You were sleeping, Mr. Uri."

He smiled. His smile always made him seem far more frail, like he was a shed skin held up only by memory.

"I had just closed my eyes. To enjoy the silence."

Grace backed up and seated herself in the chair opposite.

Mr. Uri frowned. "You look pale."

"Maybe a virus."

He shook his head. Whenever he did that, she found herself worrying absurdly that his head would come tumbling off and she would have to catch it.

"You should be in bed, not visiting old men." He laughed. It sounded more like a dry cough.

"It's Monday," Grace said. "You forgot your rent."

He straightened slightly, a dry stick unbending. "Not at all. It is on the table." He gestured, shaking.

"Admit it," Grace said. "You only forget so I have to come and fetch it."

Mr. Uri looked away. "An old man gets lonely here."

She leaned forward and took his hand again. "I know."

~

When Grace got upstairs, there were raised voices in the dining room. She thought about just heading on past, up to her bedroom. But she was still carrying Mr. Uri's rent money and she didn't want to get him in any more trouble.

Her mum sat at the over-polished table, her fingers making tight circles above the surface, as though she was polishing it still. Sean hunched in the corner, knees drawn up to his chest, arms wrapped around his knees, forcing himself into a small, shocked ball, as though if he could squeeze himself tight enough he might just disappear. Why did neither her mum nor Malcolm ever think about Sean when they had their shouting matches? He was eight, for God's sake, and he looked shell-shocked.

"What the Hell is going on here?" Grace demanded.

Malcolm swung away from the window. His hands were clenched into white fists.

"Watch your mouth. I'll have no swearing in my house."

Oh, no. Grace wasn't letting that one past. She raised her eyebrows. "Whose house?"

She saw Malcolm's teeth clamp down, like he was chewing on wood, and his face redden.

9

Her mum cut in, before the argument could really let fly. "Your dad went down—"

"He's not my dad."

Her mum let out a long, silent breath.

"Your dad went down to see Mr. Uri."

"He missed his rent," Malcolm said. "As fucking usual. Thinks this is a free ride." He slammed the side of his fist against the wall, making the pictures shake. Sean flinched. No one except Grace seemed to notice. "I know he was in there. I hammered on his door. Bastard pretended he was asleep."

"Maybe he *was* asleep," Grace said.

"Yeah?" Malcolm lifted his chin. "Then he needs to wake up. We're not a charity. He's missed his rent. That's it."

Grace shoved her hand into her back pocket where she's put Mr. Uri's money. Her head hurt, she had a sick dog to look after, and this arsehole was making everything difficult again. "He hasn't missed his rent." She pulled the money out and flung it at Malcolm. The notes scattered, like a flock of birds bursting before a cat. "There it is."

Malcolm's eyes flattened and stilled, fixed on her. Grace knew he wanted to hit her. He might even have tried to, if her mother hadn't been there. She glared at him.

He snapped away, as abrupt as a gunshot, turning on Grace's mother.

"He should be in a home."

Grace knew she should stop. She knew she had pushed it too far already. But she couldn't.

"He is in a home. His home. It's been his home for a whole lot longer than it's been yours."

In the silence that followed, the air was thick, frozen.

Pins and needles prickled across Grace's skin, and for a second she thought she was seeing through smoke. Through the soles of her feet, she felt the ground shake, like

(...*flesh splitting, boiling, breaking apart*...)

an earthquake. Fuck! She was *not* giving in to this virus. Not when she had all this to sort out.

Through dry lips, she managed, "Longer than it's been home to anyone of us. If anyone should leave, it's us. Not—"

The sharp, incongruous sound of her phone cut her off. She plucked it out of her pocket and flipped it open.

Hell.

"Dean," she said. "Hi."

BEING BEST FRIENDS WITH THE HOTTEST GUY IN SCHOOL should be fantastic, right?

Wrong.

Grace and Dean had been friends since they'd been two years old. They'd done everything together, right from the start. They'd been in the same classes right through to high school, and they still were. They'd played games together, slept over, been bathed together, holidayed together. For a few years, they'd not talked much, because boys and girls didn't, but they'd been friends anyway. And then, unfairly, three years ago, Dean had got *hot* and she hadn't. His shoulders had widened, the puppy fat had burned away over his cheekbones, his eyes had darkened. And all he would ever think of her as was his friend.

They could walk down the street, arm-in-arm, and they were only friends. They could go to movies or cafés, as friends. He would tell her about his girlfriends. She knew when he'd started having sex. She'd had to look happy for him. Be happy.

It was killing her.

Maybe she could have tried to be more like the girls he liked. Blonde, thin, tight clothes. Too much make-up. She hadn't. She'd gone the other way. She'd dyed her hair black and grown curves where she wasn't supposed have curves.

Dean wanted to talk about his new girlfriend. Rachel. Grace could have told him Rachel was a bitch. She could have told him it was going to end badly. Instead, she pretended to be pleased, and tried to think of how she could make Dean see.

2. TUESDAY

Her dog, Hope, was worse. She hadn't eaten the rice Grace had cooked for her, or touched her water. She scarcely lifted her head when Grace came over. Hope wasn't shivering anymore. Grace didn't know if that was good or bad.

Grace wasn't feeling that great either. She lay down next to Hope and wrapped herself around the poor creature's thin body.

·   ·   ·

3. WEDNESDAY

It wasn't rent day, but Grace went to visit Mr. Uri anyway. The man didn't get any other visitors. Grace couldn't imagine how awful it must be to be too old to do anything by yourself and to have no one ever coming to call. She didn't know how he could stand it.

Mr. Uri was in his chair, where he always sat. Grace had never seen him anywhere else, although she knew he must move about. He ate. He kept himself clean and shaved. He wore a clean shirt every day. It was just hard to imagine him doing any of those things. He looked too delicate, like he was made of tissue paper and could blow away or crumple up in a breeze.

His eyes opened as she came in, and he smiled. She drew up a chair next to him.

"You've got a new dog."

"Yeah... How did you know?"

"I always know," Mr. Uri said.

Grace looked down at her folded hands. Her fingers clenched each other too tightly. "She's... sick."

The old head bowed, and again Grace was scared his neck would just snap with the movement.

"I know," Mr. Uri said. "There was a time I could have done something about that."

Grace looked up. "You were a vet?"

A frown creased Mr. Uri's papery forehead. "I... I don't remember. Maybe. Something like that. But... I stopped. It wasn't worth the price. I stopped."

13

Grace leant close. "What do you mean? What price? Where are you from, Mr. Uri? Who are you, really?"

But the old man's eyes were already fluttering shut. An old man, dreaming old, confused dreams. That was all he was.

Grace adjusted the pillow under his head then tiptoed away.

4. THURSDAY

"You know what I think?" Malcolm said. They were sitting in the kitchen, eating breakfast. Grace's mum was at the stove, frying bacon. Grace hadn't eaten meat for years. Neither had her mum, before. "I think he's one of those Nazis. One of those war criminals." Malcolm had rolled up his newspaper and punctuated his words with short snaps on the edge of the table. It was setting Grace's nerves on edge.

"For God's sake!"

"Why not? He's old enough. He's got that weird accent. That's what they did, the Nazis. They ran away and hid. Pretended they were normal people. Changed their names."

Grace slapped her toast down, suddenly not hungry. "He's just an old man. Why can't you leave him alone?"

"I think we should call the police," Malcolm said. "Get them to take him away. Get him out of here. I don't want no Nazis in this house."

"Sounds like we've got one already," Grace muttered, but too quietly to be heard.

WHEN GRACE GOT BACK TO HER BEDROOM, HOPE DIDN'T LOOK up. She didn't open her eyes. She lay there, unmoving. Her chest wasn't rising or falling.

"No," Grace whispered. "Don't be dead. Don't die."

She dropped beside Hope on the pile of blankets. With a trembling hand, she touched her dog's nose. It was dry and too cold, but air feathered against her hand. Grace let out a shaky breath. She pushed herself from her knees, unfolding carefully, not wanting to disturb Hope, and crossed to the other side of the room. She pulled out her phone and punched quick-dial.

"Dean?" she said. "I need a favour. Can you come over?"

"YOU LOOK SHIT," DEAN SAID, AS GRACE OPENED THE DOOR.

"Thanks." Dean didn't look shit. He looked fantastic.

"Seriously. You're pale. Are you sick?"

"I feel

(...*the weight of rusting metal, crushing, cracking, breaking...*)

a bit... weird." Understatement. Her skin felt both hot and cold, pricked by a thousand separate needles.

"You need to see a doctor?"

"No. That's not why I asked you around." She indicated with her head. "Upstairs."

He followed her to her bedroom. If they hadn't been friends, that would have meant something.

When he saw Hope, Dean looked at Grace. "The broken, the beaten, and the damned, right?"

"What?"

"You. You want to save your mum. You want to save me from Rachel. You want to save that old bloke downstairs. You want to save this dog." He reached out a hand and touched Grace's cheek. The touch made her shiver. "You can't save everyone, Grace."

"I don't want to," Grace whispered. "Just her." But she was too quiet, and Dean didn't hear her.

Dean sighed. "So what do you need?"

"Help me get her to the vet," Grace said.

THE CONSULTING ROOM STANK OF DISINFECTANT AND FEAR. Air-conditioned coolness washed from the ceiling. Grace laid Hope on the rubber-covered examining table and stepped back.

They had started by taking turns carrying Hope, but by half-way, Dean had been doing all the carrying, and Grace had had to lean on his arm. Her legs were shaky, and she could feel sweat on her cold skin. (Weren't viruses supposed to move faster? This one had been hanging around for days.) Dean hadn't complained. Even though Hope had fouled her bedding during the night and Grace hadn't been able to get her completely clean, and even though Dean was missing school.

The vet's practiced fingers pressed over Hope's scrawny

16

body, checking her stomach and bones and skin. At last he straightened up, refolding his stethoscope.

"Well?" Grace demanded. She felt Dean's hand resting lightly on her shoulder.

The vet shook his head.

(*All will be ash.*)

Grace's knees lost their strength, and the virus kicked through her system. If Dean hadn't been touching her, she might have fallen.

"She's too sick," the vet said. "It would be kindest if you let me put her to sleep."

"No," Grace whispered. She shook her head. "No. You're a vet. She's sick. Do something about it."

The vet sighed. "She's malnourished, probably with some kind of internal injury. She's got fleas and an eye infection. That's just the start of it."

Hope turned her brown eyes up to Grace, showing the frightened whites like twin crescent moons. Grace put her hand on Hope's flank, and the dog leaned hard against her, trying to press itself into her.

"You wouldn't say that if she was a person."

"I'd need to do a full work-up. CBC to rule infections. Blood chemistry profile. Urinalysis. Some X-rays. If there's something serious wrong, the tests and the treatment could cost thousands. You can't afford that, can you?"

For once, Grace didn't know what to say. Behind her, she could feel Dean's warm body against her, holding her. Hope pressed against her stomach, bones like sticks against Grace's hand.

The vet sighed. "Look, this is what I'll do. I'll keep her here, keep an eye on her, try to get her to eat and drink something. There are a few things we could try. You can pick her up this evening. If she'll keep eating, she might regain enough strength. Then we can take another look at her, see if anything is clearing itself up. Otherwise..."

(*All will be ashes.*)

THAT EVENING, WHEN THEY BROUGHT HOPE HOME, THEY MET Malcolm on the stairs. He shouted. Grace screamed and held Hope tight.

In her bedroom, Hope lapped at the water and took a lick of the rice.

Grace cried.

5. FRIDAY

Grace had to leave school early. In her fever, she couldn't hold a pen. Dean helped her home and tucked her into bed.

She cried when he left.

She was in love. She was sick.

She shivered under her covers. Across the room, Hope stood, stumbled to the bed, and clambered on.

6. SATURDAY

The house was dark and still when Grace awoke, her

bedroom painted streetlight-yellow. Hope's warm weight was gone from her legs. For a moment, her heart stopped. Then she saw Hope curled up in her own blankets.

Grace's fever seemed to have broken some time in the night. She felt weak, but the wrongness that had swelled in every cell of her body was gone. She swung her legs over the edge of her bed, pushing off her tangled covers.

Hope was sleeping, but she'd eaten the rice Grace had left for her. Grace felt tears dampen the corner of her eyes.

"You're going to be okay," she whispered.

Hope's eyes opened, and her tail gave a single thump.

"Come on," Grace said. "Let's get you out to the garden. Then I'll find you something more to eat."

When they came back, Grace found some chicken in the fridge, warmed it in the microwave and fed it to Hope, one sliver at a time. Hope's bright eyes watched every piece. Towards the end, she started to jump for the chicken.

In the house, everyone else was sleeping.

7. Sunday

"Tomorrow," Malcolm said, "everything's going to be different."

Grace put her fork down warily. "What do you mean?"

"The Nazi. If he hasn't paid his rent by nine o'clock, he's out of here. We've got a contract. I'm fed up with him ignoring it. And you're getting rid of that dog. Take it to a shelter or put it down. Whatever. It's time this family started acting like a family, and that means you're going to learn to show me a little respect."

Grace slammed back her chair. "You're not part of this family. You're not our dad. You don't get to decide." She stood. "If you touch my dog, I'll kill you in your sleep."

She spun away, heading for the door.

"Tomorrow," Malcolm called.

"Fuck you."

HOPE WAS CURLED TIGHTLY INTO HER BLANKETS, A BALL OF patchy fur and bones. Grace could hear the sighing of Hope's breath. The bowl of chicken and rice next to Hope's bed hadn't been touched. Grace dropped down beside her and placed her hand on Hope's neck.

"You're just not hungry, right? Right?"

Hope didn't open her eyes.

8. MONDAY

Her fever had returned with a vengeance, sometime in the night. Grace's skin felt clammy, and her teeth chattered uncontrollably. She rolled over in her bed. The sheets were damp with sweat.

Ten o'clock. Shit. She'd slept in too late.

She tumbled out of bed, pulled on her jeans and a sweater. Her hair was tangled and dirty, the T-shirt she'd slept in crumpled.

Hope was lying where Grace had left her. She didn't look like she'd moved at all. The bowl of rice and chicken was still untouched. She hadn't come to Grace in the night when her fever had returned.

(*Everything will be different.*)

"Not you," Grace whispered. "You're going to be okay. No matter what, you're going to be okay."

(*Everything will be different.*)

Grace hunched down next to Hope, her body held in tight against her shaking chills. Hope's fur felt dry beneath her hand. The dog was scarcely breathing, but now they were touching, Grace could feel the shivers rippling across Hope's frail body, to match Grace's own. Hope cracked open a sticky eye. It drifted shut again, and Hope's breath sighed out. For a moment, Grace could feel nothing in Hope. Not a movement, not a shiver, not a breath. Then, with a shudder, Hope drew in another breath. Grace pushed herself to her feet.

The vet. She had to get Hope to the vet. They could feed her somehow. A feeding tube or something. Build up her strength, test her, treat her. Make her better.

And it would cost thousands. Grace had nothing. Just a few pounds. She could sell stuff. Her iPod. Her computer. Malcolm would be furious, but Grace didn't give a fuck. Except it wouldn't be enough, and it would be too slow.

(*Bones will splinter under heavy wheels. Fires will burn. All will be ashes.*)

She stumbled, the fever stealing the strength from her

21

legs. With a grimace, she forced the muscles in her legs to lock firm.

Malcolm had money. Lots of it. Grace didn't know exactly how much, but she did know he was loaded.

There was no way he would give her a penny of it. Not for Hope.

Dean would give her money. He wouldn't even ask why. But he had even less than she did.

She wanted to scream. Who else? Her mum? Not without Malcolm knowing and putting a stop to it.

Tears stung her eyes. "You're not going to die! You're not."

Who else?

Mr. Uri. Mr. Uri had money. Maybe not much. He was an old man. But he paid his rent every single week, no matter what Malcolm might say, and she knew he paid for his laundry to be done and his food to be delivered. Maybe he could lend her enough. She could work, pay it back. Even the idea of asking him made her feel sick, dirty.

(*Skin torn away. Iron jaws closing on muscle. Screams in the darkness.*)

"Stop it! Please." She could hardly stand.

(*Everything will be different. All will be ashes.*)

She had no choice. He was the only one she could go to. He was the only one who could help her.

She dropped to her knees

(*...flesh bursting with sores...*)

and scooped Hope into her arms.

"I'm not leaving you," she whispered. Tears were running

down her face. She wiped them on her shoulder, then staggered to the door.

~

MALCOLM WAS OUTSIDE MR. URI'S ROOMS, HAMMERING ON
the door. He wasn't alone. Two men – friends of Malcolm's –
were leaning against the wall, almost blocking the corridor.
They watched her as she descended the stairs, not saying
anything.

"What are you *doing*?" Grace demanded.

Malcolm turned from the door. His look of satisfaction
made his face almost pleasant. "He missed the rent. That's it.
He's out."

Grace gripped Hope tighter and felt the bones push
through her thin T-shirt. "What's he supposed to do? Where's
he supposed to go?"

Malcolm leaned in close. "I. Don't. Care. He can sleep on
the streets for all I care. And that fucking animal can join
him. It stinks."

She took a step back. Malcolm turned to the door and
shook the handle.

"Fucker's locked his door." He hammered on the wood,
the sound too loud in Grace's ears. Hope let out a whimper,
but she didn't open her eyes.

"Wake up, you old fucker, or I'm kicking this door down!"

Grace closed her eyes and took a steadying breath. She
forced the fever back a step.

"Let me talk to him. Just for a minute?"

Malcolm gave her a disgusted look. "Yeah?" He considered, then shrugged. "Please yourself. But if he's not out of there in an hour, I'm going to get him out myself, and it won't be pretty."

Grace squeezed past Malcolm. He didn't move back far enough, and she felt the hard muscle of his leg against her thigh.

"I'll tell you this much," Malcolm said. "He's awake now." He thumped once more, hard, on the door. "Aren't you, you old bastard?"

Balancing Hope in one arm, against her chest, Grace reached for the door handle.

It didn't surprise her at all that the door opened beneath her hand.

GRACE CLICKED THE DOOR SHUT BEHIND HER. MR. URI WASN'T in his usual chair. The window was open, but she couldn't hear the birds singing.

He had left a couple of blankets folded into a dog's bed by the door.

"Mr. Uri?"

He knew we were coming.

She shook her head. Maybe he had just hoped. She lowered Hope into the bed. Hope laid her head down, eyes closing.

Grace straightened, and the movement sent her fever sweeping up through her, the room spinning away.

She stumbled forward a step—

And her foot came down on a path of bones.

They were blackened, splintered and ground and crushed.

(*The bones of your family, your friends, of everyone who ever was and ever will be.*)

(*He is awakening.*)

Skulls stared blankly up, eye sockets dark and lost. Above her, a smoke-stained sky stretched from horizon to horizon.

A scream built in Grace's throat, pushing itself up, over her tongue, past her lips.

It was impossible. It was the fever. She was hallucinating.

She could feel the hardness of the bones beneath her feet.

It was real.

It didn't matter. She had to find Mr. Uri.

(*If he awakes, all will be ashes.*)

"I don't care," Grace whispered. "I don't care."

To the left of the path, a single tree, stripped of its leaves and bark, stood skeletal and white against the heavy sky. Grace saw no birds, no stars, no moon or sun. Just the shroud of smoke. She smelled ashes and rust.

"Mr. Uri?"

Something immense and metallic groaned.

(*Nothing will stand. Nothing will endure.*)

(*He is awakening.*)

(*He is awakening.*)

(*He is awakening.*)

(*Bones crack, blood turns to steam, diseased flesh burns.*)

Grace shuddered. She bowed her head and took a step along the path of bones. Then another.

Far behind, she heard the sound of a fist hammering on wood. She ignored it. She kept walking.

In the distance, something grew. First it was a line along the horizon, then a strip, then a wall. It stretched as far as she could see and cut across the path. She kept walking.

(*Blackened worlds spin in a dead sky.*)

The wall was vast, taller than a tower block. It blocked out the sky, as black as obsidian, but dull, as though the thin light from the smoky sky sank into it, unable to escape.

In the centre, at the end of the path of bones, stood a pair of iron gates.

The gates were ajar.

Bones slipped and crumbled beneath her feet. Grace kept her eyes fixed on the gates. The path rose towards them.

On the blackened earth before the gates lay the bodies of eagles. Dozens of them. Their wings were broken, their feathers charred, their eyes blank.

(*Nothing will endure. Bodies will be broken.*)

Grace stepped over the bodies, feeling her way past them. She laid her hands on the iron gates. They were cold beneath her skin.

Behind the gates, behind the wall, something was growing. A mountain of darkness. Storm clouds piled upon each other, up and up and up, leaning towards her, towards the gates. She could feel their weight and their fury even from here. Metal creaked.

The gap between the gates was too narrow for her to slip

26

through. She tugged at the gates, pulling them further apart.

Screams tore the burning air. Weight piled upon her. The clouds rolled forwards.

(*All will be ashes.*)

"Mr. Uri?" she called.

If she could reach him, he would help her. He would change everything. Fix Grace, get rid of Malcolm, save Dean. Make it all right. He could do that.

(*All will be ashes.*)

Just an inch more.

Wind howled, hot and dark and fierce.

From behind her came the sound of furious barking. Grace turned.

Running up the path of bones came Hope. Her head was down, drooping, but still she barked.

"No," Grace whispered. "Go back."

Hope stumbled, her weak legs failing her. Grace saw her dog's jaw smack into the bones.

"No!"

Hope struggled to her feet again, took another step forwards. Fell again.

Grace ran. She leapt across the bodies of the fallen eagles, raced over the blackened bones.

Hope tried to rise.

Panic gave Grace a burst of strength. She lunged forwards and caught Hope before she could fall again.

Hope's body shivered helplessly and violently. Grace gathered her and hugged her tight. Hope's head dropped and her body went limp.

Slowly, Grace rose and turned towards the gates.

Step by step she made her way back.

The storm clouds shrieked. Hot wind blasted her.

Mr. Uri could help her, but all would be ashes. He had said it wasn't worth the price. She squeezed her eyes shut, and tears spilled onto her cheeks. "Hope," she whispered.

She knew what she had to do.

She opened her eyes and leant her shoulders against the gates. Tendrils of storm clouds reached through the gap between the gates and licked across her skin like icy fire. She pushed the gates shut.

At the gates, among the ashes and the bones and the death, she slumped to the ground. She buried her face in Hope's thin fur and waited for the end.

In the dead world, all was silent.

Hope's body twitched, once. Grace's eyes popped open. She looked up.

Light streamed in the open window. She could hear birds singing. Mr. Uri sat in his chair above her. He gazed down at her with eyes of pure black. Inside them, Grace saw storm clouds churn.

"Your friend was right," Mr. Uri said. "You can't save everyone. You never can."

"I don't want to," Grace said. "Just her."

Mr. Uri's frail hand descended and rested on Hope's neck. For a moment so brief Grace couldn't be sure she hadn't just blinked, Grace saw blackness lick over Hope's skin like icy fire.

"You already did," Mr. Uri said.

Hope looked up at Grace with clear eyes. Her tail thumped against Mr. Uri's carpet.

When Grace looked back up, Mr. Uri's eyes were drifting shut.

"I'm tired," he said. "Tired."

"Sleep," Grace whispered.

GRACE SETTLED MR. URI'S HEAD ON HIS PILLOW, MAKING SURE he was comfortable and wouldn't wake with a crick in his neck.

He had left his rent money on the table by the chair. She picked it up and strode to the door, Hope dancing along behind her. The fever had gone from her body and taken her weakness with it. She pulled open the door.

Malcolm was standing behind it, fist raised. She shoved the rent money at him.

"He's paid his rent."

Malcolm's mouth opened, but Grace didn't give him a chance to answer. She remembered the storm clouds in Mr. Uri's eyes and the fire that had touched her skin. She reached out with her memory to touch them. She met Malcolm's gaze. "Everything is different," she said. "Everything. You'll leave him alone. You won't touch him."

She stepped past and left Malcolm standing there. Everything was different. It was going to stay that way.

FIVE THINGS OF BEAUTY

ABOUT THE STORY

This is a very short story, and so it gets a very short introduction; it's hard to say anything about it without spoiling it.

There's a certain appeal to stripping down a story to its absolute bones and carrying most of that story through brief hints, leaving the reader to infer or extrapolate what's really happening. It's an elegant way of telling a story. I hope you agree after reading it.

FIVE THINGS OF BEAUTY

THE MORNING AFTER VAIDWATTIE LEFT, SRILAL FOUND THE first thing of beauty. It was lying on the damp pavement outside his house, where a thousand boots trod every day. The first thing of beauty was an origami bird so delicate and fine that when Srilal lifted it on the palm of his hand, he thought it might fly away. He placed it on his mantelpiece, above the dead television, next to their wedding photo, and he cried.

Once, Vaidwattie had told him, "I can make you anything with twelve folds of paper." He hadn't believed her. "Prove it," he had said, but she had just shaken her head and been hurt.

The wedding had taken five days. There had been seven types of curry served on palm leaves, and rum until dawn faded the stars. His cousins had danced and his aunts had sung. Vaidwattie had worn a red, white, and gold sari. Srilal had worn a white sherwani.

The second thing of beauty was a poppy made from fine silver wire. It lay where the first had lain the morning before. When he turned it in his hand, the petals caught the rain-paled light and seemed to glow red.

Her lips had been brown, not red. Sometimes she had worn lipstick to make them red, because she thought it pleased him. He had preferred them brown. He had not told her that until near the end.

After he had placed the flower by the origami bird, he returned to his bed. He lay there and listened to the thousand boots of five hundred men march up the street from the camp. Always from the camp, never towards it.

"Love has a bitter heart," Vaidwattie had told him. "That makes its lips all the sweeter."

"No," he had said. "Love is war. It glorifies us all."

He did not sleep that night. He sat by the window, staring out at the street, to see who was leaving the things of beauty. Hoping it was Vaidwattie. He saw no one.

At first light, he stepped out onto the damp street and found the third thing of beauty.

It was a simple green box. He opened it and there was a bigger box within. Inside that was an even bigger box. He wondered if it would go on forever, but when he opened the third box a galaxy floated within. He blinked and it was gone.

"I love you like the stars love night," she had said.

"Like the sun loves the day," he had said.

"Like a river loves the ocean."

"Like men love the North."

"No," she had said, shocked. "Not like that. Never like that."

"One day I will march north," he had said, full of pride. "Men's souls are born in the North."

"I would hold your soul here," she had whispered.

"You could never understand."

There were a hundred numbers in her address book. A hundred places she could have gone when she left. He sat by the phone with the hundred numbers, not dialling them.

He had given her his life. He had given her his heart. She had taken it and then she had gone. And he didn't know *why*.

The fourth thing of beauty waited on the fourth morning. It was a white stone shot through with grey-blue and grey-red.

They had met when they were fifteen, Vaidwattie and Srilal. Her hair had been thick and black and oiled, and it had reached her waist. She had dived into a clear, fast stream that day and brought out a white stone shot through with grey-blue and grey-red. She had placed it in his palm, and curled the fingers of his hand over it, then curled her own over them.

"We are like this," she had said. "We are this strong."

He had kept it ever since beside his bed.

The fourth thing of beauty felt as fragile as an empty egg. He held it in his fist where a twitch of rage could crush it.

He listened to five hundred men march north between endless red brick row houses.

She was gone. The peg pinning his soul was gone.

Day grew long, became empty sleepless night. Became cold. Became hard.

He arose. Morning slipped over damp rooftops.

He opened his front door, leaving it to swing.

The fifth thing of beauty was a felt-soft heart that pulsed gently in the light rain. Srilal stepped over the fifth thing of beauty and left it lying on the wet pavement. He turned down the street towards the camp. That day, a thousand boots fell on the thing of beauty, and it died.

UNCLE VERNON'S LIE

ABOUT THE STORY

When I wrote Uncle Vernon's Lie *in 2005, I didn't have any children. At the time of writing this note it's the end of 2020 and I have two children, one twelve years old, the other seven.*

Reading back the story, I discovered that I had made Benji eight years old. I have to admit that Benji isn't very realistic as an eight year old. He doesn't think like an eight year old or talk like an eight year old. I considered leaving him at eight so the whole world could marvel at my ignorance, but in the end, I would rather the story held together a bit better.

Benji probably should be closer to four or five, although he doesn't really fit those ages perfectly either. So I've left his age out of the story and you can make your own judgements, and if you must mock me, you may.

UNCLE VERNON'S LIE

"Your Uncle Vernon will only tell you one lie in your whole life," Benji's dad said on the day he packed Benji off for his summer holiday. "Watch out for it."

Benji's mum had had to stay at home to look after the baby, so Benji and his dad were travelling together on the bus to the railway station. Benji had never been away on his own before, and he'd never met his uncle, but he wanted to look brave in front of his dad, and he was trying hard not to cry, so he just said, "Okay," and that was that.

Uncle Vernon, Benji discovered, didn't use teabags. He used whole leaves that had rolled up into tight, almost-black balls when they dried. He tipped a single teaspoonful into his teapot then poured in the boiling water. ("Always fresh, boiling water," he said as he poured. "Always.") Benji watched, fascinated.

Within moments, dozens of tiny bubbles had risen to the surface of the tea.

"Why are there bubbles?" Benji asked.

"Ah," said Uncle Vernon, leaning across the breakfast table. He had thick, white eyebrows, and these rose as he leaned forward, as though they were attached to the ceiling by strings. "Now that's a secret, but I shall tell you anyway. Then we'll both have a secret. Would you like that?"

"Okay," Benji said.

"Well," said Uncle Vernon. "There's a tiny little man wrapped up inside each tealeaf. When the boiling water hits the men, they scream. That's what makes the bubbles." He waggled his eyebrows.

Benji sat back, satisfied. He might have been young, but he wasn't stupid. *One lie.*

UNCLE VERNON'S HOUSE WAS LARGE. IT WAS MADE OF OLD RED brick, with gables and bay windows and a dozen chimneys that rose in two clumps like the exhausts of a clay rocketship.

A maze of gravel paths wound through the walled garden behind the house, between borders filled with tall flowers and thick shrubs. A single, closed wooden door in the surrounding brick wall led from the garden at the far end. Beyond the wall, Benji could see the tops of swaying trees.

Benji was walking along, feet crunching on the gravel

path as though he was walking on the crumbling shells of million-year-old sea creatures, when he heard humming from the bushes ahead.

He stopped short. How could somebody be humming in the garden? Uncle Vernon was in his study. No one else lived here. That meant it must be someone who shouldn't be in the garden. A stranger. Benji's teachers had told him never to talk to strangers. Strangers were dangerous.

He backed away. He would run back to his room, hide there.

And then what? Hide there all holiday?

If he had to.

He turned and hurried away down the path.

Do you think Uncle Vernon will let you stay in your room all the time? He'll make *you go out and play.*

The paths twisted and turned and crossed over themselves. Benji dared not look away from them, in case they writhed like worms in water. Now the humming came from the left, then the right, ahead, behind as the path wound.

When Uncle Vernon made him come out to play again, that faceless stranger might still be there, humming in the bushes, watching Benji with invisible eyes. Reaching out a hand. He would be too scared to breathe.

"Doesn't matter. I'll run back to the house again. Every time."

He'd seen this bush before, hadn't he? Just a minute ago. Maybe he had run in a circle. Benji didn't even know if he was on the right path. He couldn't see the house.

His parents' house in London only had a small garden,

just a patch of grass, some concrete, and a single tree. This one seemed to stretch on forever, and there were too many places for a stranger to hide.

The path swung suddenly around a high bed of lavender. Benji stopped.

The humming was coming from just behind the bush ahead of him, a high sound, reaching up and down, up and down.

His throat hurt like someone had hold of it.

The stranger was following him, slipping through the bushes.

Benji stared around. He didn't know where he was. He didn't—

A girl appeared from behind the bush.

She was on her hands and knees, pushing a little toy fire engine before her. Benji realised that her humming was supposed to be the sound of its siren.

The girl looked up and stopped humming.

"Oh," she said.

Benji's breath came back so quickly he coughed. The girl frowned.

She was about Benji's age, although sometimes girls grew quicker, like Matt's sister who was twice as tall as either of them, even though she was only two years older, so Benji figured the girl could have been a bit younger than him. Benji's dad had said that Uncle Vernon didn't have any children.

"You don't look dangerous," Benji said.

"Hmm," the girl said.

"I was scared."

"That's silly. What's there to be scared of?"

Benji didn't answer, although he wanted to say, "Everything," because everything was scary. Uncle Vernon's house, the wild garden, the silence, the hidden, dark corners, the strange lie Uncle Vernon had told.

Benji squatted down in front of the girl. "What are you doing?"

She rolled her eyes. "Putting out a fire. What does it look like?"

"Where's the fire?" Benji asked.

"It's not a real fire. It's just a game." The girl sighed. "Games get so boring, don't you think?"

Benji shrugged. He didn't find games boring.

"Who are you?" the girl asked.

"I'm Uncle Vernon's nephew," Benji said.

"Oh." She half-heartedly shoved her fire engine a little further along the path then left it there. "That's good. Uncle Vernon needs a friend. He doesn't talk to me very much any more. I think he's worried that I might become too grown-up if I spend too long with him."

"Who are you?" Benji asked.

"I don't really know," the girl said. "Uncle Vernon looks after me. He's always looked after me."

"Oh," Benji said, then, suddenly, surprising himself, "I didn't want to come here. My dad made me. He said I was too serious." His mouth turned down. "I wanted to stay at home."

The girl looked startled. "Why didn't you want to come? Isn't it nice here?"

Benji looked around the garden, at the flowers and statues and the big house. It did look nice, like a painting, but it was also scary.

"I didn't know it was nice."

She stared at him. "You only like doing things you already know about?"

Benji looked down at his shoes. "I get frightened."

She shook her head, and sighed. Then she looked up hopefully. "Can you think of any new games?"

UNCLE VERNON'S CAR WAS OLD, SMOOTH, AND SOLID. IT looked like a matchbox car that had been blown up to real size and polished for a year. Everything was old around here. Benji had had to change trains a couple of stations from Uncle Vernon's stop. He'd had to get on a cranky old steam train. Benji hadn't ever seen a steam train before, except on TV.

Uncle Vernon didn't have a TV. He didn't have a computer or radio or anything like that. So there was nothing to do except play in the frightening, old garden, and hope no one was watching out of the shadows. They played every game that Benji could think of, but the girl had played them all before. She did play them, but she never really looked happy.

DINNER WASN'T UNTIL NINE O'CLOCK. BY THE TIME BENJI AND
Uncle Vernon were finished, Benji was too tired even to
yawn. Uncle Vernon leaned backwards and stretched. His
spine popped, one vertebra after another.

"So, Benji," Uncle Vernon said, "do you want to go up to
the roof?"

Benji looked up at the clock. "It's past my bedtime."

"Hmph. Well, we won't worry about that. There won't be
any bedtimes here, only when you're tired, and I'm sure a boy
like you doesn't get tired very early."

A spiral oak staircase led up through the house. The
wood was dark and old, and it creaked beneath Uncle
Vernon's steps. From time to time, the whole staircase
swayed. Benji walked as lightly as he could as he followed his
uncle up.

About half way up, Uncle Vernon stopped and bent over,
coughing. Benji waited while his uncle dabbed at his lips
with a handkerchief. When he was done, Uncle Vernon
winked down at Benji.

"Not as young as I used to be."

The light had faded when they came out onto the flat
wooden platform on the roof of the house. A big brass telescope on a tripod took up much of the platform, along with a
deckchair and a coil of rope. Uncle Vernon placed his eye to
the telescope and peered up into the sky.

"What are you looking at?" Benji asked.

"The stars." Uncle Vernon glanced down at him. "Want to
look?"

Benji nodded. His uncle lifted him up around the waist.

Benji squinted. Normally, the stars were flat and small, like a faint scattering of powdered sugar on black paper. Not any more. They were round, like tiny glowing balls, and deep. They seemed to stretch back forever, in front and behind each other. And they seemed close, too. He could reach out his hands and cup them like fiery cherries.

Uncle Vernon lowered him.

"A river of stars flows over the house," Uncle Vernon said. "You have to be careful at night. If you stand on your head while you're outside, you might fall in and be swept away." He turned his eye back to the great brass telescope. "That's why I watch, so that I can see if any little boys or girls have been swept away and throw them a rope."

One lie, Benji thought. *Only one.*

That night, after Uncle Vernon had tucked him into bed, Benji snuck down to the kitchen. He found the sharpest knife in the drawer, the one that glinted like the edge of broken glass. Carefully, he sliced open every rolled tealeaf and watched the tiny men run to safety, ducking under the back door and away. It took all night, and by the end, Benji was exhausted. But he was happy.

THE SUN GOT UP EARLY. BY THE TIME BENJI HAD FINISHED HIS cereal and gone out to play, it was well up in the sky and pouring heat down into the walled garden. The shadows were deep though, and although he peered close, Benji could not see what they hid.

An owl peered at him from a tree, its eyes following him. Benji shivered. He felt cold from tiredness, despite the heat. Every time his eyes drifted shut, he remembered the tiny men running away. At breakfast, when Uncle Vernon had made tea, Benji had been so afraid that his uncle would be angry at him. But all Uncle Vernon had said was, "No bubbles today?" and raised his eyebrows.

Benji's tired mind kept trying to trick him into thinking that things were moving in the dark places, hidden by leaves. He clenched his fists, tightened his jaw, and tried not to jump. His breath was quick and shallow in his nose.

This place was too scary. He just wanted to go home.

Something rustled in the undergrowth. Benji stumbled away, his face crinkling with the effort of not screaming.

A face emerged. Benji sagged. The girl he had met in the garden the previous day frowned up at him.

"Oh," she said. "It's you."

She showed a smile that quickly faded.

"Aren't you going to help me out?" she said.

Benji offered a hand and pulled her from the undergrowth.

"Thanks," she said as she brushed off the leaves and twigs and dirt. "The bushes like to hang on."

Benji gave the bushes a wary look. *A lie? The truth?* He didn't want to find out.

"What were you doing?" he said.

The girl frowned again. Benji could see the lines on her forehead even when she didn't frown.

"I've lost something," she said. "I'm trying to find it."

"What have you lost?"

Her frown deepened. "I don't know. I don't remember."

They looked all day, behind leering statues, in pools, on paths, in bushes. Every time Benji had to part the undergrowth or lean past a statue, he was sure something cruel would reach out and grab him.

Finally, when the shadows had returned and grown late-evening-long, the girl said, "You should go. Uncle Vernon will be worrying about you."

"What about you?" Benji asked

"Oh. I'll just...just..."

She shrugged and wandered away down one of the paths.

BENJI'S BED WAS THE BIGGEST BED HE HAD EVER SEEN. FOUR OF him could have fitted in without bumping elbows. The mattress and pillows were full of feathers and soft, so that he sank deep into them. He felt like he was blinking out of a hole. The room smelled of mothballs and warm wood.

Benji could hardly keep his eyes open. He felt like weights were hanging from the skin beneath his eyes.

"You must have had a tiring day," Uncle Vernon said, smiling, as he pulled the sheet up to Benji's chin.

"Mm-hmm," Benji said.

"I suppose you've heard what people say about how cats sit on your chest when you're asleep and suck out your breath?"

Benji's eyes popped open. He had seen the cats lying in

the sun on the kitchen doorstep. His heart trembled. He pulled his sheet a little further up.

"Yes..."

"Poppycock," Uncle Vernon said. "Complete rubbish. Those people don't know what they're talking about. You don't have to worry about cats."

"Oh," Benji said, relieved, but also a bit disappointed.

"No, it's the owls you have to look out for," Uncle Vernon said. "They'll suck out your breath, peck out your eyes, and feed your soul to the things in the dark." He shook his head. "Look out for them, that's all." He got up and crossed to the door. "Shall I turn out the light?"

"No," Benji whispered.

It had to be a lie. It had to be.

He listened to his uncle walk away down the corridor. Uncle Vernon coughed as he walked, a nasty, sticky, raking, wet cough that sounded like the coughs Benji used to get when he was a kid, the kind of coughs that just wouldn't go away.

Benji couldn't sleep. He lay there in his bed and listened to the owls in the corridor and on the window ledges, listened to their beaks rattle against the windows and their claws scratch on the floorboards.

"Let me go home," he sobbed into the pillows. "Please, let me go home."

❧

IT HAD TO BE A LIE. THE OWLS COULDN'T BE LIKE UNCLE Vernon said. If they were, Benji didn't think he could ever sleep again. How could he sleep if he thought the owls could sneak in and climb onto his chest?

He pulled the sheet off and rolled to the edge of the bed.

It *was* a lie, but that meant that everything else Uncle Vernon had said had to be true. He would prove it was. Then he could sleep.

The floorboards felt rough beneath his feet. The room was filled with liquid dark so that he could scarcely see. Against the windows, hard beaks tapped.

Benji closed his hand around the door handle. Claws skittered in the corridor outside.

It had to be the lie.

He pulled open the door and slipped out into the corridor.

A white shape ghosted from the dark. Benji ducked and felt soft wings brush his cheeks.

Fear grabbed him and shook him like a rag.

He ran. His feet slapped on the floorboards and then the stairs. An owl screeched. Eyes shone like tiny moons.

Benji burst from the house, out into the garden. The gravel stabbed into the soles of his feet. Stars sparkled brightly above him.

He found a patch of grass and stood there, panting. He peered up. Were the stars flowing? He couldn't tell. *A river of stars,* Uncle Vernon had said.

The owls did not seem to have followed. Perhaps they

were waiting in his bedroom, up on top of the wardrobe or on the curtain rail. Waiting for him to close his eyes.

He crouched down and placed his head on the grass, his hands flat on the ground on either side of his head. Then he flung his legs up and stood on his head.

The world turned.

Below Benji's feet, stars flowed.

He fell.

Desperately, Benji tightened his fists in the grass. He jerked to a halt. He hung there by his burning arms. Below his feet, the river of stars rushed on.

Benji kicked his feet. If he could turn himself, maybe the world would right itself. Tears fell from his eyes, down to the river.

Grass parted between his fingers.

"Help me," he whispered. No one answered

His legs wouldn't go high enough. He was too weak to pull himself up. His muscles stretched and shook.

The grass gave way, and Benji fell, into the river of burning stars. The current swept him away.

A rope snaked down into the river. Benji flailed for it. He caught on and held tight as he was pulled from the river.

Uncle Vernon hauled Benji up onto the platform and laid him down.

Once again, the world turned, and Benji found himself lying next to his uncle's deckchair.

"Are you all right?" Uncle Vernon said. "Did you get burned?" He was busy coiling his rope again.

Benji sat up.

"I'm okay."

His tears were still falling. He reached up to brush them away. Gently, Uncle Vernon caught his hand.

"Did you know," Uncle Vernon said, "there are planets that are just made of water? The people in them are happy and sad, they love, they hate, they sing, they fight, they build the most beautiful things and the most ugly. They're selfish and generous and cruel and wonderful. They're just like us, and every tear we shed is one of their worlds. They only have the time it takes for a tear to fall to the ground to do everything, and then they're gone. Tears are never wasted, and you should never wipe them away. Be happy when you're crying."

Benji stared up at his uncle. "Is that a lie?"

"No. Of course not."

"I'm scared," Benji said.

Uncle Vernon nodded. "The world's a frightening place. But it's also wonderful. You can't have one without the other. You just have to go poking into the corners to find the wonderful things." He pulled Benji up. "The worst thing about growing up is that you stop believing things. A long time ago, I decided I would believe everything I could. That way, growing up wouldn't be so bad. Maybe I wouldn't have to grow up at all. Now, let's get you back to bed." He winked. "Don't worry. I never let the owls get into the bedrooms."

UNCLE VERNON'S STUDY WAS AT THE FRONT OF THE HOUSE. A wide wooden desk with neat piles of paper stood in front of a tall bay window. From there, Uncle Vernon could see the front lawn with its towering chestnut trees. He sat in there most of the day. Sometimes the piles of paper seemed to move around, but Benji had never seen him actually touch any of them. Whenever he had looked in, Uncle Vernon had been staring out those windows.

The front of the house would not work, then.

As soon as Uncle Vernon had disappeared off to his study, Benji headed for the back garden. He could never quite remember which path led where, but he knew that they all reached everywhere, in the end. Perhaps they were all the same path. Benji set off, feet crunching the gravel.

Butterflies swirled from flower to flower, their wings like tumbling confetti in the sunlight. The flowers were wild with colour and intoxicating with scent. Benji found his pace slowing and himself drifting towards the flower beds.

He forced himself to keep going. It would be easy to stop by the flowers. But there were shadows in the undergrowth, and bushes that grabbed. His heart fluttered like the butterflies' wings.

The path led around a final curve, and Benji saw it in front of him. The door through the wall. Out of the garden. He reached for the handle, laid his palm on the cool iron.

"What are you doing?"

Benji jerked back and around. The girl was staring at him.

"I'm running away," Benji said.

"Running away?" Her eyes widened. "Why?"

"Because I hate it!" Benji shouted. He hadn't meant to

shout, but now it came bursting out of him, he couldn't stop it. "I'm scared of it all. I'm scared of the owls and the men in the tea leaves and the river of stars. I'm scared to cry in case worlds come out my eyes. I just want to go home." He blinked. He wouldn't cry. "I don't mean to leave you on your own, and I don't mean to leave Uncle Vernon, and I know I promised you I would help you find whatever you've lost. But…" His voice became a whisper. "I just can't stay anymore. I'm too scared. It's all too horrible."

"You can't run away from the world," the girl said.

"I don't want to," Benji said. "I just want to get away from all of this. The rest of the world's not like this. It doesn't have all these horrible things."

"Are you sure?" the girl said. "Have you ever gone looking for them?"

Benji didn't answer.

"The world's full of magic and miracles," the girl said. She was frowning again. "They're everywhere around you."

"I've never—"

The girl shook her head. "It's true. That's why you're a child, so you can see and touch and know the magic and miracles. If you don't, what's the point of being a child? You might as well grow up."

She came along the path to him and took his hand.

"Yeah, some of them are scary," she said. "Some of them are dangerous. But things have to be dangerous when you're a kid. It's part of being a kid. Otherwise you're just an egg all wrapped up in cotton wool, blind and suffocating instead of being young. You have to believe in the magic and the miracles. You have to stop being scared."

"It might hurt," Benji said.

The girl shrugged. "It might. But it'll also be wonderful. And if you don't, you'll be scared all your life. In the end, you'll just wither away like a stick all burned up and falling into ash. Being scared hurts more than anything."

Spots of sunlight scattered across the gravel between them, like dust on water.

"I don't know what to do," Benji said.

"You have to choose not to be afraid anymore."

Benji stared into the girl's eyes. She stared back. He didn't remember when he hadn't been afraid. Except...now, he wasn't sure he was afraid at all. Not here.

"I'll try," he said, and it was as if until that point he had been a bird trapped in a net, afraid to move in case he broke his wings.

He smiled. The girl returned his smile, although Benji thought that her smile wasn't as happy as his.

"So," Benji said, his wings beating inside him. "Are we going to look for whatever you've lost?"

The girl nodded. "I always look. Every day."

"We'll find it. What does it look like?"

"I don't remember," the girl said. The corners of her mouth turned down. "I just know I lost it."

"Was it big or small?"

"Big, I think," she said. "It must have been, because when I think about it I feel very small."

"Then we should be able to find it, shouldn't we?" Benji said. "Come on."

~

THEY LOOKED ALL MORNING UNTIL BENJI STARTED TO FEEL hungry.

"Aren't you coming for lunch?" Benji said. "Uncle Vernon won't mind."

"No," the girl said. "I'll just keep looking."

Benji's stomach rumbled.

"Okay," Benji said. "I'll come back afterwards."

He turned and raced back to the house.

The food was already spread on the table: gently steaming bread, salads, cheese, soup, pickles. But Uncle Vernon wasn't there.

"Uncle Vernon?" Benji called.

There was no answer. Benji crossed the room and opened the door to the corridor. At the far end of the corridor was Uncle Vernon's study. The door was ajar.

"Uncle Vernon?"

Perhaps his uncle had fallen asleep. He was very old, after all. Old people seemed to fall asleep all the time. Benji hurried along the corridor. He paused for a second then pushed through into the study.

Uncle Vernon was there, hunched up under his big desk.

"Get down!" Uncle Vernon whispered the moment he saw Benji.

Benji dropped to his stomach and wiggled his way across the carpet to the desk.

"What's wrong?" he asked.

"Shh!" Uncle Vernon hissed.

Someone hammered on the front door. Uncle Vernon screwed up his eyes and hunched deeper.

They huddled under the wide, heavy desk. Outside, there was silence.

Eventually, Uncle Vernon said, "Take a look out. See if he's still there."

Benji inched his way up until he could peer over the windowsill. A man was pacing up and down outside the house. He wore a brown hat and a long brown coat, despite the heat, and he carried a leather bag.

"He's there," Benji said.

"Oh, God."

The man pulled a watch out of his pocket, looked at it, and shook his head.

"He's going," Benji said.

The man strode off down the path, beneath the chestnut trees, to the road. There he got into a car and, moments later, drove away.

"He's gone."

Benji scrambled out from under the desk and reached back to help his uncle.

Uncle Vernon's eyes were watering, and his face was red. He started to get to his hands and knees, then stopped. His chest spasmed, his back kicked, and he began to cough. His whole body shook. He coughed and coughed, unable to stop. His head bounced against the underside of the desk.

"Uncle Vernon?"

Uncle Vernon grabbed a handkerchief from his jacket pocket and pressed it to his mouth.

Eventually, his coughing subsided. He wiped his lips and then balled the handkerchief and shoved it into his pocket. He crawled out from under the desk and straightened, throwing a nervous glance out the window.

Benji stared at his uncle.

Uncle Vernon caught Benji staring and gave him a water-colour smile.

"Just a bit of a chest," he said.

"What did that man want?" Benji asked.

Uncle Vernon grimaced. "He's a doctor."

"Then why didn't you let him in?"

"In?" Uncle Vernon's face whitened. "No, my boy. That would never do. Doctors make people ill."

"What do you mean?" Benji said. "They make people better."

"They don't, whatever they might tell you," Uncle Vernon said. "They make diseases. They make cancer and bad backs and in-grown toenails and colds and the Black Death and the dreaded lurgy. Doctors go poking around looking for new illnesses. They find someone who's a little under-the-weather and say, 'Ah-ha, you've got lung cancer'. Then, ever-after, people have to suffer from lung cancer, and the doctor gets a medal or certificate." He shook his head. "I let a doctor into my house once, and he made me a new disease. That's why I never let doctors in anymore." He glanced out the window. "Doesn't stop them trying. Meddlers."

Benji considered that. "The dreaded lurgy isn't a real disease," he said.

"Ah!" Uncle Vernon leaned down. "Not yet, it isn't. Stay away from doctors, and it might never be. See?" He peered out the window again. "Are you sure he's gone?"

Benji took his uncle's big hand in his own. "You can't be afraid forever," he told his uncle.

Uncle Vernon smiled down at him. "What's that, my boy?" To Benji it looked like his uncle wasn't really smiling, not like he meant it.

"You can't be afraid forever."

Uncle Vernon cleared his throat. "Why don't we go and have lunch before it gets cold?" he said. "There's cake." He placed his hands on Benji's shoulders. "Don't tell your mother I gave you cake for lunch, or I'll never hear the end of it."

BENJI HIKED HIMSELF UP ONTO HIS CHAIR WHILE HIS UNCLE heaped salad onto his plate.

"Tell me something," Benji said.

Uncle Vernon's eyebrows rose. "Something?"

"Something amazing," Benji said. "Tell me about the magic in the world."

Uncle Vernon gave him an enormous smile. "I wondered when you'd come around to that. What to tell... Ah. Did you know that there's a big spring in the middle of the Earth? Well, there is. A man has to go down there every month and give it a wind, otherwise the world would stop turning and everybody would fall off. It's true. There's a coil sticking up through my garden. I keep asking for someone to come and tuck it back in, in case something goes wrong, but you know what it's like trying to get things fixed. One of these days I'll have to go and tuck it in myself. Maybe you can help me."

"Okay," Benji said, then, "Is that true? Would we really fall off?"

"Oh, yes. Have you ever been on a roundabout when someone suddenly stops it? Everyone falls off."

Benji stared with wide eyes. "Tell me something more."

They sat there for an hour while Uncle Vernon told Benji about satyrs who weaved stories into the air on their looms made of moonbeams so that children would have something to dream, and pools where every time you skipped a stone an eye was opened for the water to stare out, and the shadows that shadows cast when the sun turns its face away, and a dozen other hidden miracles that Benji had never seen.

"I wish I could stay with you forever," Benji said.

"For a while," said Uncle Vernon. "Just long enough to be young, not long enough to grow old." And he looked sad again. "Now, why don't you go out and play? A flower has just opened in the garden. Every time a new flower opens, it lets out a kiss. If you hurry, you might manage to catch it before someone else does."

SHE WAS OUT IN THE GARDEN, SITTING ON A STONE BENCH FROM which carved faces leered. Benji came around and sat down next to her. She turned as he sat, took his face in her hands, and kissed him gently on his lips. Benji's chest stuttered and stalled. Kisses had never felt this way before.

At last, she released him.

"I caught the kiss," she said. "I wanted to share it. To say thank you. For helping me search."

"Thank you," Benji said.

She smiled. "You taste like bees."

"Like honey?" Benji asked.

"No. Like bees." She jumped up. "Shall we keep searching?"

THE DAYS PASSED, FULL OF SUMMER AND LIFE AND MIRACLES. Benji listened to the tales the satyrs wove, and skipped stones on pools of silver, and played hide-and-seek with the shadows of shadows. He tucked the spring coil back down into the Earth and felt it thrum under his hands. And still they both searched for whatever the girl had lost.

As time drew on, the girl's frown deepened. "Why can't we find it?" she said, over and over again. "It's big. I know it is."

Eventually, Benji's last day arrived. He rose early, before breakfast, and went down to the garden. The sun was low and cast long, feeling shadows across the garden from the trees beyond the walls.

The girl was curled up beneath a mulberry bush, frowning even as she slept. Benji touched her shoulder. She blinked awake. Her face was so serious, so down. But she smiled at Benji.

"Come on," he said. "Let's start looking. I'm sure we're going to find what you lost today."

Yet when the bell rang for breakfast, they had found nothing.

"I'll be back as soon as I can," Benji said. "I don't have to leave until two o'clock."

"Yes," she said. "Yes."

Uncle Vernon had made a pot of steaming, hot porridge. Benji could see the currants in it, and the pools of thick condensed milk. Uncle Vernon sprinkled brown sugar over it, and Benji watched the sugar melt.

After they had eaten, Uncle Vernon leaned back and patted his stomach. "Now that's what I call breakfast."

"Uncle," Benji said. "Who's the girl in the garden?"

"Her name's Aimee," Uncle Vernon said. "She fell into the river of stars and was swept away. I pulled her out forty years ago, and she decided to stay. Such a sweet girl. She

brings me berries from the raspberry bushes every summer."
He smiled happily to himself.

"She's sad," Benji said.

"Sad? How can she be sad when the world is full of wonder?"

"She is."

Uncle Vernon's mouth worked, but for a minute he couldn't make a single sound. He looked like he was going to cry.

"I showed her every miracle and all the magic in the world." His voice sounded empty, like an echo in an old bucket.

"Even so," Benji said.

Uncle Vernon turned away. "I thought she would never grow old." His voice was as weak as a winter leaf. He coughed, hawked something up, and wiped it away with his handkerchief. "Never."

Quietly, Benji slipped from the table and snuck out of the room.

Behind him, he heard his uncle start to cough. The sound did not end until Benji was halfway down the garden and the bushes had hidden the house from view.

The girl, Aimee, was sitting on the stone bench, crying. She glanced up as Benji approached.

"I don't think I'll ever find it," she said. "I've looked everywhere."

Benji crouched before her. "Do you believe in miracles and magic?" he asked.

Aimee looked down. "Not any more," she whispered.

"Then I know what you've lost." Benji took her hand. "Come on."

"Are we going to find it?"

"No," Benji said. "I don't think you can ever find it again. You just have to stop being scared."

He led her along the winding paths through the garden until they reached the door in the wall.

"I can't—"

"Shh," Benji said.

He pulled open the door. A path led through the woods ahead.

"Go on," he said.

She glanced at him.

He nodded. "It's okay."

She gave him a smile, then turned, and walked through the door. Benji stood there and watched her walk away into the trees. Although she was walking away from him, she seemed to be growing as he watched. By the time she disappeared from sight, she was as tall as Benji's mum, and her stride had become determined and firm. She didn't look like a little girl anymore at all.

UNCLE VERNON WAS TALKING ON THE PHONE WHEN BENJI GOT back to the house. He covered the mouthpiece with a hand.

"Why don't you go and pack?"

Benji hurried upstairs. When he got to his room he started to stuff all of his things into his bag. It didn't feel like he was going home. It felt like he was leaving. The feeling hung heavy in his throat and chest.

Part way through, he stopped by his window. From here he could see the front garden and the road beyond. A car had pulled up, and as Benji watched, a figure emerged.

At first Benji thought it was the doctor again, and he was ready to race downstairs to look after his uncle. But this man was different. He seemed to be made of shadows: he wore a long, black cloak that reached down to his black shoes, and a wide, black hat hid his face. He started along the path beneath the chestnut trees towards the house. When the man's cloak flapped in the breeze, Benji thought he saw dark wings flutter beneath it.

Benji shoved the last of his clothes into his bag and raced downstairs. Uncle Vernon was waiting by the front door. He had donned his hat and his driving gloves. He gave Benji a wink.

"If I didn't know better," he said, "I'd say you were trying to be late and miss the train. Eh?"

"I saw a man outside," Benji said. "He was wearing black."

Uncle Vernon's face softened, so that despite his white hair and wrinkles, he looked like a child to Benji.

"He's the raven."

"What does he want?" Benji said, heart hammering.

"I called him," Uncle Vernon said. "You were right, Benji.

I've been afraid too long." He straightened. "The raven is a great doctor. He's not like other doctors. He doesn't make people ill."

"Oh," Benji said. For some reason, he felt sad. Things shouldn't change here.

"Come on," Uncle Vernon said, and led Benji out.

They drove to the station in Uncle Vernon's Bentley, sliding almost silently along the tree-lined lanes to the town.

The train was already at the station, puffing smoke-signals of steam into the blue sky. Uncle Vernon helped Benji up into his compartment and passed him the bag.

"Give your parents my love," Uncle Vernon said. "I miss them."

"Why don't you come with me?" Benji said desperately. "You could stay in my room."

"I can't," Uncle Vernon said. He smiled. "The raven's waiting to take my illness away. It would be rude to keep him waiting any longer."

"Can he do that?" Benji said.

"The raven can take it all away," Uncle Vernon said.

"I don't want to go home." Benji stared down at his uncle. A tide seemed to be rising within him. "I don't want to leave you."

Uncle Vernon kissed him. "You have to. Don't cry."

But Benji couldn't stop. Worlds tumbled from his eyes and fell to break on the stone platform. Uncle Vernon's mouth turned down at the corners. Benji thought his uncle was going to burst into tears too. Then his uncle stiffened his shoulders. He gave Benji a wink.

"Don't cry. I'll see you back here again next summer. I promise."

Benji sniffed. He could wait that long. "Okay, then."

The whistle blew, and the train pulled away. Benji watched his uncle slip further and further behind, until the steam hid him from view, and Benji's perfect summer holiday was gone.

BENJI'S FATHER WAS WAITING AT THE STATION. THEY WALKED silently across the platform out to the car park.

"Sit by me," his dad said.

Benji slid into the passenger's seat.

"What lie did your uncle tell you?" his dad asked.

The lie. Benji had forgotten about the lie.

He looked down at his lap.

"He said he would see me back there again next year," Benji whispered. "He promised."

"Yeah," Benji's dad said, and the word came out as a sob. "Yeah."

This time, neither of them even tried not to cry.

FINISTERRE

ABOUT THE STORY

British people of a certain age – and sailors – will probably be familiar with the shipping forecast. It's basically a weather forecast for the sea, but it has its own very particular format, with sea areas given odd names. The shipping forecast was (and may well still be) broadcast on Radio 4 just before the station went off the air for the night, and I would often be listening at that time. It was a comforting, almost hypnotic listen.

Then, one day, whoever was in charge of the shipping forecast decided to rename the shipping area Finisterre (meaning 'end of the Earth' and situated, I believe, off the coast of Spain) to the more mundane FitzRoy and stole all the magic from it.

I started thinking: what if, when something changes its name, the original still remains somewhere, somewhere mysterious, beyond the end of the world...

FINISTERRE

SHE'S SITTING THERE ON THE UNDERGROUND, HEAD NODDING to whatever industrial grind she's got playing through her headphones, and suddenly for the first time in years I'm reminded of Jorge, and I miss him like God just tore out a chunk of my heart.

She's not much like Jorge really. She looks like she'd be a vampire if she had the imagination for it. All black makeup and pale skin. Jorge's skin was so rich I could have planted a seed in it and it would have grown. I think it is her eyes, the colour of raw sugar, that remind me of him, although Jorge never had that blank, hopeless expression. Not even when they hung him.

Even so, for a moment I'm tempted to get up and go over to her, just to talk, to remember his voice. Hey, but how would that look? Forty-eight year old man, not shaved for a week, not changed his clothes for as long, smelling of old beer goes up to a teenage girl on the subway. What would you think if you saw it? So I don't. I just close my eyes and remember Jorge.

Jorge with his guitar, singing revolutionary songs under the banana trees by the river.

Jorge with a rifle, in the jungle, waiting for the troops to pass.

Jorge drinking and laughing in the town square while Somoza's National Guard were gathering in the hills with their CIA friends.

Jorge in my arms.

Jorge between my thighs.

Ah, God.

Jorge hanging from a rope in the town square.

It was just a little town, about thirty miles east and ten miles north of Matagalpa. Maybe you wouldn't even call it a town. But to Jorge and his friends it was like heaven. *Corazón de la Revolución* they called it, Heart of the Revolution. They put up signs all around town with that on, *Corazón de la Revolución*. Then they sang and laughed. It was 1976, and the National Guard were moving towards us with their American weapons. And there were Jorge and twenty of his friends with rifles that only worked two times out of three, and me, straight out of college, writing articles that would never be published for newspapers that didn't care.

Jorge didn't die when the National Guard took the town, but the Heart of the Revolution did. When we saw we had lost, we hid. They tore down the signs around the town and put up their own. They called the town San Lorenzo. Their captain's name was Lorenzo. Perhaps he thought he was a saint.

American money bought Jorge from the people who had hidden him. The National Guard hung him in the town square as a lesson. And I watched. I watched, that's all. I didn't help him. I didn't even have the courage to take a photograph. And then he was dead. Jorge. God, I miss him. I should have saved him.

I open my eyes.

I've missed my stop and the girl's gone. In her place is a man. He looks a bit like me. Dirty, unshaven. But he looks happy. He's smiling.

"Finisterre," he says.

"What?"

"The end of the Earth."

I shake my head and look out the window at the darkness, hoping he'll go away.

"He died, didn't he? You lost him."

My head jerks around. "What did you say?"

"You lost him. I know. I can see. You're like me. I recognise you. I lost someone, but I found them again."

He's got that unhealthy glow of enthusiasm in his eyes. For a moment, I think he's going to offer me a copy of *Watchtower* or something. But he doesn't. Instead he pushes his hand through his thinning hair. "Her name was Jennifer. I loved her, but I lost her."

My neck reddens. "But you found her again," I say, almost shouting it. "Jorge is dead. He's been dead for twenty-six years. I'll never find him again."

I subside back in my seat. The train is pulling in to Kings Cross. I wonder if I should just get out and change trains.

"Tell me," he says, his voice soft, persuasive.

And, to my surprise, I do. The hole in my heart demands no less than this drawing out of quarter of a century of pus.

"What do you think happened to *Corazón de la Revolución*?" he says when I stop.

"They burnt it down a month later," I tell him. "Somoza depopulated Matagalpa province. That was his lesson to the peasants."

The man shakes his head. "No they didn't. They burnt down San Lorenzo," he says. "There is a difference."

"Some difference."

He smiles again. I want to punch his smug face, but I don't have the strength. Remembering Jorge has left me weak.

"Do you think *Corazón de la Revolución* just disappeared when they changed its name to San Lorenzo?" he asks.

I sigh. I should have got off at Kings Cross. "No. It became San Lorenzo. To the National Guard, anyway. Not to me."

He nods, as though somehow I've proved his point. "*Corazón de la Revolución* didn't go away because they changed its name. It is still alive." His voice drops, and I have to strain to hear it. "In Finisterre, at the end of the Earth."

A train passes us, going the other way in the darkness of the tunnel. I see strobes of light from the windows, and faces flashing past too quick for me to distinguish.

"So what if it is? Jorge is still dead. I don't care about *Corazón de la Revolución*. I only care about Jorge. He's dead."

74

The man frowns, like I'm some remedial student struggling over an algebra problem.

"Your Jorge wasn't killed in *Corazón de la Revolución*. He was killed in San Lorenzo. In *Corazón de la Revolución* he may still be alive."

I'm shaking my head, but my throat is tight because I want to believe him. "How do you know this?"

"Because," he says, "Jennifer was killed in Avon just after its name was changed from Somerset. I went to Finisterre, and I found her there. Alive."

My scalp is aching like every hair in my body is trying to pull itself out of my head. A pulse is throbbing somewhere behind my eyes. I'm cold and sweating at the same time. Jorge. I can see him laughing, see that gap between his front teeth.

This man is mad. But I don't think I care. Not anymore. Better to be mad than lost like this. His madness is a sea. I plunge in, let the waves wash over me.

"Where," I say through a sticky mouth, "Where is this Finisterre? How do I get there?"

"I told you," he says. "It's at the end of the Earth. It is where places go when their names are changed. In Finisterre are Constantinople and Rhodesia, Petrograd and Somerset, Babylon and Thebes. And there is *Corazón de la Revolución*. It's easy to get there." He leans towards me, eyes flicking from side to side, as though he thinks someone might be listening. Then he whispers, "Just change your name."

❧

I'm feeling stupid and angry and hollow. I'm sitting in front of the desk, my paperwork all filled in, my money order lying there. Forty pounds doesn't come easily to someone like me. Maybe I won't eat next week. All because I wanted to believe the story of some madman.

The lawyer glances up. "It all appears to be in order, Mr Carlyle," he says. His smile is weak, like he used to practice it but doesn't bother any more. After the revolution, we used to say, there would be no more lawyers, no more bureaucrats. After the revolution. Today, I don't think I even remember what the revolution was about.

He picks his stamp up, inks it on the pad so slowly that my muscles are burning with lactic acid from the tension. So this is all it takes. A few bits of paper, some money, and Thomas Carlyle is gone, replaced by Evan Harris.

The stamp lifts, descends towards the paper...

And I'm on my knees in mud. Cold water seeps over my hands, through my threadbare jeans. I push myself to my feet and stumble away from the stream.

Where the Hell is this?

Well, I know one place it isn't. It isn't *Corazón de la Revolución*. The trees around me look like British woodland. There are oaks and chestnuts and some others I can't name, and tangled brambles and ivy choking the ground. The trees are that dark, heavy green of late summer, and I hear birds hidden in the foliage. I can smell smoke from somewhere not far ahead.

I push through the undergrowth, and the trees end. Up ahead is a steep, artificial hill topped by an earth and wood wall. I recognise the construction from my history lessons as a kid. It's a motte and bailey fort. The smoke is coming from the top, not the gentle smoke from a cooking fire, but a roiling, rising, uncontrolled black mass.

There's a wall at the bottom too, stretching out to surround a cluster of low buildings, but it's been shattered in several places leaving craters in the soil. I hear voices shouting from the top of the hill. There's a standard up there, too, but even when I squint it's just black shapes against the bright blue sky.

If I were sensible, I would go around, head back into the trees and avoid this place. But I need to know where I am and where *Corazón de la Revolución* is.

I ease myself through one of the gaps in the lower wall. There's a body lying in the mud nearby. I try not to look.

I'm about half way up the mound when I hear a sound in the sky above me, a sound that tears the sky, that rises to a shriek. I look up and see a jet banking, a streak of light detaching itself, falling.

The explosion shudders the mound. The earth beneath me slips then bucks, and I find myself face down. Earth hammers down around me, on me, thumping in clods like fist blows. Something more solid smacks the ground by me. It's the standard: a series of metal discs, crescents, half-discs, and wreaths along a pole, topped by a cracked eagle clutching crossed bolts of lightning. It looks Roman. I didn't think the Romans built forts like this. They certainly didn't use jets.

A hole has been torn in the top of the hill. The jet turns

in a wide arc, coming around again. I struggle to my feet, my heart drumming. Sweat mingles with dirt on my face.

I can hear the jet again now.

Something streaks from the trees, racing towards it. Fire blooms in the sky, followed a second later by a shockwave of sound. Fragments, like black confetti, scatter from the sky.

I half walk, half fall down the slope, away from the shattered summit. There are no voices up there now.

As I reach the gap in the lower wall, I see the body in the mud twitch, and hear a low, ragged moan. Reluctance weights my legs with lead, but I force myself over to the man.

A wet, almost black stain shows through a rip in his khaki fatigues. It bubbles when he breathes.

His face is hidden by tumbled black hair. A rifle is trapped beneath him. I kneel beside him.

He twitches again, his arms convulsing as though he is attempting to push himself up, and as he does so, I see the armband. It's a double band, red above black, with white letters on it. An FSLN armband. Jorge used to wear one of those. For a moment I can't breathe. It's like someone's grabbed me by the throat with stone fingers. Jorge's hair was black like this.

Not caring about his wound, I turn the man onto his back. His head lolls back, the hair slipping free of his face, and I gaze down at him. He doesn't look Central or South American. I would guess Slavic if I had to, but even that isn't quite right. His eyes are open, but unfocused and glistening feverishly. He whispers disjointedly in a language I don't recognise.

There's nothing I can do for him. Even if I had medical training it's obvious he needs a hospital. But maybe he knows about Jorge, or where I can find the FSLN.

I bring him water in my cupped hands from the nearby stream, a trickle at a time. I see no one else in that time.

Late in the afternoon, his eyes clear a bit to focus on my face. I kneel down over him.

"Who are you? Where am I?" I repeat it in my rusty Spanish.

Eventually he replies, his English heavily accented. "You're new." Then he laughs, but it is more of a cough, and his face lines with pain.

"Where am I?"

"Finisterre," he whispers. "Took the fort for two days. Captured their standard. Great victory. Until that damned jet."

His eyes close again, and I shake his shoulders. He winces, but his eyes open again.

"What's happening?" I say. "Where did you come from?"

He runs a dry tongue across his lips. I should bring him more water, but I dare not lose this chance.

"Attacking us for ten years. Trying to crush the revolution." He pushes himself painfully up on one elbow. "Never."

"Where is the revolution?" I say.

"In our hearts," he says, and tries to smile, then, "Inwards. West."

He doesn't speak again. He dies sometime in the night. His consciousness runs away from him like the water through my fingers, and I don't know when he dies.

79

In the morning, I walk away from the rising sun, towards the west.

I don't know how long I walk in this woodland before I reach the river, but the joints in my legs are aching. The river is slow and a thick brown-green, and there is a rich, sickly smell of rotting vegetation.

I dip my hand into the water. It is warm, not like a British river. It reminds me of the *Rio Tuma* that ran near *Corazón de la Revolución*. If I threw myself in, would I find myself there? But this river is wider. Some tropical beast of a river whose name has been changed and which has found itself here, like me, in Finisterre. How many hundreds or thousands of such rivers are there in Finisterre? How many name changes? How many cities and towns and villages? How many countries? I finally realise the enormity of this place. It must be many times the size of the world I know, and *Corazón de la Revolución* is no more than a hundred small buildings. But I will not despair, not again. *Inwards. West.* I will find the revolution, and I will find Jorge.

I follow the current, and soon the river curves to the west. Beyond the curve, I see a city.

It is such an incongruous sight that for a moment I forget my exhaustion and the hunger burrowing in my stomach. The bridge on the edge of town could be from Renaissance Italy. It dead-ends in the wall of a pagoda, and behind that looms a medieval cathedral that I could swear I've seen somewhere before. On the other side of the river, a Victorian terrace forks into a line of Dutch colonial wooden houses on stilts and a concrete high-rise. Eras, architectural styles, nationalities are thrown together with no thought or planning, glass offices against mud huts, country bungalows shadowed by a Japanese temple.

I am so astonished that at first I don't notice the bullet holes that pockmark the pagoda, nor the way the bay window of one of the Victorian houses has slumped into a crater in the road, nor the silence that smothers the city.

In front of the city is a strip of fields, carved from the woodland. When I reach the fields, I see the furrows ripped into the earth by tank treads that approach the city.

The damage is worse close up. Walls are blackened, windows smashed, houses no more than shells. Everywhere are bullet holes.

In a square a couple of hundred yards beyond the cathedral, where the signs of battle are scarred deep into the stone, I find the bodies. They have been crucified, in rows three deep, around the entire square. Each of them wears the black and red FSLN armband. The last of my strength fails, and I fall to the flagstones.

I wake to the buzz of flies. It is evening, and the crosses cast long, emaciated shadows across the square. Shaking, I lever myself to my knees, then my feet. I leave the way I came in, circle the dead, patchwork city, and follow the river again, west.

Two defeats, I tell myself. Two defeats for the FSLN, for Jorge's revolution. It means nothing. Finisterre is enormous. There is no reason to think that the FSLN are losing where Jorge is, nor that there is even fighting. But as I stumble on, my imagination plagues me with the image of Jorge nailed to one those crosses, or hanging as he did before in the town square.

The river ends in a lake that stretches almost to the horizon. It takes me two days to reach this lake, two days scavenging berries and sometimes fruit from the woodlands until my stomach never loses that bitter pain of indigestion. Clustered around the shore, as far as I can see, are tents and lean-tos, and huddled figures. Even from where the woodlands end, a couple of miles from the lake, I can smell it. Raw sewage, dirty water, sweat. I have seen refugee camps before, in Palestine, but nothing like this. There must be hundreds of thousands of people here.

Roads lead from the lake, splaying out to every horizon, and on the roads, streams of people are making their way towards the lake. On one road, I see a convoy of trucks trailing trains of dust like stretched, dirty cotton wool behind them.

The shelters are clustered into blocks, separated by muddy thoroughfares. At intervals are spaced medical posts and feeding stations. Through it all are the crowds, washing tides of thin, wounded, and despairing humanity, dozens of races, hundreds of languages.

I would have recognised the woman sitting on the upturned crate at the back of the medical post anywhere. The braided cord of her hair that almost reaches her knees is more grey than black now, and someone has broken her nose, but the eyebrows like wings and the wide, solid shoulders are the same, and the lopsided smile that widens when she is angry. Inés Rivera. She was one of Jorge's closest friends.

I hurry across to her.

She looks shocked, afraid, but then understanding smoothes her features. She stands, knocking back the crate, and I feel the fire, the passion, from her that I had forgotten. She clasps my hand.

"Thomas, my friend. You have come to the wrong place."

My forehead creases like old paper in water. "What?"

"Women. This is place is full of women." She laughs, throwing back her head, a rolling, deep sound that stirs even the despondent crowds around us. I had forgotten that laugh. "These women. They marry. They change their names and they are suddenly here, without their husbands, with their old names, all alone and lonely. Paradise for most men, eh? But not you. How long have you been in Finisterre?"

"Three days, maybe four." My heart is thumping like a steam engine.

"Then it is a miracle that we have found each other. You could walk a hundred years in this place and never see a face you know." Her smile widens slightly, and I know Finisterre angers her somehow. "Or perhaps it is not a miracle. People can be drawn to places in Finisterre. Perhaps there is a purpose, perhaps a sympathy, a resonance between the person and the place. Sometimes it is weak, sometimes strong. Sometimes it does not appear to happen at all. I do not understand it." Inés has never liked things she cannot understand.

She shakes her head sending waves along her braided

hair. "But you were never interested in thoughts like that," she says. "You cared only for the revolution. I remember. I admired you."

"You?"

Things have changed, I want to say. I no longer know what I believe in. I haven't for a long time. For a while, after *Corazón de la Revolución*, I travelled the world, looking for other revolutions. But I could never regain the fire.

"And so did Jorge."

"Tell me about *Corazón de la Revolución*," I say. "What happened when you found yourselves here? Did..." I have to talk around the stone that's in my throat. I hear the pathetic desperation in my tone. "...did they still hang Jorge?"

"Hang Jorge?" She sounds shocked. Then she laughs again, and the crowds draw away, as though the sound scares them. "No, they did not hang him. They were confused. Most of their men were outside the town when it happened. We fought our way out. Jorge led us."

Us. It has not occurred to me until now. If Jorge and Inés and all the others are in this place while also being in the world I knew, then so should everyone who was in *Corazón de la Revolución* when its name changed. Captain Lorenzo, the soldiers, and the peasants. And me. Me. A version of me should be here. Is that me with Jorge even now?

"And me?" I croak. "What happened to me? What did I do?"

Inés turns away.

"Tell me."

She sighs, and places a strong hand on my shoulder. "You

would not come, my friend. You were afraid. You stayed behind. When we retook the town, later, you...." Her eyes slide away from mine. "You were dead. The soldiers had killed you."

Dead. What does that mean? All it means to me is *twice*. I let Jorge down twice. Once in each world. Despair pulls down on my throat, my stomach. My limbs are too heavy, my head unsupportable rock. I fall.

"Is Jorge in *Corazón de la Revolución*?" I ask. It is later. Night has fallen and we are sitting by a fire, eating a bowl of stew Inés has found for us.

She shrugs. "Twenty-six years ago, Jorge was there. Today? Who can say? We left, to spread the revolution, each of us apart. I came this way. Jorge went north, I think. I have not seen him since, although I've heard tales of him, as we all have."

He will be there. I am sure. *Corazón de la Revolución* was Jorge's town, his dream. If the troops are heading towards it, Jorge will be there.

"Who is fighting against the revolution?" I ask. "Is Somoza here?"

She shakes her head. "No. They call themselves Romans, although I don't know if they are." She rests her chin on the palm of her hand. "This place is not like the world we came from, Thomas. Most civilisations collapse when they arrive here, particularly advanced ones. Imagine that you are

85

suddenly in this place, your power, your water, your source of food, and your trade routes, all gone. And it is not easy to re-establish them. One day you may be drawing water from a river or trading with a neighbour, the next there is a hundred miles of forest or a new city between you and them. In many ways, primitive civilisations survive best. The Romans have been here a long time.

"They say they are the descendants of Roman legions who were campaigning in Africa when they found themselves here. They were ideally set to take power from the chaos of tribes that existed here before. They have dominated newcomers to this part of Finisterre ever since." Her eyes flick up to mine. "Until the revolution. The revolution is within us. It has no leaders, no capitals. This place was made for the revolution." She sighs. "Perhaps we were lucky. *Corazón de la Revolución* did not arrive in Roman lands. It appeared surrounded by towns and cities that paid tribute to the Romans, but which were not ruled by them. We helped them free themselves from their local oppressors, because oppression lives everywhere. We brought freedom to millions."

"But what happened to the revolution?" I ask. "I've seen so many FSLN bodies here."

"And you'll see more. I don't know what happened. The Romans usually care little who rules outside their borders, as long as the tributes continue. But even before we approached the borders of the Roman lands, they attacked us and the newly freed lands. They are worse than Somoza ever was.

They will kill a thousand peasants to kill a single revolutionary."

I point at the crowds around us. "But how about this camp?"

"They let these people be fed. They want grateful subjects, not just bodies. But if they knew we were here, they would destroy this place."

I started to push myself to my feet. "Then we should leave. We can't risk that."

The look on her face stops me dead.

"We will not run from oppression," she says. "You believed that once. You wrote it down. Have you forgotten?"

"I...."

Her smile could crack her face in two, could swallow me.

"You look like shit," she says. "You look old. I never thought you would look old."

She doesn't look old. Despite the grey hair and the wrinkles she looks young. Her fire has sustained her. Mine died with Jorge. No, I realise, as I think it. That is wrong. My fire died when I failed Jorge.

"Come with me to *Corazón de la Revolución*," I say. "Let us find Jorge, save him, and start again."

She shakes her head, pity in her deep eyes. "*Corazón de la Revolución* does not matter. Jorge does not matter. The revolution is wherever the people's hearts yearn to be free. You believed that once too. I will be where the revolution is. Where will you be?"

I do not know. All I know is that twice I let Jorge down. Twice is enough.

Stealing a truck is easy. No one is guarding them now that they're empty of food. Refugees drain into this place, fleeing from the relentless march of the Roman troops. There's nowhere else for them to go, and no reason for them to take a truck. But I can't flee from the battles. I know the troops are heading inwards, towards the heart of the revolution, towards Jorge. I won't let him down a third time.

Crowds form a wake behind the truck, hands stretched out, faces upturned, pleading. I have nothing for them.

THE DIESEL IN THE TRUCK TAKES ME CLOSE ON THREE HUNDRED miles. All the way I pass the ruins of towns and cities and villages, and camps or columns of troops. But there is no fighting. The war here is over. Even so this is not a land at peace. Victorious Roman troops stand ominous guard over the ruins. Several times, my truck is stopped and searched, but I am carrying no weapons or fighters and they let me pass.

The truck finally fails on the edge of a bombed-out fifties housing estate that skulks before a range of sharp hills. There is a mass grave just outside the estate. It's an old grave, maybe months old. As I stand before it, wondering whose bodies it contains, I realise that I am going to be too late. I will not be able to reach *Corazón de la Revolución* before the Roman troops do. They are probably there already.

But even so, I cannot stop. I cannot turn away and abandon Jorge again. I set out into the hills.

For two weeks I hike, avoiding habitations and people, following the sun west. Once I see an almost brown ocean and hear seagulls. Another time I skirt the edge of a burning desert. At the beginning of the third week, I find a bicycle and follow a rutted track through a humid rainforest. Through the trees I glimpse a line of temples carved from a golden cliff of sandstone. An enormous Roman eagle has been painted crudely on the stone above them.

Sometimes now, I hear gunfire and explosions or see a speck of a jet or bomber overhead. I cycle faster. There is a smell in the air now, of the river, of banana trees. I know I should stop more for food or rest, but I cannot. The spinning of my feet is all that keeps the Roman soldiers from Jorge.

The track ends abruptly in hills five days later, as evening falls. I reach the first ridge in full darkness, and see flashes of light, tracers, hear rumbles of sound, the rustle of gunfire.

By the time I reach the second ridge, my clothes coated in mud, my hands scraped and bloody, I can only hear the odd, weak pop of a rifle. Silence accompanies me after that.

Panting, I struggle up one last ridge. Far below, I see *Corazón de la Revolución*, the buildings silhouetted by scattered fires.

There are bodies here in the trees. I kneel by one, pull off the red and black FSLN armband, and pick up the rifle by the body.

I see the men before they see me. They are limping towards me, supporting each other. They stop when they see me, but they don't raise their weapons.

"It is too late," one of them says. "They have taken *Corazón de la Revolución*. The resistance is over. We have lost."

It is too dark to see their faces.

"You cannot fight them," the man says. "You must go, take the revolution elsewhere."

I no longer care about the revolution. I care for nothing except Jorge.

I walk past them. I knew one of them once, I realise as I pass. I don't remember his name.

"If you go down there you will die," he calls after me.

Die? I have been dead for twenty-six years.

I raise my rifle, and walk down the slope towards *Corazón de la Revolución*.

THEY DON'T SHOOT ME. MY RIFLE JAMS WHEN I TRY TO FIRE IT, and they laugh when they disarm me. I am grabbed, pulled, punched, kicked to the town jail. I don't feel pain.

There is only one cell. I know. I stood outside this place once, while Jorge sat inside, waiting to die. I stood, and then turned away.

Not this time.

I am flung into the cell, landing on my face on the flag-stone floor.

Strong hands help me to my feet.

"Thomas," he says. There is no surprise in his voice. Jorge. I stare at his silty eyes, made dark by the shadows, his earth-rich skin, the gap between his teeth. Age has hardened him, cut away the softness from his flesh. But he is still Jorge. We embrace.

Later, he says, "I think the revolution might have been won. If not for our friend, Captain Lorenzo."

"Is he here?" I say, the familiar fear squeezing my stomach.

Jorge smiles. "He is. He could no more stay away than you or I could. But this is still *Corazón de la Revolución*, not San Lorenzo. It isn't safe to change the names of places here. Names define Finisterre. So perhaps we have won after all."

I cannot take my eyes off the way his lips move. "But what went wrong?" I say.

Jorge shifts, grimacing at some old wound. "Captain Lorenzo fled from *Corazón de la Revolución* when we broke out. He left his men here and ran, like the coward he is, to the Romans. He convinced them that the revolution would come to them, and when it approached, they were ready. They let him join the forces of oppression against us."

I look around the little cell. If there were a way out, Jorge would have found it last time.

"Then it was all for nothing," I whisper. I wanted to save Jorge, to get him back. But instead we will both die at Lorenzo's hand, like Jorge did twenty-six years ago.

"No," he says. He crosses his hands behind his head and smiles. "I have learnt something about Finisterre, my friend. Every day new places arrive here. The Romans can subjugate some of them, but not all. *Corazón de la Revolución* is lost, but one day there will be a new heart." He looks straight at me. "The revolution will come again."

Fuck the revolution, I want to say. But I can't. Not to him. Instead I stare through the tiny high window, waiting for the morning light. And Jorge sings soft songs of revolution, until dawn.

The sun has not yet risen when the soldiers arrive at the cell. I see the Roman eagle embroidered on their breasts. Jorge touches the FSLN armband on my biceps, and smiles.

As the guards lead us out to the town square, I take Jorge's hand. There are hundreds of soldiers in ranks around the square, and two scaffolds, side by side. Jorge leans close to me, his lips brushing against my ear.

"I knew you would come," he says. "I knew you would not leave me to hang alone."

I meet his eyes. "Never," I say.

The rope is softer than I expect around my neck.

THE LAWYER LIFTS HIS STAMP, INKS IT TOO SLOWLY, AND THEN brings it down on the paper. He looks up at me and smiles his weak smile.

"Congratulations, Mr Harris," he says. "You are a new man."

He stands, pushing out a hand. I rise and take it. Nothing has changed. The office is the same. I am still here.

What did I expect? I was so desperate to believe the story of a madman. But there is no forgiveness in fantasies. I bite down on my lip.

The madman from the underground is waiting outside.

Fury surges in me like a beast beneath my skin. I grab him by the throat and slam him against the wall.

"Where the Hell is this Finisterre? Where is *Corazón de la Revolución*? Where is Jorge?"

He swallows beneath my tight fingers. "Did you change your name?"

I don't loosen my grip. "Yes."

"To what?"

"Evan Harris," I say.

"And what happened to Thomas Carlyle?"

I let him fall. He is mad. I should blame myself for my stupidity, not him. "I am Thomas Carlyle. I am here."

He looks up at me. "No. Evan Harris is here. Thomas Carlyle is in Finisterre. Just as when your *Corazón de la Revolución* had its name changed to San Lorenzo, San Lorenzo stayed in this world and *Corazón de la Revolución* went to Finisterre. It's the way it works."

My anger fades as he speaks. Softly, I say, "You said you lost your Jennifer but you got her back. So where is she?"

He smiles. "In Finisterre, with me."

"And," I say, almost too quiet for even me to hear, "what use is that?"

"Tell me," he says. "How do you feel?"

His words are soft, but they stop me. I have been so engrossed with my anger that I have not looked at the wound inside me. Now I do.

The hole is filled, the wound healed. I feel good. I feel happy. He is right. I no longer miss Jorge. I smile.

Somewhere, I know, I am out there, with Jorge. We are

singing songs by the river. Our skin is brushing, touching, pressing...

On the way home on the underground, I see a man slumped in his seat, eyes pressed closed, the familiar misery of loss as strong as a fluorescent light around him. I sit opposite him, leaning forward, and wait for his eyes to open.

A VEIL, A MEAL, AND DUST

ABOUT THE STORY

*Look! A science fiction story amongst all this fantasy. Well, kind of.
A science fantasy, let's say. Actually, I don't think I'd be accurately
able to identify a science fantasy story if it ambushed me in the
full light of day.*

Science fiction. That's what we're going with.

Possibly space opera.

Or fantasy.

*This is the oldest story in the collection. I wrote it in 2001
during my second week at the Clarion West Writers' Workshop in
Seattle, USA (a workshop I thoroughly recommend to new writers
of science fiction and fantasy). It was an experiment for me, but it
worked.*

A VEIL, A MEAL, AND DUST

THE TIME HAD COME FOR THE CATECHIST OF YERATET TO choose a new spouse. The final candidates knelt at three corners of a blanket, heads bowed, while the priest kneeling at the fourth corner recited the ritual questioning of God. Ivory pillars, inlaid with gold and jade, reached to the high domed ceiling of the Catechilis. Outside, sand whispered against the thick stone walls. The air tasted dry and smelled of dust.

Parteeka Ren Sussu took the opportunity to size up the other two candidates. The man on her left was tall and solid, with skin the colour of slate dust. Scars seamed his arms and neck like zippers, and one very old scar crossed his nose and his left cheek, just below the eye.

The supreme leader of Yeratet would never choose this scarred thug as his spouse. He had chosen but two men in seventy-two spouses. Parteeka struggled not to show her contempt. She must not underestimate the thug. He had made it this far through the selection. And showing the wrong emotion at the wrong time could undermine her entire carefully designed strategy.

The young woman on Parteeka's right presented a more serious challenge. She was dressed cheaply but was small, with long brown hair, a tough body, and taut, tanned skin. This Catechist was known to like tough women. Indeed, his last wife, Turana, had been very similar to this girl. Well, Parteeka thought, there were more ways of being tough than having a hard body.

There had been a thousand candidates at the first round of selection; now there were only three. Parteeka had spent most of her fortune and called in favours gained over twenty years to get her this far, but here her influence had ended. The Catechist could not be bought. Still, if all went well, she would soon be the Catechist's new wife.

The priest finished the ritual and drew out a cloth bag. "In this place you will speak only the truth." He offered the bag to the young woman, who reached in and brought out her fist with something clutched inside. The bag passed to Parteeka, and she too reached in. There were two smooth balls. She ran her fingers over them, trying to feel a difference between them, then selected one at random and pulled it out. The scarred man took the last ball.

The priest folded the bag into his robe. "In this place, God and the Catechist hear all, see all, know all. Do not lie, for no one may lie in this place and live. Speak true, speak well, and you will become the spouse of the Catechist." He stood, and strode from the Catechilis.

Parteeka looked down at the small black ball clutched in her hand. *Two.*

The scarred man rose. Tinted light from the stained-glass windows high above fell on his black skin. Muscles tensed beneath his clothes as he spoke. "Dorat has number one." Parteeka did not recognize his accent. "Dorat tells you how he saw the Catechist of Yeratet and fell in love.

"In Serinda, on the other side of the world, the flame-spike trees flower for fourteen months a year, and the blossom is as thick as oil in the air. At dusk, the sky is filled with silver bats flickering among the towers. Some have said that it is the most beautiful city in the world. Perhaps they are right. It did not seem so to Dorat.

"Those who say it was beautiful have not seen the hanging square where crowds gathered to cheer the death of their neighbours, nor the way Serinda treated those who seemed different. There was beauty, yes, in the flowing water and the trees and the flowers and the golden temples, in the syrupy smell of figs and the dry spices, but a homeless child cannot appreciate that beauty when the militia are hunting him down."

Tears began to flow down the man's cheeks. Parteeka smiled to herself. This man was weak. The Catechist would not choose a weak spouse.

"Dorat does not recall his parents. He thinks they must

have died when he was too young to remember, although they may have abandoned him. He imagines they were like him, for that is the way of such things, but he cannot know. He did not see any others like himself in Serinda, so maybe he was a freak of nature.

"Serinda was a beautiful city, they say, and a homeless boy did not look beautiful. His childhood was a fearful fusion of thievery, pursuit, and beatings. When he was hungry he would sometimes climb the flame-spike trees and gather their bitter, unripe fruits to sell at the market for a few pennies. It was poor work, and the thick pollen of the trees choked him and made his skin erupt and his eyes run tears. To Dorat, this was life.

"Come Septimaltide one year, Dorat made a mistake. Maybe you do not know, because in this part of the world it has fallen from use, but Septimaltide was a great feast in Serinda. On that day no man worked, and the Catechist arrived to celebrate with his people. Dorat believed that on this day, too, the militia would celebrate, so Dorat joined the crowds. He saw the Catechist's glistening silvery ships descend from the sky, saw the flight-fields snap off, and the ramps descend. Saw the Catechist in his purple veil walk out in front of the crowds. And felt a hand clamp his arm, jerk him back, and turn him around. He looked up into the face of a militiaman.

"Here is what the militia did to a small, strange boy called Dorat in far Serinda: They took him to the palace. They stripped him, beat him, burned him, electrocuted him, kicked him, cut him, and left him on the cold stones. Dorat remembers all of this. He wishes he did not, but he has no choice."

So, Parteeka thought, settling back on her heels, this Dorat would try for sympathy. It was an interesting tactic. She had considered it herself then discarded it. The Catechist would not choose from sympathy, her advisors had told her. He wanted ambition, success, influence, and ruthlessness. All of these she could offer.

Dorat was still speaking. "Eventually the lure of drink led his captors away. They thought, perhaps, that Dorat was dead. But he was not. In agony he pulled himself across the stones, up endless steps, and out of the palace. Dorat does not know how he managed this; he could not do it now.

"In the palace grounds he saw flame-spike trees. It seems unlikely that Dorat was thinking clear, but no doubt he recognised these as safety. He decided that if he could just climb one of these ,the militia would not catch him. He had done such a thing before.

"Dorat could not use one leg, and the fingers of his left hand had been crushed, but he was an agile boy – and so, with tears of effort and pain, he dragged himself into the stinging blossom. The branches were sticky beneath him. It may have been sap. It may have been blood. The ghost wind of evening was rustling the fire-spikes."

There was something wrong with the man's story, Parteeka thought. It had been nagging at her for a while. Some detail. Something she once knew. Ah, but she had seen so many cities on so many worlds. What was Serinda among them? But if she could remember, if she could prove he was lying....

"Eventually his eyes cleared and Dorat realised he could see straight into a room in the second story of the palace. This room was ornamented with gold and silks and glittering stones. A great bed sat in the middle of the floor. As he watched, Dorat saw the Catechist of all Yeratet enter the room. Before Dorat's frightened eyes the Catechist removed that purple veil. As all men know, as Dorat knew, anyone who sees the face of the Catechist, save his spouse, must die. But Dorat thought then that it was worth the price. Dorat, injured, weak, and bloody, saw the only thing of true beauty that he had ever seen in his short life: the uncovered face of the Catechist of Yeratet. In that moment, Dorat fell in love. There is little more to say except that Dorat never lost his love for that Catechist.

"So Dorat is here."

The man sat. *Love!* Now Parteeka did sneer, raising her hand to cover it. Did the fool think that the Catechist required love from his spouse? This was even weaker than the sympathy ploy. The Catechist required power and ambition from his spouse, nothing else. With a quick movement she stood and cast her ball onto the blanket.

"I will speak," she said.

The man, Dorat, sank slowly back to the blanket. Tears still rolled from his clear blue eyes.

"I think I was about five when I first tasted Jondian wine-truffles," Parteeka said. "At the time I thought they were the finest food in the world. I was stupidly naïve, of course, but I was young, and the experience was enough to set me on my life's mission. It was the first time that I truly understood the sacred nature of food, how a taste is more powerful than a gun and more important than life, love, or truth." She glanced at the others. Neither of them seemed to be paying her any attention. That didn't matter. She wasn't speaking for their benefit. "I doubt that is a lesson either of you have learnt.

"I learnt to read in little more than a month to discover more about food. My parents were too ignorant to be able to tell me anything worth hearing, and what they cooked shouldn't even have been thrown into a pig's trough. They might have been decent people by other standards, I suppose, but by then I had learned what was truly important.

"In a book that my parents had obviously never opened I found a description of Hadiyan melting cake. The words were plain, but they were great poetry because in my mind I could see the cake, and I could already taste it dissolving on my tongue.

"I searched the city, walking from bakery to bakery, when my parents thought I was at school. It took me five foot-worn weeks to cover them all. At last, in a tiny shop I had walked past several times without noticing, I found the true Hadiyan melting cake. One look, and a hint of the spices in my nose, and I knew I must have it. But there was one problem. The baker wanted a quarter ounce of gold dust for it, and where does a five-year-old child find a quarter ounce of gold?"

The girl on the blanket looked up, frowning, as though

Parteeka were addressing the question to her. Parteeka rewarded her with a thin smile.

"She steals it of course. That is not wrong. It is far less of a crime than denying your passion, and passion for food is a true passion: it brings suffering and struggle, pierced with moments of purest light. That is passion.

"I had long known where my parents hid their money. It was easy to steal a quarter ounce of gold dust. No doubt each assumed that the other had taken it, if they noticed at all.

"Over the next four years I searched out every delicacy our city could offer, plundering my parents' savings when necessary. It was inevitable that one day I would be caught, but I had planned ahead. When, at the age of nine, they found me taking a diamond for a pie of jade-bird kidneys, and they beat me and removed what was left of their savings to somewhere safer, I had already gathered my own little hoard, skimmed off from the money I had stolen over the years. At this age I was already cleverer than my parents."

Parteeka was striding around the blanket. She didn't stop herself. Her advisors had told her to let her passion show. The Catechist would be listening, somewhere, judging them. She would show how driven she was. Let the others try to match her.

"In the meantime, my school had discovered my love of food and were trying to teach me cookery. Cookery! As though a true gourmet would cook her own food. I knew I must escape.

"I left home at eleven and never returned. I do not know

what became of my parents. I did not care. My fate, my passion was more important.

"It was not difficult to find groups who shared this passion. We travelled the continent, dining on exotic feasts and treats that would cost an emperor his wealth if he tried to buy them. Sometimes we stole, sometimes we dealt, always we pursued the finest foods. We chased down legends and myths. We had many disappointments and wasted trips, but these were more than paid for by the delights we found. It was a golden time for a child, and I still have some gratitude to these people.

"But eventually I grew tired of them, too. Their ambitions were too mundane. They did not understand that there must something more. The dishes we ate were good, maybe even sublime, but they were not perfect. The perfect food should overwhelm the gourmet, not by force, but by seduction of every sense. It should leave her complete, her life over, with no more to experience. I had not yet found this food.

"I took what I could of their money and moved on. Do not misjudge me here. They would have done the same, had their ambition been sufficient." This was important. The Catechist must understand that she would do anything for an important cause. He would want that in a wife. The Catechist's wife must be ruthless.

"I began to dig deeper.

"I have eaten eyes from a live Yenus monkey, swan stuffed with a hundred hummingbirds and basted in secret spices, and eggs of the now extinct sighing owl.

"At the age of seventeen I joined the Lænon Mercenaries'

raid on Saphith Tertiary because I had heard that the natives had a unique method of preparing veal, and I wished to taste it before their civilisation was destroyed entirely. Later that year I organised and led an attack on the Gordonian Heretics, on what turned out to be a false rumour of a fragile secret wine. So it went.

"If it was that people died, then it was a price worth paying." *Ruthlessness and dedication again.* No one could rule Yeratet's stagnant empire without it.

"As I penetrated further into the mysteries of food, I started to hear whispers of one dish so astonishing that any who ate it would never be able to eat other food again. At first no one could tell me what it involved, but as I picked up fragments from those who had heard of it in passing, whispered from generation to generation of gourmet, the concept began to form in my mind, until after half-a-dozen years I knew this food. It was based on the liver of a bird so unusual it did not even have a name. I aimed my entire, now considerable resources at finding this bird. I hardly cared to eat, such was my passion. I travelled from continent to continent, and even from world to world to find one. But each time I found either no trace, or merely that the information was so out of date that the birds were long gone. On Gentale I almost reached my goal, only to find that the last bird had been slaughtered the day before and boiled in a common soup. I killed the man who had committed this crime. He deserved worse.

"Now I am convinced that these birds are extinct. All save one. I have discovered the last of the species. It is owned by the Catechist of Yeratet. It is the right of the new spouse of the Catechist to demand any dish for her wedding meal. I will marry the man, and I will eat the dish. Then my life will be complete." It was a calculated risk, that truth. But above all, in this place, truth was essential. By now the Catechist would know her determination and power. That she would risk rejection by telling this truth could only confirm her qualities to him. He would choose her.

Dust swirled in the light. The others seemed deep in thought. Parteeka watched them carefully. The man, Dorat, was staring far away, as though locked in his memories. She wondered if he had even heard her story. She didn't care. Her passion was stronger, *more worthy*, than his mere love of the Catechist.

Finally, the young woman sighed and lifted her head. Her gaze flitted around the open space of the Catechilis, like a bird trying to flee.

"I don't want to tell my story," she said. "It hurts, and I have had enough of pain. It hurts like you cannot imagine." She fixed Parteeka with a glare. "You know nothing of pain and not all of the words in the world could show it to you." She stopped for a long while. A smile formed on Parteeka's lips. The girl was not going to speak. She would lose by default.

Again the girl sighed. "How to tell it? How do we tell any tale? My name is Martia Ponacia Quendente. I guess that doesn't mean much to you. Why should it? Why should you care?" She ducked her head, her cheeks flushing. A flush of anger not embarrassment, Parteeka thought.

"My people are Gordonian Heretics." She glared at them, perhaps expecting comment. When none came, she continued. "No doubt you think us evil. We believe that the Catechist of Yeratet is an abomination before God. No man should stand between the people and God. It is for a man to learn through suffering. The Catechist prevents this. Abomination! My people have suffered much and so we have learnt much." She shook her head, and her long hair shimmered across her back. "Maybe I should thank you for that. You have given us the suffering, but I find I cannot do so. Can I thank you for Prestat's death? You do not even know who Prestat was, but you killed him. He was my brother. I found him dead on the sands. Do you care yet?"

Martia's hands balled into fists in her robes. Why should they care? Parteeka wondered. Why should the Catechist care? People died.

"Let me tell you of the Hander Wastes. In the evening, the winds throw dust into the air, and the setting sun turns the sky a heavy red. The storms can strip skin from your face in seconds, and the howling winds force sand into your mouth and nose and fill your lungs with choking dust. It is our place.

"We fled there to escape the Catechist's persecution, and we made it ours, with its bitter beauty that suits us so well. The ever-present dust is our friend and our enemy. But they – you – followed us even to the desert. For a dozen generations, the Catechist has pursued a campaign against my people in our desert retreat. At first we were unprepared, and his troops drew lines of blood across the sand. We, a peace-

108

ful, contemplative people, were faced with the heavily armed soldiers of Yeratet. They were merciless. They killed all they found and swam in heretic blood. We were almost wiped out.

"Eventually, we learned to fight back. If we can learn from suffering, so can you. We swore to make your people suffer, to cut the Catechist at his heart, to make him bleed as we bled. So he would learn. And so we did. We became as dust in the wind, creeping into cracks in your cities and towns. We were everywhere, but uncatchable. We killed and we killed. I myself have cut the throats of the Catechist's soldiers and bureaucrats and people. I have placed bombs in his cities. Blood for blood. Do you care yet?" Martia glared at them. Her eyes had gained a fire.

"My father was captured by soldiers and burned alive. My mother died when your razorships came across her party on the open sands. My brothers died with guns in their hands. I am proud of them all. I have seen your soldiers murder children, rape women, torture men. The Catechist did this because we challenge his right to rule.

"We live beneath the sands and in huddles in the rocks. No flame-spike trees and running water and playing children for us." That was it! The flame-spike trees. Suddenly Parteeka realised what was wrong with Dorat's story. A smile broke over her face. It enraged Martia. "You think you have suffered, but you do not even understand my words! How can you smile? I have told you how my father died. That means nothing to you. To me it is beyond words, it is pain and longing and despair and you do not even care." She took a calming breath.

"We have fought for over a hundred years and we have learnt well how to fight. Now your soldiers do not dare to enter the Hander Wastes except in their ships and armoured creepers. Your people cannot rest easy in any city because we can come there and kill you. And we have. And heretic blood has soaked into the wastes.

"In two generations, nothing has changed. You do not advance nor retreat. We bleed each other.

"The stalemate has gone on too long. Our peoples have died and died and died, and the sands are darkened with blown blood. It is time for peace between our peoples. I will bring peace." Her skin was flushed. She ducked her head. When she spoke her voice was almost a whisper. "I ... I will marry the Catechist."

"And then?" Parteeka asked.

Silence.

"And then?" Parteeka repeated, her body thrumming with tension.

"And then I will kill him."

Parteeka laughed. She had won. Already she could taste that perfect meal in her mouth. Her heart thundered beneath her breast. The Catechist would never allow someone who wished to kill him to become his spouse. And as for Dorat, he had made a mistake. This was the place of truth. No one could lie and hope to live. She knew his lie. She faced him, triumphant.

"You lied, Dorat. I have been to Serinda. I have seen it. There are no flame-spike trees, nor golden temples. No running water and flowers. There are only age old ruins, and dust. The Catechist destroyed Serinda a thousand years ago." The fool had not even been able to get his story straight.

Dorat stood again and lifted his chin. "I never lie. I saw the flame-spike trees in Serinda bloom. I saw the Catechist of Yeratet remove his veil, and he saw me. And it was a thousand years ago.

"No person can see the Catechist's face and live, except for his spouse, and this Catechist was only half way through his forty-fourth marriage, so I could not become his spouse. He could have had me killed; he should have. But he did not. Perhaps he was tired. That comes to us all. He chose to step down from his calling and return to the seas of youth. He chose me as his successor.

"I am the Catechist of Yeratet."

Cold sweat broke from Parteeka's skin. She heard Martia gasp, then spit and come to her feet.

He was the Catechist. And Parteeka had seen his face. If she did not become his spouse, she would die.

"I am the Catechist, and I am tired. Today I have not come to choose a spouse, but to choose a successor. You are the final candidates."

Parteeka saw Martia's hand dart for her belt, as though to draw a weapon that wasn't there, then drop away. She saw fury and betrayal cross the girl's face. For a moment, Parteeka thought Martia might attack the Catechist with her bare hands, but then a look of resignation replaced the anger.

"Know this, Martia," the Catechist said. "Serinda was the original city of the Gordonian Heretics. It was they who tortured and nearly killed the boy Dorat, and when I became

Catechist I swore that the first thing I would do was wipe out these people. In that I have failed. It will be up to the next Catechist to decide what to do in this matter."

He bowed his head.

"I have asked myself for a thousand years how I should choose my successor. What makes a Catechist? They should be strong, supple, determined, brave – both of you are that. They may be just, although that is not so important. They must be a leader. I could find a thousand men and women like that. But they would not be the right person. So, what makes a Catechist?"

He looked at both of them, as though expecting an answer.

Martia trembled with fury beside Parteeka. The girl wouldn't answer. But Parteeka would. What made a Catechist? What answer did the man expect? She would tell any lie he wanted to hear. No less than her life was at stake. Her story rushed through her mind. Whatever she said must not contradict that. She could not risk being thought a liar.

Or could she contradict herself? Was that the key? The Catechist was waiting for something that wasn't in either of their stories. She and Martia were both still here. Neither had yet ruled herself out. So what was he waiting for? There could be only one thing. Take the risk.

She cleared her dry throat.

"Is it that a Catechist must compromise?" she said. The Catechist's blue eyes turned to her. Yes. She was right. "Is it that a Catechist must give up her desires, her beliefs, her previous life to dedicate herself to Yeratet?"

The Catechist seemed to incline his head, ever so slightly. She smiled. She could tell this lie. She could make him believe it.

"Parteeka Ren Sussu. Would you give up your desires, your beliefs, and your previous life for Yeratet?"

She held his gaze. It was easy. "I would."

The Catechist turned to Martia.

"Martia Ponacia Quendente. Would you give up your desires, your beliefs, and your previous life for Yeratet?"

Parteeka couldn't breathe. How well could the little heretic lie? Would she lie at all?

Silence stretched between them.

Parteeka dared not move. The sand was rough against her soft skin. Sweat soaked her shirt.

Then Martia turned her head and spat. "Never."

Parteeka's heart leapt. The stupid girl!

She stepped forward, bowing her head. "Catechist. I will always—"

He cut her off with a raised hand.

"Above all," Dorat said, "a Catechist must be true to herself."

He reached inside his robe, pulled out the purple veil of the Catechist, and stepped past her. He placed the veil over Martia's head, and then whistled sharply. Doors burst open around the Catechilis. Armed soldiers ran in. Martia tensed, then relaxed.

"I lied," Parteeka said, desperately. "I lied. I would never give up my desires and beliefs. You must believe me. I lied."

Dorat, the old Catechist, stared past her. The tears that

had begun when he told his story still flowed from his blue eyes, but he was smiling, smiling. Parteeka could hear the scratch of every grain of shifting sand.

Then Dorat faced the soldiers.

"We have seen the face of the Catechist," he said.

A FIELD GUIDE TO UGLY PLACES

ABOUT THIS STORY

For me, fantasy has always been the wildwood, the untamed, magical, uncontrolled wonder of nature. But nature doesn't always mean the countryside. There is wildness and magic among crumbling concrete and brickwork.

I grew up in a variety of places, but the greatest part of my childhood was spent in the inner city, among the roads, close-packed houses, industrial units, and decaying remains of previous ages. My parents believed in taking us out of the city to the countryside, but the wildness in my childhood manifested itself equally in among the traffic, people, and collapsing buildings of the 1970s and 80s.

A Field Guide to Ugly Places, although it's set in a different country at a different time and to someone quite different from the child I was, is about the type of magic you might find there.

A FIELD GUIDE TO UGLY PLACES

The Friday after Marlene upped and went, Jamie Barton sat on an overturned barrel in the midst of the abandoned industrial park, feeling more lost than he had ever believed he could be. The bones of the dead factories – sagging asbestos and rusted iron spars – threw cold shadows onto the cracked concrete, loose bricks, and thin, black puddles that surrounded him. Scarcely twenty feet in front of him, a dozen kingfishers skimmed low over the chemical-streaked water in the culvert. He'd never seen even one kingfisher before; now there were a full dozen. If his heart hadn't been broken, Jamie reckoned he might have been amazed.

The sky had been grey and wet until that moment, but as the kingfishers darted by, a crack of pale blue split the clouds. From each bird's beak, something fell. Something that flashed silvery and sleek in the air before hitting the foamy, yellow water and slipping from sight.

Fish, Jamie thought, and then didn't think much else for a while.

He'd had his first job over there, in the factory on the other side of the concrete culvert, sweeping metal turnings and oil from under the lathes, eight hours a day for $3.35 an hour. The factory had been closed these last four years, of course, left to decay like the rest of the industrial park, and the building had slumped into sad ruin. Its corrugated metal roof had collapsed, and black squares gaped where panels had fallen in. The walls were scrawled with graffiti; the doors had been boarded over, then later kicked in. Water pooled between the heaps of bricks and the rusting fossils of machinery.

Recession, the bosses had said as they'd closed it all down and driven away in their slick BMWs, leaving Jamie and two and a half thousand others with far more leisure time than any politician had ever promised. Truth was, Jamie had spent most of that time in one bar or another.

When he'd been twelve, Jenny Harris had shown him her bra. She'd done it in the shadow of the industrial park's truck depot. Jamie had wanted to see what was *under* her bra, but she hadn't let him see *that* until five years later. Once, he'd thought he would marry Jenny Harris. Then Marlene had come along, and he'd forgotten all about Jenny. Last Jamie had heard, Jenny had shown what was under her bra to one of the suits in a BMW and found her way right out of town.

Now Marlene was gone too. Fifteen damned years of graft and compromise, then *bang!* she was gone. He felt like a balloon with half its helium gone, limp and caught on thorns.

"You come here often?"

The voice had come from behind him. Jamie twisted his neck to see who had spoken. Sunlight had snuck in through that crack in the sky, so he had to squint to see.

A woman was standing there, looking down at him. She stepped around the barrel so he didn't have to squint anymore. He guessed she was in her mid-forties, ten years older than Jamie. Maybe a bit more. She was wearing blue overalls. They were streaked with oil. The oil had gotten into her hair, too. Jamie figured her hair might be brown like old wood under that dirt, but he couldn't quite tell. It hung loose and ragged to just below her neck.

"From time to time," he said. "You?"

"Not for a while." She lifted a paper bag and opened it, showing him sandwiches neatly wrapped in waxed paper inside. "Mind if I join you?"

Jamie scooted along the barrel. "Please yourself."

She sat close. Their hips just touched. She was soft beneath the overalls in a way that Marlene, with her four days a week down at the gym, never had been. A real woman, Jamie's mother would have called this one. A woman who wasn't afraid to put on a few honest pounds.

"I used to work around here," the woman said by way of explanation. "Before your time, I'd guess." She softened it with a smile.

"So where do you work now?" Jamie asked.

"Round about. I'm thinking about starting here again."

Jamie frowned. "There's work here?"

"God, yeah." She unwrapped her sandwiches with hands that still showed oil beneath the fingernails, and offered him one. "Hungry?"

He was. He hadn't eaten all week. He'd drunk a fair bit, but that didn't fill a man's stomach the same way.

Jamie took a bite. Cheese and pickle on white bread.

"The food of the gods," he said.

"Cheap," she said.

ABOUT A YEAR AFTER HE AND MARLENE HAD MARRIED, JAMIE had had a few too many to drink with the boys. Marlene had come in and found him draped across some blonde. He didn't remember the blonde's name and wasn't sure he'd ever known it.

"Give me a chance," he'd whispered when he and Marlene had gotten home.

"A thousand chances," she'd said, and kissed him.

He had thought that would be enough.

He had never figured she would be counting.

MARLENE HAD NEVER DONE CHEAP. SHE WORKED HARD FOR IT, she'd said, so why should she do cheap?

She had worked hard. Plenty of work for a social security manager to do in this town. Plenty of broken people to pick up. Plenty who'd be right back down there again the next day. She must have got good with all that practice. "No, there's no jobs. Here's your check. It won't take you far." Far as the nearest bar, mostly.

Worst thing about it? Marlene had *cared*. She'd cared about every damned lost soul out there. It broke her heart every day. And the person who should have picked *her* up hadn't been there. He'd been lost in a wilderness of bars.

JAMIE HADN'T SLEPT MORE THAN A WINK IN THE FIVE NIGHTS since Marlene had left. For fifteen years, he and Marlene had never spent even one night apart. An empty bed wasn't a bed at all. It was just somewhere to lie and pray that the hole inside him would fill. The dark ceiling had become his most intimate companion.

Dawn touched the sky with a watercolour stroke of grey at six. Jamie levered himself upright, stopped off in the bathroom for a piss and a glass of water, then headed out along the dead streets. Marlene had taken the car when she'd gone.

"It hurts," he whispered to the streets as he walked. The apartment blocks with their peeling paint and broken windows, the abandoned gas station, the McDonalds wrappers creeping like tumbleweed along the gutters, the rusting fence around the cracked basketball court, none of them disagreed. "Yeah," they whispered. "It hurts. It hurts."

Far away, a siren rose and fell. Jamie kept walking.

Even the bars were closed at this hour of the morning, neon dulled, signs tatty in the unkind dawn glow.

All that Jamie had ever had or been lay in a wasteland now; it called Jamie home.

He turned down River Street, then squeezed through the loose siding into the industrial park. Abandoned factories and warehouses loomed in the murk.

It was just light enough for Jamie to see where he was putting his feet. Within a couple of paces, he realised the ground was coated in moths, hundreds upon thousands upon millions of them, settled over every brick, every girder, ever stained patch of asphalt. They spun away where he stepped, before his feet could crush them, like snowflakes falling upwards.

The ground beneath his feet felt odd. He crouched. The ground was dusty and dry. He reached down and ran a finger over it, then lifted it to his lips. His tongue flicked over his finger. Dirt. And something else. Something sweet, like flowers. Pollen?

He stared at his finger. For a moment, it seemed like something alien. Then he shook his head, and moved on.

He reached the culvert and sat himself on the barrel. A halo of moths rose around him, then settled again further away. The barrel, too, was covered in the layer of dirt and pollen. Jamie took a deep breath. For the first time that he could recall, the air in this place wasn't stagnant and laced with degraded oil. It was almost intoxicating.

The sun showed at last above the cluttered horizon. The moths rose like a lifted shroud with the first rays of sun. For a moment the air was dense with them. Then they were gone, as if a magician had snapped his fingers.

Jamie sat there, watching the islands of foam spin on the water as the culvert washed them down. Maybe it was his imagination, but the water didn't seem so yellow today.

"You're here early."

This time, Jamie wasn't surprised to see the woman standing in the sunlight.

"So are you."

She seated herself next to him.

"I got the job," she said.

"Early start."

"Tell me about it."

She'd washed her hair last night. The oil streaks were gone. He hadn't noticed before what great hair she had. She had lush, slipping waves of it that he could have lost his fingers in. There were touches of grey in it, but none of the dry brittleness age sometimes brought.

"So what's the job?" Jamie asked.

"Clearing up this place."

"On your own?"

She laughed. It was a deep, rich sound. It made him smile. "God, no. What do you take me for?"

He sighed. "So, any vacancies?"

She looked at him. Her eyes were the colour of fresh earth. "Uh-uh. I'll let you know if anything comes up, though."

"Right." He'd heard that enough times before. Sometimes they'd even meant it. Most times they'd meant "piss off."

"Don't look so down," she said. "Might be I'll put in a good word for you."

"Yeah," he said. "Say, you want to get some breakfast?"

She smiled again. It was good to see her smile. It made the day feel warmer. "Sure," she said.

THERE WAS A MALL A MILE OR SO AWAY. THEY WALKED THERE IN the growing light and traffic. There wasn't much open at the mall, just the diner, but that was what they wanted. They took a table by the window and waited for the waitress to come over.

"So, what are you doing hanging around that place?" she said. "Young guy like you ought to have better places than that to go."

Jamie gazed down at the plastic tablecloth. "My wife left. Fifteen years and she left."

"Ah."

"Only good things that ever happened to me happened in those factories."

"You met Marlene there?"

Jamie looked up at her, a frown forming. "Yeah. She had a job in the office."

The waitress approached, flipping open her pad.

"What'll it be?"

She was tall in high heels, with bleached blonde hair piled above a tired face. Jamie thought he might have dated her back in high school, but he couldn't be sure.

"A bagel and coffee," he said. "Black."

The waitress grunted and scribbled.

"I'll have a glass of milk and chicken salad on nine-grain bread," Jamie's companion said.

"I don't think they do that," Jamie started to say, but the waitress had already closed her pad and was heading back to the bar.

"You'd be surprised what people will do if you ask."

She might have showered and washed her hair, but there was still oil under her fingernails. Jamie remembered what that was like. The oil stuck deep in there and wouldn't shift. He would have given anything for a job that dirtied his fingers. If he'd had that, maybe Marlene would have stayed.

"Tell me about her."

Jamie blinked away tears. They were the first he'd shed for Marlene.

"I loved her," he said through dry lips. "I loved her with everything I am. Now she's gone, and I don't think there's anything left in me."

"You know what, Jamie?" the woman said. "There's two types of marriages. In one, everything you do and everything you are magnifies what the each of you is. Yeah, you make sacrifices. Yeah, you make compromises. But, afterwards, they leave both of you more. They make both of you more *you*.

"The other type" – she shook her head – "the other type, see, every time you make a sacrifice or compromise, it erases something of you. It diminishes you. After a while, there's nothing of yourself truly left. It's not because either of you is a bad person. It doesn't mean you don't love each other. It's just the way it goes.

"I think you and Marlene, you had the second type of marriage. I think she knew it. She loved you all the way to the end. Still does. But I think she figured you could both only lose a thousand pieces of yourself before it was too much."

"No," Jamie whispered. "She loved me. She—"

"Ah, look." The woman smiled. "Breakfast."

She said grace over her chicken, head bowed, hands together. Jamie watched her face, his eyes dwelling on the lines, the roundness that was sinking into jowls, every pock and pore, the deep smile lines, the crow's-feet around her eyes, the grey at her temples, every mark that love and life and laughter had set on her features. He watched and listened to her praying and thought, *This is good. This is right.*

She opened her eyes. "You eating or letting it spoil?"

Jamie took a bite, chewed. "You didn't say grace with the sandwiches yesterday."

She laughed. "I say it when I make them. It saves time."

They ate in silence, chewing and swallowing, biting again. At length, it brought a degree of peace to Jamie. He couldn't remember the last time he and Marlene had eaten together. Evenings, he'd been in the bar by the time Marlene got back. He'd rarely been awake when she left for work.

"When we were first married," Jamie said, "we used to watch every crumb the other ate. I could have watched the way her lips moved when she chewed for hours." He dropped his head.

The woman chewed, swallowed, and then wiped her mouth with a napkin.

"Have you ever watched when it rains hard on a pond?" she asked. "Every raindrop forms a bubble that floats on the surface of the water."

"So?" Jamie said.

"We're like those bubbles. All of us."

"I don't understand," he said.

She leaned across the table and kissed him on the forehead. "Don't worry about it."

The kiss spread warmth through him. He felt his tense skin relax.

"Look," she whispered.

Jamie twisted to follow where she was pointing. Out the window, in the washed morning sky, three tiny specks circled.

"Eagles," she said.

"How can you tell?"

"Trust me." She slid out from the table. "Want to go and see them?"

THE EAGLES WERE CIRCLING IN THE BREEZE ABOVE THE industrial park. In the fuller light, Jamie saw more clearly the thin layer that coated every surface, from the bent-backed roofs to the fractured pavement. It was fine, rich earth. He rubbed it between finger and thumb.

"You'd pay a fortune for a sack of stuff like this for your plants."

The woman flashed him a wonderful smile. "Isn't it great?" She looked up. "The eagles are coming lower."

Jamie tilted back his head. The eagles were enormous and lushly feathered. The sun glinted and slipped on their wings.

"Golden eagles," the woman said.

"We don't get golden eagles around here," Jamie said. "Not that I've heard."

"Uh-huh?" She looked delighted.

The eagles were clutching things in their claws. As they descended, they released their grips. Tiny shapes rained down and pattered onto the ground. Then the eagles were beating their wings and rising into the perfect sky.

Jamie knelt, picked up one of the shapes. "A seed."

"Strange days," the woman said.

Jamie couldn't have said he disagreed.

SLEEP WOULDN'T COME. NO MATTER HOW HE LAY OR WHAT HE tried, Jamie remained exhaustedly awake.

"Let me sleep," Jamie muttered in a voice that threatened to become a sob. "God, just let me sleep."

He had loved her. She had left. Sleep would not come.

Eventually, Jamie hauled himself out of bed. The clock said twelve-thirty. He'd only been in bed for two hours. It felt like most of the night. He pulled on jeans and shoes, ran a hand through his hair, and headed out.

The night was humid, the air low and too close. He felt like his body wanted to sweat, but couldn't.

A couple of blocks up, neon flickered. The bar was still open. There was nowhere else to go.

"Been a while," the bartender said, as Jamie pulled up a stool.

"Two nights," Jamie said. He'd been coming here a year, and he'd never learned the man's name.

The bartender slid over a bottle. "Like I said. A while."

"Yeah," Jamie said. "What's your name?"

The man frowned. "Tom. What's it matter?"

"It doesn't." Jamie pushed himself off the stool and slapped a couple of dollars on the counter. "Take my advice, Tom. Don't take anything for granted. You can think you know a person, then you find out you just don't. Fifteen years, and you don't know shit."

"Whatever you say."

"Yeah. Whatever I say."

He carried his beer under the creaking ceiling fan to the corner table.

Bobby and Cole looked up as Jamie plumped himself onto the frayed stool at the end of the table. Bobby had been at school with Jamie. They'd chased after the same girls, maybe even caught the same ones, for all Jamie knew. Not that he did know. He himself had claimed to catch some who'd never even looked his way, and Bobby had been full of it since they were both eleven.

"Been a while," Cole said. Cole he hadn't met until the factory. Cole had worked on one of the machines near where Jamie swept. They'd discovered a shared love of Van Halen and *Knight Rider*. *Knight Rider* was long gone and Van Halen hadn't been the same for years, but the three of them had found beer filled the gap pretty well.

"Yeah."

"So what's up?" Cole said. "Don't tell me you're still pining over Marlene? Listen to me. They come and they go. One's pretty much like another, and there's a hundred 'nothers out there."

Jamie's hand froze to his bottle. A drop of dew touched his index finger, rolled over the knuckles. It seemed to take forever.

"You're being a jerk," Jamie whispered.

"No," Bobby snapped, cracking his own bottle down on the plastic tabletop. "He's not. He's trying to help you."

"Help me?"

"Yeah. Help. Look, Jamie. Marlene's gone. She ain't coming back. You need to accept that." Bobby turned his bottle in his hands. "Have you even looked at yourself recently?"

"No."

"You look like shit. You're dirty. You've lost weight. You stink. It's only been a week."

Jamie swayed back on his stool. "I don't have to listen to this."

"Yeah, you do. You need to listen and you need to hear."

After that, no one said anything for a while. Jamie drank his beer, but he didn't taste it. They played some cards. Jamie couldn't remember who won. He guessed it wasn't him.

Some time later, Cole levered himself out. "Wife's waiting."

"Right," Jamie said.

"Don't stay too long," Cole said. "Feels like rain's coming. Maybe a storm. Air's tight."

"Maybe," Jamie said. "But not yet."

"PLACES LIKE THESE," THE WOMAN SAID, TAKING A BITE OF HER sandwich. "They're like a pin through the heart of a butterfly. They hold a town down. They kill it. A town can't recover until you pull out the pin. Then it might fly again. It might live."

They were sitting together on the barrel, staring across the culvert at the twisted metal and sagging factories. Everything was covered still by the thin layer of rich, brown earth, as though a sandstorm had blown in one night and dumped its cargo over the wasteland. If anything, the layer was deeper today. But there had been no storm. The air was heavy with unbroken humidity.

"Seems like it's a tough pin to pull," Jamie said. "Site like this, it's not going anywhere."

"No?"

"Nah. See, you'd have to bring in the heavy equipment. You'd have to pull it all down and cart it away. Then you'd have to take out all the soil and replace it. Been a lot of chemicals spilled here. The ground's poison, all the way down."

The woman rolled her shoulders and gave him a grin. "Yeah, it's some job."

She swallowed the last of her sandwich, then brushed the crumbs from her lap. Jamie liked the way this woman moved. There was no prissy elegance to her, just like she wore no makeup. Everything about her was right-down-to-the-soil simple.

He caught himself staring at her and looked away. "I hope they're paying you good."

She didn't answer.

Jamie pushed himself off the barrel and stretched. His eyes felt as heavy as iron balls. Even the beer hadn't helped him sleep. He felt like one of those walking wounded, like the photos he'd seen in some magazine a couple of years back of men with shell shock, or like one of the zombies in *Night of the Living Dead*, the original black-and-white version, not the 1990 remake. This woman, he bet she slept like a baby.

He strolled over to the culvert, then stopped, frowning.

He must have been half-asleep all morning. He hadn't even noticed the change.

The foam that had coated the thick water was gone. The yellow stain had washed away, and the water was as clear as a freshly cleaned window. Within it, tiny silver shapes flashed and darted.

"What?" the woman said, so close to Jamie's shoulder he almost missed a breath. "You thought it would stay bad forever? You thought it'd never come clean?"

"No," he said.

But he had. He'd been sure of it.

WHEN THERE'D BEEN THE TWO OF THEM IN THE APARTMENT, IT had been just the right size. Now Jamie was on his own, it was too damned small. He couldn't walk half a dozen paces without coming up against a wall. Half a dozen paces, six seconds. Turn and back. Another six. Five times there, five times back, a minute. Just one stupid goddamned minute, until he wanted to scream and punch the door, and the goddamned night would never goddamned END.

Movement outside caught Jamie's eye. The street seemed to ripple, like the wind over black grass. He stopped at the window, frowning. It was night, dark beneath heavy clouds, so it took his eyes a moment to adjust.

The street was alive. Hundreds – no, thousands – of creatures. Mice, rats, snakes, a pair of dogs, rabbits. All sorts. All of them flowing down the street like a drunkard's dream.

Jamie grabbed up his jacket and took the stairs.

The beasts didn't make much sound, just the tiny scrabble of claws on asphalt, the dry slither of scales, and the hush of fur. Jamie stood on the doorstep for a while, watching the flow slip by.

In due course, the flow thinned and trailed away, leaving a ragged tail: a fox tiptoeing past; a couple of nervous mice zigzagging along near the gutter; a three-legged dog; something furry that was God-knows-what. Jamie stepped out into the street and followed them, already sure of where they were going.

They were pressed up against the fence around the industrial park, milling around the gap. Jamie picked his way through them. They hurried and scurried away from his feet. Jamie saw a rattler among them. It curved lazily aside.

He grabbed hold of the siding and tugged. It creaked, then *spanged* open in a shower of rust. The flow resumed, and the animals swept through into the industrial park.

In the poor light, Jamie could only see the shift of bodies for a dozen feet or so before they blended into the night, but he could hear them beyond: little squeaks and barks and the ghost-call of a fox. From somewhere deep in the clutter of ruined factories, a wolf howled.

The animals were dropping things as they ran. A pine cone from a rat. A bundle of worms scattered from a raccoon's mouth. Soil and seeds and dung, rotting leaves and twigs. Jamie walked through the detritus. It was soft and giving beneath his bare feet.

It took him a while to find the barrel by the culvert. It was almost buried in the gifts the creatures had left. In the end, he only found it because she was there.

Even in the dark, she looked glorious.

She smiled at him.

"You never told me your name," Jamie said.

"No, I didn't," she said.

And that was that.

Jamie sat himself on the soil-covered barrel. Some creature had dropped moss on top of the soil. Jamie sank his fingers into it.

"Looks like your job's nearly done."

"Yep," the woman said, settling herself next to him. "Nearly. By tomorrow, I reckon. If all goes well."

"Don't seem like you'll have a problem."

The woman smiled. "Still got the hard bit left to do. Or maybe the easy bit."

Jamie sighed. In front of him, clean water washed through the culvert. The smell of fresh soil made the night air rich.

"She was perfect," Jamie said. "Marlene was perfect."

The woman got up, crouched in front of him, and took his hand. Jamie saw that her fingers were clean, even right under the nails.

"Yes, she was. But she wasn't perfect for you."

"I don't think I can go on anymore," Jamie said. He was too tired, too heavy inside.

The woman straightened. She unzipped her overalls and let them fall to the ground. She wasn't wearing anything underneath. Jamie wasn't surprised.

"You never cried for Marlene," the woman said. "Not properly. You know that?"

"I know."

She took him in her arms. She pulled him down onto the soft earth. His clothes loosened, then were gone. He rested his cheek on her left breast.

"Cry," she said.

He did. He sobbed until the rain came down and thunder cracked the sky like an archangel's sword. He cried until tears spattered his bare back and soaked the fresh ground. He cried, and when he was done, he was clean.

JAMIE AWOKE IN BRIGHT MORNING SUNLIGHT. HE WAS LYING, naked, in a field of flowers and fresh grass. Twenty feet beyond him, the culvert had become a bright stream. Pillowed beneath his head, the barrel was a fairy mound of lilies of the valley.

He squinted. A stag was bent over the stream, drinking. It lifted its head and watched him for a while. Then it leaped the stream and cantered around the small hill that had once been the factory where Jamie Barton had once earned three-thirty-five an hour, eight hours a day. Fresh-leaved saplings poked from the soil that covered it.

Jamie sat up. His clothes were lying on the grass. Reluctantly, he pulled them on. He realised he was smiling.

"You did well."

Jamie turned. The woman was alive in the sunlight. It sliced gold through her hair, caressed warmth deep in her bare skin.

"I knew you would," she said.

"Stay with me," Jamie said desperately. "Stay with me." He started towards her, hands reaching forward.

She gave him a sad smile. "That's not the way the story goes."

Jamie stopped still.

"What do you mean?"

"Bubbles on a pond," she said, coming close to him. "You float around. Sometimes you touch and join for a while. Sometimes you drift apart. Some bubbles pop. New ones form. That's the story the rain tells."

Jamie looked down. His feet sank deep in the silky new grass. "And what happens when the rain ends?"

She shrugged. "It ends. But if we work hard, it won't end anytime soon."

Jamie took a breath, then looked up. "What now?"

She took a step and kissed him on his forehead. "There's always work to do. There's always another pin to pull, another heart to mend." She stepped back again. "I said I would put in a good word for you. I did."

Jamie turned from her and gazed out over the industrial park. If he hadn't known better, he would have thought this had been wild forever, a corner of lush wilderness fenced off from the town. Where there had been concrete, there was now rich earth and grass, caught fresh in the morning sunlight. Where broken bricks had once piled over collapsed iron, carpets of flowers spilled. Jamie could smell something he thought might be wild garlic. Birds called in the chilly, damp air. Beyond the collapsed siding that surrounded the meadow, he saw windows opening in the nearby apartment blocks.

When he looked back, the woman was gone.

THE STREETS WERE WASHED CLEAN. THE RAIN HAD SWEPT AWAY every trace of dirt and trash. Windows glittered in homes and shops. The air was as pure as spring in the mountains.

From an apartment, Jamie heard laughter.

A group of kids raced around the corner, shouting joy.

Around him, as he walked, the town came to life.

He walked until he reached the edge of town. There he waited until a truck came by. He thumbed a lift and climbed in.

"Nice-looking day," the driver said.

"The best," Jamie said with a smile.

"So, where you going?"

"Somewhere ugly," Jamie said. "Anywhere."

SLIPPER OF GLASS

ABOUT THE STORY

I don't write a whole lot of fairy tale retellings. In fact, I think this may be one of only two I've done, the other being The Frog King, *which is not in this collection, but which you can read for free by subscribing to my newsletter. Fairy tales are living stories, retold over and over again to new generations, with new meanings, new angles, and new messages that fit the times and situations their readers find themselves in. This story takes the idea of living fairy-tales rather literally...*

SLIPPER OF GLASS

YOU NEVER KNOW FOR SURE WHAT A FAIRY TALE'S vulnerability is going to be. Yeah, sometimes you have a pretty good idea. With a fairy tale like this, nine times out of ten, if you take out the Cinderella, it all falls to pieces. Take her out, take her place, don't go to the ball. No Cinderella means no dance, no glass slipper on the step, no search through the country for the One True Foot, and – this is absolutely the key – no happily-ever-after. Job done. Town saved. All of that.

This time it isn't going to be that simple. I know that the moment they call me in on my night off. I've been out with Sian – she's our Snow Queen specialist, just like I'm the Cinderella specialist, and we only get the night off together once in a blue moon (and don't get me started on Blue Moons) – and we've both got pissed out of our skulls. When the F.I.S. drag me out of bed, I've only been asleep for a couple of hours and I'm at that midway point between drunk and hungover when you don't know whether you want to dance or hide under the covers but you do know you don't want some asshole in a suit interrupting you. I pop a couple of painkillers, down a bottle of water (refillable; I'm not a fucking monster), and lie out as comfortably as possible on the back seat of the car as it carries me into the night.

The official name of the F.I.S. is Department 23. Unofficially, and out of our hearing, we're known as the Little Bo Peeps. As far as I know, there are no departments one through 22. We aren't part of MI5 of MI6 or the Met Police or any of the other security services. Rumour has it that we're run out of a small, unassuming office somewhere in Whitehall with only 'Private' on the door. The story goes that if you're important enough to need to visit, you already know where it is.

I sleep intermittently on the car journey, helped by the fact that my driver and his companion insisted on talking about football for the entire journey, but it's still dark when we arrive. That isn't a good sign, either. Cinderellas are best handled in the daytime. By the time it reaches night, things are getting out of hand.

The F.I.S. have set up base in a couple of trailers a mile from the exclusion zone. Sometimes zones grow, and the last thing you want is to get the whole operation sucked in. There's something naggingly familiar about the lay-by we've occupied, but in the dark I can't pin it down. I've done enough insertions that by now they blur together.

The command trailer is already packed when I push the

door open. White walls, screens, people desperately poking at laptops. It isn't what a girl needs with a hangover.

"So," I announce. "Who fucked up?"

Marty Harrison looks up from where she's leaning over the shoulder of a tech. She's middle-aged, shaven-headed, and dressed in the kind of suit that could cut flesh. Marty was a Red Riding Hood specialist until the wolf took her arm off at the shoulder.

"Local," she says, shooting a glance at a balding man hunched in front of a laptop at the far end of the trailer.

I thought I looked bad after my night out, but this poor sod looks like he's falling to bits. It isn't hot in the trailer, but he's sweating.

"It came on fast," he protests.

"Of course it came on fast," Marty says. "It's the fucking Path." She turns back to me. "Stupid bastards missed the whole first day. By the time they cottoned on, the Cinderella was already on her way to the ball."

"Fuck," I say. It's not much of a contribution, but it sums it up nicely.

"Sorry I had to call you in. I know it's your night off."

"Yeah, no. I get it." Most of the time, any agent can do an insertion, but this late in the game, you need a specialist. "I bet the boys and girls with the guns are just itching to get involved."

The second trailer will be filled with the tactical squad. If everything else fails – and I mean *everything* – they will get their chance. But it's a last resort. Things can go very bad, very quickly when you send them in. The Path doesn't like it when you go hard against the story. That's why people like me exist. As far as I'm concerned, the tactical squad can stay in their trailer, fondling their weapons.

Marty looks me over. "You up to it?"

I nod, wincing as the movement sends pain spearing through my skull. "Nothing a few painkillers and a bit of makeup won't solve. And when I'm on the Path…"

"Yeah."

When I'm on the Path, none of it will matter anymore.

Everyone knows fairy tales. Cute, bedtime stories for kids. They've even made movies out of them, the stupid bastards. What people don't know and what the F.I.S. sincerely hope they never realise is that fairy tales aren't over. They keep coming back, like a bad case of herpes. Humanity is fertile soil. Fairy tales sprout over and over again. If they're allowed to play out they can take over completely. We call it the Path, because, left alone, the fairy tale will play out along a predetermined path until that's all that remains. At a best guess, we lost several dozen small European countries and a whole bunch of towns, cities, and counties to the Path before anyone figured out what was going on. The job of the F.I.S. is to get in there, disrupt the Path, and make the fairy tale collapse before it's too late.

Which, in this case, it almost is already.

I join Marty and peer over the tech's shoulder. The map of the town hits me like a bottle across the back of the head.

"Fuck me. Is that Bedford?"

Marty nods. "I know it's your hometown, and we wouldn't normally take the risk, but…" She shrugs.

"You need a specialist."

"We double-checked your file against our best intelligence," the tech says, without looking up. "You're clean."

The Path is dangerous for any insertion. An agent can get swept along and become part of the fairy tale, and the risk is only greater if there's some emotional attachment. That's why the F.I.S. makes sure they know everything there is to know about an agent. The interviews were ... extensive. The F.I.S. know every damned thing about me. Almost everything. There are a few things in my past that I keep to myself. Things that are just too traumatic to dredge up again. But they're nothing to do with my home town, and a girl has to have some secrets.

Attachment to the town I grew up in won't be an issue. I was never happy there. It isn't a bad town, I just didn't truly belong, and I don't have any family left. It's the kind of place to leave rather than come back to.

"Who's the Cinderella?"

The tech pulls up another screen.

"Maria Elaine Cole. Twenty five. Café worker."

I look at the photo. It's from a driving license, but there's nothing that stands out about her. Blonde hair, good skin, attractive in a bland sort of way. I don't recognise her. Cinderellas are always of a type. I don't look so different myself, when I'm not hungover. That's why I can insert into this fairy tale so well. The Path has its preferences.

"We think it's about nine o'clock in there right now," the tech says.

I grunt. Time runs oddly in a fairy tale. Nine o'clock

means three more hours of fairy tale time before the stroke of midnight when the Cinderella flees the ball. After that, the job will get a whole lot more difficult.

"Better get in there, then."

One of the things I like least about Cinderella insertions is the outfit. Don't get me wrong. There are times when wearing a dress in the shape of a wedding cake is appropriate, and I've learned how to move in it. It's the fucking slippers that do my head in. Who would wear slippers of glass? They're a fucking hazard. One wrong step, one slip, and you could end up with shards cutting right through your foot. How is that sexy?

Even if you don't slice yourself up like sashimi, the blisters will be something to behold.

"I know it's late in the game," Marty says as I pull on the layers of tight, frilly dress, "but it's still the usual run. Extract, replace. Don't fall in love."

I snort again. "Have you seen these guys?"

"And don't get cocky."

THE POLICE HAVE SET UP A ROAD BLOCK ON THE A6 ON THE edge of the exclusion zone. A tired looking copper holds up his hand as I step out of the car and approach.

"Road traffic accident," he calls. "Both directions. You're going to have to go back." He looks me up and down. "Hen night end early?"

"Fairy tale Investigation Squad," I say, holding up my I.D.

He smirks. Big mistake. He isn't taking into account my throbbing hangover. I push right up to him, ignoring the pain in my feet.

"You know what, kid?" He's the same age as me, maybe older. "There are things in fairy tales that would tear you and your fellow uniforms into bloody shreds. I've met them. I'm still here. Now step out of the way or you can be the one explaining to the Home Secretary why Bedford is no more than a footnote in some myth. Got me?"

I don't know if he's been briefed on the F.I.S. or whether he isn't up to dealing with angry, hungover refugees from a long night out, but he steps aside and lets me past.

You can always tell when you cross over the boundary into a fairy tale. There isn't necessarily any immediate change in the landscape, but there's a quickening to the air, a draw like something is plucking at you. Everyone in here will be feeling it. You don't have to be one of the principals in the story that has taken over the zone. You don't even have to feature in the fairy tale at all. But the Path still sweeps you along. Not many people can resist it, but I've had training.

By the time I reach the edge of town, the fairy tale has taken full grip. The brick and concrete houses that used to line the road have become cottages, barns, and pigsties. Pebbledash has become flaking, whitewashed daub. Garages, industrial estates, and car dealerships have become farms and mills. The tarmac road has narrowed to cobbles and mud. I can hear chickens complaining in a nearby coop and a cow lowing from what was an ALDI a couple of days ago.

My borrowed car fades as I reach the town. I know better

than to push my luck. I pull over and watch it fade to an abandoned cart slouched one wheel in a ditch. If I succeed, the car will be waiting. If I don't, well, it's not my car.

John Bunyan – the guy who wrote *The Pilgrim's Progress* and who made my life a misery one long summer holiday when I made the mistake of packing the damn book – was born in Bedford. Bet you didn't know that. In school, I never heard the end of it. Where he was born wasn't even part of Bedford back then, although the town has pretty much engulfed it now. People still go on about it. That tells you all you need to know about Bedford. Almost 400 years, and that's still the most exciting thing that's happened here.

Until now.

The Borough Council is usually an uninspired building on the banks of the Great Ouse. Not anymore. The Path has transformed it into a fairy tale castle, all spires and arches. Lines of carriages wait beneath bright lamps to one side of the flagstoned courtyard. I wonder idly which one of them is due to turn into a pumpkin in a couple of hours. It doesn't really matter. I will either have succeeded before then or the Path will have become unstoppable.

Men in elegant, long jackets and women in sparkling robes move elegantly up the steps or stand on balconies. I can hear the orchestra inside and the sweep of the music. Bedford has never been so glorious.

No. That's the Path speaking. I push it away. I'm not part of this story. I'm the stick in the bicycle's wheel, the screwdriver dropped into the cogs.

Inside is a whirl of movement, dancers spinning and

dipping, liveried servants moving through the crowds as elegantly as the dancers themselves. Until tonight, most of those people have probably never danced, but tonight the Path has them and they are as hypnotic as leaves in a gale.

I move around the edge of the grand ballroom. There are the two ugly stepsisters watching the dance with sour expressions. They probably aren't sisters. They probably never even met each other until the Path drew them into their roles. Tomorrow, they will cut off their own toes to fit into the glass slipper. It won't do them any good.

And there is the Cinderella, dancing with the long, tall figure of the Prince Charming. I can't see his face. He's staring down at her, black hair hiding him from view.

This is exactly why I was dragged out of bed on my night off. This is why it's a job for a specialist. The Cinderella has met her Prince Charming. They are dancing. The Path says they have already fallen in love. At midnight she will flee, leaving behind a glass slipper, and he will search the countryside – or the former Bedford, anyway – until he finds her. They will marry. The Path will have this town. It will be a fairy tale land. Everyone here will be trapped in their roles.

Not on my watch. I haven't lost one yet, and this isn't the first late insertion I've done. There will still be an opportunity to replace her. Most people would think it impossible. The Prince Charming and the Cinderella have been dancing for hours. Surely he will notice if his Cinderella is replaced? What's he been doing all night? Staring at her tits? But the truth is, she's just the role. The Path doesn't care who the Cinderella is, as long as there is one, and so neither does the

149

Prince Charming. I mean, despite supposedly falling in love, he won't recognise her tomorrow unless he can jam her foot in a glass slipper.

And while we're on that, take a hint, asshole. She runs away – literally flees – not even stopping to pick up her shoe, and you still don't leave her alone?

I draw closer to the dancing couple, taking care not to be seen. In her driving license photo, the Cinderella was someone you would pass by on the street. The Path has transformed her. She doesn't *look* different, but she is. There's an undeniable electric attraction that makes her the centre of the room. I study her, the way she moves, the way she glances at her Prince Charming, the curve of her lips. The Path won't give me many chances. They won't stop dancing to get a drink or take a piss. There's none of that in the fairy tale. They will dance until the chimes of midnight.

But every tune stops. It won't be a ball if there isn't that break for the dancers to change partners, return to the side lines, enter anew. In one of those breaks, the Prince Charming will lead his Cinderella out to the balcony to look out over his whole, glorious, glittering realm.

Soon. Soon. I haven't missed it yet. After that visit, she will dance closer, her eyes will be wider. Time will fade for her. The glass slippers will fly over the floor.

I cross to the double glass doors that lead to the balcony and stand, back towards them, listening to the music reach a crescendo then break. There is laughter, applause. And foot-steps approaching. A breathy laugh. The Path reaches past me, almost pushing me aside. I let myself move a step.

Then the Prince Charming is at the doors, leading the Cinderella.

Wait.

He takes a step through, then I move. I shove him, hard enough to break their grip, push the Cinderella backwards, and slam the doors closed between them, dropping the latch.

For a second, everything freezes. Dancers, music, the air in the room. But the Path won't be stopped so easily. I have only seconds before it finds a new way, before someone opens the doors, or the Prince Charming finds another route back, or the Path rearranges everything and they are dancing again.

In the stillness, I pull the Cinderella away, ducking behind drapes. Then I reach into my dress, pull out the syringe, flick off the protective cap, and pump enough tranquiliser into her to kill an elephant.

The first time I did that, I worried it would kill the Cinderella, but the Path is strong and it isn't her destiny to die this night. The Path *will* have her marry her prince.

I leave her there, unconscious, out of sight, and step back into view. The scene is coming back to life. Men and women are moving towards the closed doors. I get there first. I pull the doors open and step through to meet my Prince Charming, hand held out, lips slightly parted in laughter the way *hers* were, moving as elegantly and as smoothly as the fucking glass slippers and my fading hangover let me. For a moment, everything holds suspended. And then the Path begins to flow again. Later on, the Cinderella will wake, head aching from the tranquiliser and she will no longer be a

Cinderella. She will be part of the background. The Path has accepted me as a substitute. All I have to do is play out the role until I find the point of weakness, and then I can break this.

I feel the Prince Charming take my hand and I look up towards him.

This job is hard, stressful. No one can do it forever. The mental strain of resisting the Path takes its toll. I've heard some of the older agents talk about the Path turning its gaze upon you, as though it recognises you and finally decides to move against you. Until now, I thought that was superstition.

Dark eyes meet mine, and suddenly I realise I should have listened, because I know those eyes. I know them. Somewhere deep in the back of my head, I'm screaming, but it's too late. The Prince Charming has led me back inside. We are dancing, and the Path has taken me.

When you join the F.I.S., they find out everything about you. Everyone you ever knew, everything you did, everywhere you've ever been. You can't be sent in to a fairy tale if you have a personal connection to any of the principals, because that leaves an opening for the Path.

I told the F.I.S. everything. Everything except this. I didn't tell them this, because the memory hurt too much. And because Ryan Paxton is dead.

The Path has turned its gaze on me. It has been waiting. It has been ready. And now I belong to the Path.

I have often wondered what it is like to be taken by the Path. Is it a dream, or a blackness you never notice? Is it death? Now I know. I'm still there, in the back of my head, but all I can do is scream silently, while my body dances, glowing, hangover forgotten, pressed close to the Prince Charming, smiling, laughing, following the Path all the way to the end.

You're dead, I scream into my mind. *You can't be here. You're dead.*

I met Ryan Paxton when I was nineteen years old. I was studying geology and we were been on a field trip to the Isle of Skye. I met him there, and he died, and I only knew him for four days.

Now he is here, dancing with me. The Path can't do that, it can't bring someone back from the dead. But somehow it found him and brought him here to wait for me. The Path is a snake, twisting out through the world, sliding, searching, its coils engulfing.

We dance, flowing like water, like candle flames. I don't feel tired, the hard glass slippers don't hurt or slide on the polished floor. The Path won't allow it. We swoop away. It's seductive, encompassing, inevitable.

I don't know if I was in love with Ryan Paxton. Four days is too short for love. Not for passion or for idiocy, but for love, I think. But we clicked. He was American, on vacation, he said, tracing his ancestors, but there was something else there. He didn't want me to tell anyone about him, and I never did. It was on the night before the last day that he finally told me he was fleeing an abusive family and it all made sense. But he was poor. He had run up debts to get out of there. He didn't know how much longer he could stay away. I believed him. I had money, inherited from my grandmother to pay for my education. I paid off his debts, helped him out. Why not? We had time. He would pay me back.

And then he was gone. I was out, doing fieldwork. He went kayaking, intending to paddle up the west coast of the island. He was an experienced kayaker. But the day was rough, the tides and currents could be challenging, and he never returned.

Later – much later – I sent a letter to the address I found in his belongings. I only received a terse note in reply instructing me never to contact the family again.

I respected his wishes and never told anyone about him, not even the F.I.S., even though I should have told them everything.

And the dance goes on. It doesn't matter that inside I'm screaming, raging, confused. The power the fairy tale feeds on is deep in the roots of every person. When it takes you, there's nothing you can do. So we dance. Around us there are glittering lights, bird-bright dresses, the flash of jewels. I don't notice any of it. I am the Cinderella. He is the Prince Charming. We have a story to tell. You can never underestimate the power of a story.

Then I hear it. The first chime of midnight.

The dance breaks. I step away, one hand still clasped in his, pulling, our fingers brushing like razorblades.

I'm running through the ballroom, out the doors, down the steps. My foot slips. One of the slippers flies free. I don't stop to grab it. The bells are chiming. My path is set.

As I reach my carriage – I no longer have to wonder

which one it is – the Prince Charming appears at the top of the steps.

"I will come for you," he calls after me. It sounds like a threat.

The carriage turns into a pumpkin and a cluster of confused rodents a mile from the palace. I trudge the rest of the way back to the Cinderella's home. I doubt I could place it on a map. Both time and space deform under the primal power of fairy tale.

I often wondered what it would be like in here if the Path was allowed to reach its conclusion. I know what it will be like from the outside. The town will be gone, removed from reality as though it never existed except in a fairy tale. You could drive up the A6 or boat down the Great Ouse and it just won't be there. It never will have been. Hell, maybe that will mean no John Bunyan and no tedious *Pilgrim's Progress* to suffer through. A win for the wider world. But in here? Will it just fade, whispering away like mist? Or will it continue on, all happily-ever-after, drifting, loose from its moorings, untethered from the world?

I guess I'll find out.

MY BODY AWAKES TO A VISCERAL EXCITEMENT. THERE ARE voices downstairs. The Path is nearing its end. My mind has been awake, thinking, impotently.

The Path cannot bring back the dead. It is the power of fairy tales, but Ryan Paxton died in the real world, not in a fairy tale.

The Path couldn't change that. And that leaves me with one very clear conclusion, no matter how hard I try to avoid it: Ryan Paxton didn't die in the harsh Atlantic waters. He didn't die at all. He preyed on nineteen-year-old me, took my money, and faked his death. I gave him almost fifty thousand pounds and I didn't suspect a thing. I didn't even mention him to anyone. I thought I was protecting him. But now he is here, swept up by the Path, just like me, and our parts in this tale are almost done.

By now the F.I.S. will know I've failed. They will have sent in the tactical boys and girls. People will die. They will fail, too. The Path will reach its end.

They teach you to resist the Path when you join the F.I.S., to anchor yourself in reality so the fairy tale can't take you. It's brutal. It's psychological torture. But if you survive it, you can do this job. Unless you have a vulnerability, that personal connection that twines between reality and fairy tale. In my case, it's Ryan Paxton, the Prince Charming.

Oh, but the Path is clever.

From the kitchen downstairs I hear one dull thunk, a scream, then another thunk and another scream.

I know what that is. It's the first of the ugly stepsisters having her toes cut off. The Cinderella's stepmother is so desperate for one of her daughters to marry the Prince Charming that she'll mutilate them for the chance. If only the Prince Charming could remember his Cinderella's face, none of this would be necessary.

In the fairy tale, the Cinderella is up early every day, cleaning, cooking, mending. But on the morning after the ball she is allowed to sleep in. The stepsisters have to face the Prince Charming first and fail. It has to be bloody and painful. Fairy tales aren't for kids.

My body dresses. It's all rags and worn cloth slippers. Soon, against her will, the Cinderella's stepmother will be forced to bring out the Cinderella, too, to be tried for the slipper.

A wail of anguish sounds as the first stepsister is rejected. Two more thunks of the heavy kitchen cleaver. Quiet voices. Time passes. A scream. Voices arguing, then a reluctant tread on the stairs.

The Cinderella has been waiting. I rise, descend the stairs, serene despite the rage inside me.

I wonder if Ryan Paxton is looking out of the Prince Charming's eyes, too. Or is it just the remnants of my F.I.S. training that keep me aware in here, locked in, a prisoner behind the iron bars of my body? Would he even remember me?

He is standing in the entrance hall of the house. The two step-sisters are huddled together to one side, arms around each other, sobbing. Bloody footprints cross the floor to where the Prince Charming stands, smiling, tentative. Charming. I'm not feeling fucking charmed. The Cinderella is, though. She's not noticing her bleeding step-sisters. She only has eyes for the Prince Charming.

Our eyes meet. Is that recognition or just my imagination? If it is, there's no regret or guilt. I wonder if he ever feels those.

If the slipper is placed on my foot, this is over. No intervention will be enough to stop it.

Somewhere, distant, I hear gunshots. The tactical team. They won't reach here in time, if they reach here at all. The Path has its defences.

The Prince Charming is holding the glass slipper towards me like a pizza delivery.

I never liked pizza.

Ryan Paxton didn't die. He charmed me, he got me to pay off his debts, then he disappeared and let me think he was dead. I feel the rage growing in me, unable to get out. I wonder, helplessly, whether I will explode like a pressure cooker without a safety valve. Splatter my blood and flesh and skin over his smug, expectant face. I would like to see the Path deal with that.

He kneels in front of me, holding the glass slipper up, waiting for me to offer my foot.

The Path found my weakness, the one connection I never told the F.I.S. about, and it used it. But it made a mistake.

My connection was to the man who died in the sea, swept to his death, the man I had almost fallen in love with, who I tried to save from an abusive family. He had been my weakness. But now the Path has done me a favour. Ryan Paxton was never my Prince Charming. The man I was connected to never existed. This man in front of me, this Prince Charming chosen by the Path, is not someone I'm connected to. He's not my weakness.

I am an agent of the F.I.S., an accredited Little fucking Bo-peep. I have been trained for this.

I channel my anger into a single blow that sends the glass slipper spinning from his hand. It hits the floor and shatters.

For a moment, again, the Path freezes as it looks for a new way through the fairy tale. It will find one. I don't give it the chance.

I grab a shard of the broken slipper.

"You're dead," I tell Ryan Paxton. I don't know if he can hear me in there. "You've been dead for ten years." Maybe this is justice, karma. Maybe it's another Path.

I plunge the glass into his neck.

IF THERE'S ONE THING I'VE NEVER ENJOYED, ESPECIALLY WHEN A job goes wrong, it's the debrief. The truth is, you never know what a fairy tale's vulnerability is going to be when you go in. People die. People get hurt. But more often than not, we stop the Path.

This time we lost half a dozen of the tactical boys and girls in a firefight with ... something ... three streets away. The Path has a lot of nightmares to draw on. That's why we go with insertions rather than brute force whenever we can.

"His name was Simon Eagleton," Marty says, looking up from her file. At my confusion, she adds, "The Prince Charming. He was a conman. Half a dozen warrants out for him. He conned young women out of their savings. No one is going to miss him."

Except me. I won't miss the conman who left me guilty and bereft, but I will miss the fairy tale of Ryan Paxton.

Marty slaps her file closed. "Considering how late the insertion was, you did well." She must be able to tell something of what I'm feeling, because she tilts her head to one side. "We all get caught by the Path in the end." She indicates her missing arm. "Not many of us have the discipline to get ourselves out unharmed." She pushes her chair back, looking exhausted. "Get some rest. Back to work tomorrow. Something's brewing in Leeds. We might need you up there."

THE EQUATION

ABOUT THE STORY

This story started out as a dream I had just before Christmas in 2010. Dreams don't often stay with me, but this one did, and I couldn't shake it. My wife, Steph, had been asking me to write her a short story for Christmas, and now it was Christmas Eve, so I sat down, put Freebird *on repeat, and wrote* The Equation. *(Its original title was* The Cold Equation, *but it turned out that there's a super-famous-if-ethically-dubious story with that title already, so I went with* The Equation.*)*

Steph and I have a long tradition of writing stories for each other for Christmas, although we've managed it less often since we had kids. This is her favourite of those stories.

THE EQUATION

"Oh. My. God!"

I'm standing in the Fire House Café, ordering a pot of tea – Sencha, one teaspoon, steep for three minutes – when the voice speaks right behind me.

I turn and she's standing there. Rachel Clay.

I'd be lying if I didn't say my heart stopped for just a second.

I haven't seen Rachel for eleven years. When we were sixteen, we were in Miss Haversham's science class at school. Rachel was bright, top of the class, small, cute, with blonde hair that was never really under control. We shared a kiss one night on the way home and danced together in the moonlight. What can I say? It was 1999. It was the best kiss of my life.

I left school soon after, and we never met again.

Now here she is, right behind me. I didn't think it would

be such a shock, so visceral. If she was cute when she was sixteen, she's as hot as fire right now. She's wearing geek glasses, but she still hasn't got that hair under control.

I'm too dumbstruck to say anything, so it's a good thing she just keeps on going.

"Cameron Everett. Oh my god. I was standing there in line and I saw you and I thought it can't be but... Hi."

She's blushing now. God, I used to get so turned on when she blushed.

Looks like she hasn't lost that magic.

I hurriedly turn away and scoop up my tea.

"Hi," I say. Original. "Look, can I get you a drink?"

WE FIND A TABLE UPSTAIRS, AWAY FROM ANYONE ELSE, ALMOST enveloped by an overgrown pot plant. I like to be close to living things. I sink back into the soft chair and look up at Rachel.

"So, do you keep in touch with anyone else?" I ask, more for something to say than because I'm interested. I never wanted to keep in touch with anyone from school, myself. Except Rachel, that is, and I didn't have the nerve for that back then.

Her answer knocks me back for the second time today. "Everyone," she says.

"Everyone?" I say. "Everyone in our class?"

She looks at the table, as though there's something interesting written there. "Yeah. Everyone except you." She fires a little, nervous glance.

I don't know what to say. "Okay," fills the gap.

"You disappeared," she says. "I wanted to, but..."

"It's okay," I say. "I had ... things to do. Like in the song."

"The song?"

"*Freebird.*"

She looks puzzled.

"Don't worry about it," I say. I played that song to her on the night we kissed, when we were sixteen and the moonlight was shining down and I'd just discovered Lynyrd Skynyrd. Guess it didn't make the same impact on her. Maybe I should have played her some Thin Lizzy instead. "So," I say. "What are you doing these days? Are you married? Kids?"

She blushes again. "Me?"

I can't help but feel a slight flush of warmth, but whether it's from her blush or the fact that she's not married, I'm not sure.

"How about work? You must have gone to Uni, right?"

She nods. Then she glances around. No one is close enough to hear, but she leans forward and drops her voice anyway.

"I'm working for Miss Haversham now."

I act surprised. "Miss Haversham? Our science teacher? Doing what?"

"Oh, computers," she says vaguely.

I grin. "Well, that figures. Science was always your favourite subject. Computers are the new science, right?"

She laughs. Her fingers brush back her loose hair. It's the same nervous gesture I remember from that night we kissed. I experience the overwhelming urge to lean forward and kiss her again. Somehow, I control myself.

But she's not finished with the shocks for the night.

"We all work for Miss Haversham."

That one does hit me with genuine surprise. "Excuse me?" I say.

"All our class. Well, except you." She glances around again. "I shouldn't be telling you this."

"Except me again, huh?" I grin, but it feels lopsided. I feel obscurely offended that I'm the only one not to be offered a job. Not that I'd work for Miss Haversham in a million years, but it's the principle of the thing. "What on Earth does she want everyone for? John Peters, too? He could hardly tie his shoelaces."

I should have known this. I thought I knew enough. For the first time today, I feel nervous.

"There's stuff he can do," Rachel says.

"So, what, is Miss Haversham running the school now?"

"Something like that."

Something like that. It's one way to put it. "Huh. She never really liked me, I guess."

"It was the leather jacket," Rachel says.

"This?" I still have the jacket. I'm still wearing it. It fits better now than it did when I found it in the market twelve years ago. "What, is she some kind of vegetarian or something?"

"No. It's just..." Rachel shakes her head. "She likes

166

smartly dressed. You never did smart. Look, can we talk about something else?"

"Sure, sure," I say, then, "What, even Harriet Martin?"

"Cam..."

"Sorry. So you're all working for Miss Haversham. A bit weird, but..."

"And how about you? What have you been up to?" She cups her hands around her latté, and leans forward, eyes fixed on me.

"I travelled around a bit," I say. "Peru. Georgia. Zimbabwe. Tibet. Kashmir. The Balkans. You know."

"Wow," she says, and she sounds impressed. "Doing what?"

"This and that," I say. Not a lot of details, admittedly, but details are exactly what she's not getting. Not one of Miss Haversham's brood. She'll figure out what she needs to know soon enough. I'm hardly going to help her along.

"Sounds fun."

I shrug. "It's been interesting."

"I've thought about you," Rachel says. "From time to time. We had...a good time."

I grin, and it's genuine. "Yeah. We did."

She pulls out a pen and starts doodling on a napkin, not really watching what she's doing. I can't see what she's drawing. Her hand is in the way.

"So, do you still live here?" I say. "In Bristol?"

"Yeah. I've got a little flat in Clifton. It's not much, but it's cosy. Maybe sometime..." She doesn't finish the sentence.

"Miss Haversham must pay well," I say, not answering the unspoken question. "I should have got into computers."

There are other people in the café, at other tables, talking and laughing, but I scarcely notice them. Normally I notice everything.

"It's never too late to learn," Rachel says. "I could give you some pointers. You'd be good at it."

"I don't think so," I say, smiling to show it's not a rejection. "I've got wandering feet." I whistle a couple of notes from *Freebird*.

She frowns, but she still doesn't get it.

"And you wandered back this way," she says. "Any reason?"

I shrug. "Curious, I guess. I haven't been back here for years."

"Been past the old school yet?" I'd forgotten how intense her eyes could be, even behind her glasses.

"Not yet," I say.

"I could show you."

"Is that where you work?" As though I don't know.

"No," she says. "Miss Haversham's got her own place now."

"Sounds interesting."

She sighs, and her pen stills on the napkin for a moment.

"We know who you are, Cam," she says.

Ah.

I guess we're done dancing.

She must know almost all she needs to. She wouldn't let on otherwise. She's quick. I shouldn't be surprised.

For a moment, I'm hit by a feeling of inexpressible sadness. This has been good. It was like these last eleven years never happened, like we were back in the moonlight, just before we kissed, standing only a centimetre away from each other, the air between us electric and frightening and raging with teenage desire.

"Why?" Rachel leans forward, her face genuinely anguished. "Why would you do it, Cam? They call you 'Dark Angel', you know. You were never cut out to be a villain."

"Is that what you think I am?" I say, hurt, even though she could hardly think anything else if she's with Miss Haversham. "A villain?"

"What are you then?"

"I'm a fucking hero."

She winces. I'd forgotten she hated swearing.

When she speaks again, her expression is more distant, more...professional. I don't like it. If I've made the wrong move, this could all be over. "The world's all grown up now, Cam," she says. "You're not sixteen with Che posters all over your wall. Everything's changed."

"Has it?"

"Yes. I've heard about you. I've heard what you've been doing. They say you were there during a dozen bloodbaths." Her hand clenches into a white fist. "I know you wanted to save the world, but all you're doing is getting people killed. Maybe you don't mean to, but it's what happens. Those places you go, those trouble spots, you make them worse." She's earnest, flushed, leaning towards me. Her eyes are oak-brown behind her glasses. "There are other ways of saving the world, Cam. Our ways. Ways that work. It's time to come in from the cold."

I laugh. "Do people actually say that?"

"I'm serious!"

"I know." I wish she wasn't. She didn't used to be. Back then, back when we were sixteen and in the moonlight, I loved Rachel Clay.

"Your coffee's getting cold," I say. I lean forwards and touch her cup. A spark jumps from my fingertip to the cup, and the next moment, her coffee is steaming again.

It's not much, but she yelps and jumps back. "Don't do that!"

I shrug. "Why not?"

"It's *wrong*."

"It's just coffee," I say. "I promise."

Slowly, she picks it up and takes a sip. "It's good," she says, reluctantly.

"Nothing to do with me," I say. "They make good coffee here."

"Cam," Rachel says, unwilling to let go, "We're doing important work. You could be part of that. Miss Haversham won't hold grudges. She can give you a clean slate. That's what she always used to say in class, remember? We start with a clean slate?"

I'm shaking my head before she finishes.

"You said those places I go to are trouble spots, and I know that's how Miss Haversham sees them, but they're not. They're places where people haven't forgotten their culture and traditions." I hold her gaze. I can't afford to lose her now.

"There's still magic in those places. Real magic. People like Miss Haversham can't stand it. They want to crush it and make it as though it's never been. Are you surprised there's conflict? It's the Miss Havershams of this world who are to blame, not me."

This time, Rachel is the one shaking her head.

"You're wrong. We just want peace. Those superstitions, those legends, those myths, they're what make people hate each other." She's forgotten her coffee again. "They're not worth it. All Miss Haversham wants to do – all any of us want to do – is make people see the world in a rational light. Can't you see that if people give up on those myths, they won't have any reason to fight anymore? They'll have better lives. Happier lives." She draws a breath. "You could help us."

She's intent, determined, passionate, focused on me, but the whole time, her pen is still rushing across the napkin.

"The world used to be different, you know," I say.

I ease back, feeling the leaves of the pot plant brush against the nape of my neck. I can taste the energy in them, still wild, but hidden, almost crushed.

"Magic used to be everywhere," I say. "In the streams and the woods and the villages. Everyone was full of it. Every*thing* was full of it. Gods cracked the sky with thunder. Wild spirits hid in the bark of trees. When someone spoke, magic flowed. Every myth and fairy tale was alive. Glance around, and it was glittering, wild and untamed. Until the Miss Havershams killed it, made it just stories for children, to be laughed at and forgotten."

"Sometimes..." Rachel starts, her voice quiet. "Sometimes

there's a price for peace."

Right on cue, *Freebird* starts playing over the café's speakers. I hum along to the first few bars. This time, now that it's playing, Rachel recognises it. Her eyes widen.

I chose this café for a reason. Alex Cornwell, the owner, is a friend of mine. I don't have many of those. He knows the truth.

"That time," I say, "in the moonlight, when we danced and kissed. That was the first time I felt magic. You felt it too. I *felt* you feel it."

"They'll never let you walk out of here alive," Rachel whispers, and there are genuine tears in her eyes. "Not if you don't come in with me. Not even you can escape this one, Cam."

"I can if you let me," I say.

"What?"

"Don't do it," I say. I lay a finger on the hand holding her pen. It's not enough to stop her if she doesn't want me to, just enough to make her pause.

I know what she's been doing here. She's been watching. She's been learning me, understanding my magic, working it out, seeing how it all fits together. And she's been writing it down. The cold equation.

Magic can't survive logic. It can't survive explanations. Once it's understood, it's not magic anymore. It's dead. That's how people like Miss Haversham have killed magic, by writing it down and turning it into something that makes sense and can be understood. They've turned it all into numbers and logic. Into cold, hard equations. One piece of magic at a time, they've written it down, until almost all of it has gone.

Rachel has been creating my own cold equation, the one that will rob me of magic and make me ordinary, turn me into another Miss Haversham.

"Miss Haversham chose you because you knew me," I say.

Rachel shakes her head. "I volunteered."

I smile. Over the speakers, that blistering guitar solo kicks in.

"Miss Haversham never knew, did she?" I say. "You didn't tell her that you tasted magic that one night."

"No," Rachel whispers.

"She never found out that magic was within you."

"No."

"She never wrote down your cold equation. She never knew she had to."

"No." I can scarcely hear her now.

"From the moment you showed me magic that first time," I say, "I've travelled the world, gathering every shard I could find, all those last fragments hidden out of sight of the rational world." There's magic in hate and love and passion, in awe and fear, in a baby crying, in an old man's last breath. It hides in the rawness of the world. Little, lost fragments, holding on. Without it, there's nothing. No beauty, no music, nothing to truly live for. "I can bring magic back to the world," I say. "I'm ready. But I can't do it alone. I need you, Rachel." She was my source, the core on which all the rest has grown.

With a twist of my fingers and a couple of words muttered under my breath, I cast a cantrip. Something I learned in a small Siberian village that the rest of the world had forgotten, an unveiling charm. It spreads out, unnoticed, passing like a sigh through the walls of the café.

The charm shows them to me. Two hunched in the doorway of the Starbucks opposite, trying to keep out of the cold wind. Another couple in an empty office above the Starbucks, peering down their rifle sights. Three of them out the back, in the shelter of the bins. Others mingling with the shopping crowds, trying to look inconspicuous. Even a few in the café downstairs, pretending to read papers. The whole of Miss Haversham's science class is there.

For a time, when I was sixteen, I could have been one of them.

The cantrip shows me Miss Haversham too, cold, featureless, white ice against the wintry day, not trying to hide. They are all waiting for that one last stroke of Rachel's pen that will finish the cold equation.

That cantrip may be the last magic I ever do.

"I can bring back the moonlight," I say. "With you."

For a moment, the world waits, not breathing.

Then, slowly, without looking at me, Rachel's hand closes over the napkin, scrunching it up. She lifts it and drops the cold equation into the still warm coffee.

She takes my hand, tears in her eyes.

I open a door in the air. There's moonlight behind it.

We step through, leaving the music behind us, playing to our empty table.

WHEN THE DRAGON FALLS

ABOUT THE STORY

Oddly, I have no recollection of what inspired me to write When the Dragon Falls, *nor what I was doing at the time. I was writing quite a few short stories during the period that this was written, and a lot of them were being published by the late, lamented magazine* Realms of Fantasy.

Sometimes you come across an editor whose taste matches yours perfectly, and Shawna McCarthy, the editor of Realms of Fantasy *was that editor for me.* Realms of Fantasy *stopped publishing about the same time as I mostly stopped writing short stories. We'll all just pretend that was a coincidence.*

WHEN THE DRAGON FALLS

I.

TAM FOUND THE FOSSIL JUTTING FROM THE CRUMBLING SLOPE above the lake.

The day was hot, the air thick with humidity and gnats. Chasing along the trails had left Tam red faced and sweaty. So he thrust through the tangle of hawthorn and started down the slope towards the glass-flat lake.

The fossil was in full view. The slate had slipped away, and the long, fossilised bone stared up at him.

The others gathered around quickly.

"A dragon," gasped five-year-old Rosie, wide-eyed. She was the youngest of them, and she had tagged along all morning like a burr in a dog's tail.

"A dinosaur," Josh said. At thirteen, a full year older than Tam, Josh knew everything.

Tam wasn't so sure. He didn't know what it was, but he did know one thing. He had found it. It was his.

Lisa rolled her eyes and stepped over the fossil. "Are we going swimming or not?" Her long hair was stuck to her sweaty neck.

"Not yet," Tam said, dropping to his knees. The fossilised bone ridged from a bed of dark grey slate. The same bed disappeared beneath the loose scree a couple of yards further up the slope. Tam brushed the fragments away with his hand. "There could be more of it."

"God, who cares?" Lisa said. "It's just a bone."

2.

There were sounds in the night, and shapes that flitted across Tam's peripheral vision, and lights that blinked and were gone before he could focus on them. *Bats chasing fireflies across the lake*, he told himself. But he got up from his sweat-damp sheets and crossed the room to the window, and watched the flickering lights and flitting shapes and listened to the sounds, because they might not be. They still might not be.

3.

"Who's for swimming?" Tam's dad said.

Rosie jumped up from the breakfast table, sending eggshell scattering across the wood. "Me. Me. I'm going to wear my mermaid costume and swim *under*water for a mile."

Tam's dad laughed.

"Anyone else? How about you, Tam? Lisa? Josh?"

They all nodded.

"Good," Tam's dad said, rubbing his hands. "It's going to be a scorcher. We'll swim and play football and see who can build the biggest sandcastle."

Tam's mum eased herself from the table. "Not me and Dan," she said. "We're going for a hike."

"Again, Maria?" Tam's dad said.

Tam's mum tightened her lips. "Yes, again. We *like* hiking. At least Dan doesn't just sit around all day letting himself get fat."

"Maria..."

Rosie pushed in between them. "Can I come hiking too, Mum? Oh, please."

"No, petal," Tam's mum said. "You go to the beach with your father."

Rosie's face fell, her round cheeks pouted out. Tam knew what would happen next. Tears and a tantrum and a day of sulks. "Why not?" Rosie said.

"You couldn't keep up. Not where we're going."

"Yes, I could, I—"

Tam's dad scooped Rosie up. "The lake'll be more fun, rosebud." He rubbed his greying beard against her neck until she giggled. Then he looked across at Josh and Lisa's mum. "Just you, me, and the kids, Annie. Again."

4·

"Why does my Mummy keep going for hikes with your daddy?" Rosie said.

Josh splashed water at her. "You're too young to understand. You're just a kid."

"I am not!" Rosie shrieked, her face turning red. "*You* don't know *either*."

Tam glanced up the beach to where his dad was sitting a couple of feet from Josh and Lisa's mum. They were talking quietly, staring out over the silver-rippled lake, arms wrapped around their own knees, not touching, not looking at each other.

"Tam knows," Josh said. "He's not a sprat anymore. Don't you, Tam?"

Tam felt his cheeks redden. "Of course," he said, furious that he didn't. "I'm not a kid." He splashed towards the shore. "It's too hot down here. I'm going to ask if I can go and look at my fossil."

5.

The fossil was dark grey on dark grey rock, but Tam could see it clearly, nonetheless. When he ran his fingers over it, he could feel the grain in the ancient bone-impression. A bit at a time, he cleared away loose stone and dirt with his fingers.

The bone was thicker than his arm, and the exposed section was as long as Tam if he lay down and stretched his arms over his head. It must have been an enormous beast, whatever it had been. And still the bone sank into the slope.

He stuck his fingers into a crack in the slate and tried to lever it up and snap it off.

His nail bent back, and Tam let out a pained gasp. A drop of blood welled from beneath the nail. Tam watched, fascinated, as it fell from his finger onto the fossil and spread along the grain.

The fierce sun beat on his bare neck and thin T-shirt. Sweat dripped over his nose and into his mouth.

"It *could* be a dragon," Rosie said.

Tam looked up. His little sister came slipping and sliding down the scree slope, still in her swimsuit with the little mermaid waving from it.

"Maybe," Tam said. "Does Dad know you're here?"

"They're *all* coming," Rosie said. "Dad says you've been here for too long, and it's time for lunch. You've been *hours*."

Tam took one last look at the fossil. Where it entered the rock, it seemed to widen slightly, as though the bone was coming to an end.

6.

"I dreamed about the dragon," Rosie said. She was tucked up in her bed, her sheet pulled up tight beneath her chin.

"When?" Tam said.

"Last night," Rosie said. "And when I woke up, there were dragons flying over the lake."

Tam ruffled her hair. "You were still dreaming."

"No I wasn't. If you'd been awake you would have seen

181

them too, but you weren't. You were probably snoring with your mouth open wide to catch the moths."

"Go to sleep," Tam said.

"I will," Rosie said. "And I'll dream of the dragon again. It was defending its eggs against the fairies. *That's* how it got caught and died. The fairies have got teeth like pins, and there's thousands of them, and they like to bite. But the eggs hatched and the babies swam away while the mummy dragon stopped the fairies from catching them."

7.

Tam dreamed, but in his dream there was no dragon. The dinosaur was vast, longer than a bus, heavier than a whale. Its long neck arced over the swamp, dipped down to strip the leaves from a low fern. Its eyes, small and half blind, did not see the quick movements among the deep vegetation beside the swamp, but Tam did. He wanted to shout out. He wanted to tell it to fly and to breathe fire, but it could not. It was only a dinosaur, a slow, dull dinosaur.

"You're a dragon," Tam yelled, while his sleeping body dripped sweat. "You're a dragon."

Something came rushing from the vegetation, something smaller, with tearing teeth and long jaws. Its teeth sliced into the dinosaur's leg, ripped. The dinosaur let out a moan like a slow foghorn and took a plodding step forward. Its massive tail lashed around, but by then there were a dozen more predators upon it, shredding, slicing, biting. Blood slipped into the stagnant Precambrian water.

8.

"Do you remember how we caught a fairy last year?" Rosie said.

Tam wiped his sleeve across his forehead. The heat was near unbearable, the humidity total. When he tugged at the splintering rock, his fingers slipped.

"No, we didn't," Tam said. "There's no such thing as fairies."

"We did," Rosie insisted. "You're just saying that so Josh and Lisa won't laugh at you. It was floating through the woods near the stream. You caught it by the back of its neck so it couldn't bite you, and you made it give you a wish. You wished you could be all grown up like Josh and Lisa. That was silly. Why would anyone want to be grown up and *boring*?"

Now Tam remembered. It had twisted and turned and darted, even though there had been no breeze. He had chased it and leapt and laughed and then trapped it between his fingers. He had breathed upon it, kissed it, wished...

"It was just thistledown. It's a seed. I learned that in school. We pretended it was a fairy. It was a kids' game."

9.

He cracked away the layers of slate with a knife he had snuck from the kitchen. The large bone ended, but there were other fossils in the same bed of slate. There was something that could have been a claw, and some thinner bones that stretched back further again, into the slope.

"That's its wing," Rosie said confidently from where she lounged higher on the slope.

"Go and swim," Tam said.

Rosie made a face. "Dad made Mum go to the beach with him today, and she's being all grumpy. It's no fun. Anyway, I want to see the dragon."

10.

He had never noticed how they looked at each other before, but he noticed at dinner that night. His mum kept sneaking glances at Josh and Lisa's dad. Tam's dad was growing steadily more pale. His knife and fork clattered and clashed on the willow-pattern china.

Rosie didn't notice any of it. She just kept chattering on about her dragon.

Tam's dad slammed down his cutlery. "For Heaven's sake, Rosie, shut up."

"Don't take it out on her," Tam's mum flared up.

Rosie burst into tears.

"Rosie!" both parents snapped.

11.

Tam tucked Rosie into bed.

"Why are Mummy and Daddy being so mean?" she said.

"They're having a few problems," Tam said. He brushed a

hand over her light hair. "Nothing to worry a sprat like you. It'll all be all right." It had to be. Tam curled himself up beside Rosie on the bed and closed his eyes.

"If *I* was a dragon," Rosie said, "I wouldn't let anyone be mean to anyone, and if they were I'd gobble them up."

12.

A warm breath woke Tam. At first he thought it was just the stifling night air, but then it seemed more than that. It felt like heat from rock in the midday sun. The lake would have cooled quicker than the surrounding earth. The breeze should have been cool.

Strange light strobed the cabin, cold sounds shivered into his bones.

He pulled up his sheet. He didn't want to know, wanted to know.

The angry heat was like a fever.

That was all it was. A fever. No more.

13.

"I saw your mum with my dad last night," Lisa said. "Outside."

They were standing in the shallows of the lake, up to their waists in the warm, still water. The hard sun beat upon Tam's bare back.

"Do you want to know what they were doing?" Lisa said.

"What?" Tam said, not wanting to know.

Lisa's tight arms wrapped around him. "This." She kissed him.

14.

He worked like fire in dry grass, fast, angry, violent. Chips of slate flew from the screwdriver he had taken from the cabin. *Din-o-saur, dra-gon, din-o-saur, dra-gon.* His blows hammered down to the beat of the syllables.

The slate was hard but brittle, cracking along its faults, coming away with every blow.

A larger bone was emerging. His screwdriver should have shattered and scarred it, turned the fossil into unrecognisable fragments. But fate and need and fury guided his hand. Inch by inch, the giant fossil emerged. Inch by too-slow inch.

15.

A small hand tugged Tam awake. Night was thick upon the cabin. The shy moon flirted behind slipping clouds.

"I want to show you something," Rosie whispered.

"Go back to bed," Tam muttered, turning over.

Rosie persisted. "You need to see it. You need to believe." Then, "I can stay here all night."

Tam sighed. He swung himself out of bed, pulled on a T-shirt, jeans, and sneakers.

Rosie was still dressed in her nightshirt. A dry leaf was caught on it. Her bare feet were dirty.

"Where are we going?"

Rosie held up a finger to her lips. "Shh. Outside." She turned and padded from the room. Tam followed her.

She was quick in the night, like a will-o-the-wisp, as she threaded her way up the slope behind the cabin.

Eventually, they reached the ridge. Rosie motioned him down. He dropped into a crouch.

"There." Rosie pointed.

Through the dark trees, sharp lights slipped and rose.

"And there." She directed his gaze up.

Black shapes moved across the face of the moon, like the flap of giant wings.

"The fairies are hunting the dragons again," Rosie whispered. "They want to steal the gold in their eyes and the gems in their scales."

Still the lights flowed, hurrying through the trees, rising towards the sky, red and white slivers in the night. Tam heard a breath like wind in the trees. The treetops shook and bent. For a second, the moon was obscured. Sharp teeth and scales glittered in the sky. Tam dared not breathe. His heart thundered like the hooves of fairy steeds, like—

Raised, angry, adult voices came from the cabin behind them, then footsteps on floorboards. The cabin door slammed. Car doors opened, thumped shut. The engine, starting loud, headlights springing on, the engine fading into the distance.

Tam stood there, staring down at the cabin, his eyes wide and spilling tears. "Mum?" he said.

Rosie tugged at his T-shirt. "You have to see. You have to believe."

Tam turned. He took Rosie's hand. "I'm not a child anymore, Rosie," he said. "I'm sorry." He squeezed her pudgy hand. "Look."

The lights through the trees were car lights on a nearby road, climbing up the valley side. The wings in front of the moon were simply gathering clouds. "I'm sorry," Tam said again.

16.

The weather broke that night. The heat shattered before the pounding rain.

In Tam's dream, the dragon fell, like a dark sheet from the sky, tumbling, twisting, bunching. And then it was gone.

17.

In the sad, unbending humidity of the day, Tam walked from the cabin, where his father and Josh and Lisa's mother sat, unspeaking and hollow. He followed the trail that led up through the trees, around the lake. He pushed through the hawthorn thicket and came out onto the cracked slate slope. Beyond, the lake lay flat and glassy.

He started down the slope.

The bed of slate that had held his fossil had broken off in the night and fallen into the deep lake. The fossil of the dinosaur was gone.

DAWN, BY THE LIGHT OF A BARROW FIRE

ABOUT THE STORY

Dawn, by the Light of a Barrow Fire *was one of my early stories, written soon after I had left Clarion West. At the time, my younger brother, Ben, was studying for an archaeology degree, and prehistory is something I've always loved. It's something about the possibilities inherent in a time that we only have scraps of evidence for, mystery blended with magic, fact with myth. And, hey, what better way to avoid having to do research than to have someone you can just ask?*

In retrospect, I probably should have asked about a few more things, and any archaeological or historical errors here are entirely mine.

DAWN, BY THE LIGHT OF A
BARROW FIRE

I KNEW SOMETHING WAS UP AS SOON AS I SAW FRANK TRUDGE
out of Bennett's trailer. Twenty years of working in mud and
dust and dirt beside him meant I could read him the way he
could read a pile of ancient bones. Anyway, something was
always up when Bennett asked to see one of us.

This last year, since David died, had been Hell, and
working under Bennett had only made it worse. If the
university department hadn't been so short of cash, we would
have quit in a week. Instead, we had gritted our teeth, bowed
our heads, and tried not to scream, praying for the next
funding round.

Marcy straightened beside me, and brushed her hair
back with a muddy hand.

"I'll bet you a tenner at three-to-one Bennett's decided he
wants a long barrow instead," she whispered.

"Do you think he knows what a long barrow is?"

Marcy, Frank, and I were the consultant archaeologists on this project, although Bennett did far more instructing than consulting. We were reconstructing a Neolithic settlement and round barrow for an English Heritage project – one of those projects where you're supposed to work using the same techniques that were used for the originals. In other words, it was pretty much guesswork from start to finish. We were the second team to work on this; Bennett had fired the previous team when they had refused to comply with one of his more ridiculous whims. We had avoided that fate so far, if only because we couldn't afford to lose the project.

The whole project was supposed to be for Ancient History Year. Only Ancient History Year was ancient history four months ago, and we still couldn't agree a design for the huts. Frank and I were for the standard rectangular, thatched design, wooden posts at the corners, and stone walls, a single room centred around a hearth pit. Marcy was holding out for circular with a partitioned interior. We were all trying hard not to let Bennett have a say. He would probably want a two-up, two-down with a conservatory on the back.

Frank reached the top of the hill, and collapsed into the bracken.

"Well?" Marcy said.

"He wants a trench."

I looked across the hillside, past the half-finished earth mound of the barrow, to the open moor of bracken and brambles. A hawk hovered in the blue air. There was nothing out there for miles. "Where? It's solid rock up here."

"He doesn't care," Frank said, wearily. "There's a TV crew

coming. Apparently 'everyone knows archaeologists dig ditches', so he wants one."

I groaned.

~

It rained most of the next day, a cold spring rain that threatened to turn to sleet several times. The water poured in rivers down the hillside, submerging the proto-trench we had started to dig in the valley where the ground was softer, and threatening to wash Bennett's trailer away. But no such luck.

By three o'clock, the rain had eased and Bennett sent us back to work, armed with a rusting pump. In minutes we were soaked and frozen. Thank God for students. We sent two of them into the deepest part of the trench to flail away with mattocks and shovels, while me and Marcy hunched over damp cigarettes. Frank was assiduously, and pointlessly, examining a pile of stones some distance from anything wet. Two minutes in the trench had been more than enough for him. No wonder. The whole thing was a façade. We had no reason to believe there had ever been a settlement in the valley. After all, who would want to live in a quagmire? And even if there had been, what did it have to do with building the barrow?

"Hey, look at this," one of the students shouted. He was crouched to his waist in the brown water of the trench. I pushed myself up. Mud squelched beneath me. No doubt some innocent flint was being mistaken for an axe-head again.

"He's found an ancient plastic cup," Marcy whispered, and I covered a grin.

He hadn't.

He'd found a bone.

He was waving it around, spraying water in his excitement.

Frank came wandering over and relieved the student of his find. "It's definitely human," he said, turning the brown bone in his hands. "A tibia, probably from a juvenile. Pretty old, I'd say."

A child. A cold stone dropped into my belly. I pushed past the others and dropped to my knees, scrabbling about in the lowering water.

Within moments my hands caught on something hard and curved. I pulled it free from the peat, not caring that I might be damaging it. I knew it was a skull the moment I touched it, but I didn't admit it to myself until I had it out the water. It was small. I turned it in my hand. Most of the left side was missing. Smashed away.

I felt a hand on my shoulder.

"Are you okay?" Marcy asked. I nodded, not trusting myself to speak.

"We should do this properly," she said. "Come on. Leave it to Frank and the students."

I followed her out of the trench. I was starting to shiver. Maybe it was the cold water.

A child. David had only been a child, just nine years old. My son. A boy chasing his ball. The car hadn't even stopped.

Marcy sat me down on a stone as the sun emerged from the black clouds. My knees were weak.

I sat and watched them uncover the skeleton, a bone at a time. The skeleton of some poor dead child. Maybe one who had been chasing his ball. Then a car hit him leaving a hole like a fist in his skull.

No. I shook my head to clear the memories. These bones were too old. They weren't David. David's ashes were scattered across the field behind my house. No one had scattered this child's ashes. No one had buried him.

"I'm okay," I said to Marcy, getting to my feet. "I'll be fine." I'd dealt with David dying. But it would be the anniversary of his death in three days, so it was natural that I should be thinking about him. It had been a moment of shocked memory, that was all.

"I'm going to carbon-date the bones," Frank said, looking up as we approached. "I'd bet they're at least a couple of thousand years old." He showed us one of the bones. "Look, they're in pretty good condition. We might be able to get some DNA."

I nodded, trying not to feel queasy.

A loud tooting made us all turn. A van had pulled off the road near the trailers.

"That'll be the TV," Frank said. "Last chance to hide."

I tried to smile, but it came out like a grimace. Like a skull.

The back doors of the van opened. Two men emerged

carrying a film camera and a microphone. A third man, wearing a flying jacket and dark sunglasses, and carrying a clipboard, got out the passenger's side. The wet ground had begun to steam slightly in the hot sun. I was still cold.

"Into the bunker," Frank called.

"Hush," Marcy said. "They're coming over."

I was feeling sick and weak, as though I hadn't eaten for days.

"You must be Bennett," the man in the flying jacket said when he reached us, extending a hand to Frank.

Frank started to choke.

Marcy stepped forward quickly. "I'm Marcy Raney. The comedian is Frank. The cute one is Cameron." She pointed at Frank then me. "What do you want to film?"

"Any swords, armour, stuff that'll look good on TV," Flying Jacket said. "No rocks though. People don't like watching rocks."

Marcy stared at him for a moment, then, "You know this is a Neolithic project?"

"Cool."

"You do know what Neolithic means?"

Flying Jacket frowned. "Huh? Yeah, yeah, of course."

"It means stone age."

Flying Jacket frowned. "So no swords?"

My head was throbbing. All I could see was David's body, lying by the side of the road, bleeding. I was choking.

"You're not from the BBC, are you?" Marcy said.

"Satellite," Frank whispered.

"Hey," the cameramen called. "They've got a skull over here."

"All right!" Flying Jacket shouted. "Let's get—"

"Leave the fucking skull alone!" They all turned to look at me. "Just ... just ... leave it alone." I remembered the journalists when David was killed. Wanting to see his room, his clothes, his photos. Hanging around outside the house, night and day, pointing their cameras. It had been a politician's car. It hadn't stopped.

"You okay?" Marcy whispered.

I nodded. "Just don't touch it," I said to the TV crew. "It's ... it's not been catalogued yet." It was pretty lame, and we all knew it. Maybe even the TV crew knew it.

I walked away.

HE HAS SEVENTEEN SCARS ON HIS CHEST. HIS SON HAS ONLY THREE. The boy is young. Too young to be out alone at night when there are bears and wolves around.

He walks from his hut to the barrow. The boy has too great an interest in the barrow. Maybe he will be there.

The ancestor-bones are bright in the sky tonight. The ground is white and the trees are flat against the sky. It is not a good night. Spirits can see too easily on a night like this.

He grasps the bones around his neck and hears them click together. Protect me, *he thinks.*

He wants to call out for the boy, but he does not want the spirits to hear. Nor the other men. They will think him a woman for worrying about the boy.

I have the soul of a bear, *he thinks. He wears its teeth sewn into the hides of his cloak.* I fear nothing.

The boy is not at the barrow.

I AWOKE FROM THE DREAM, SHAKING. IT HAD BEEN COLD, AND my son had been lost near the barrow. David had been lost. I had been looking for him. But that hadn't been me, had it?

Dawn was close.

I got to the site early, when the mists still cloaked the hills and turned the barrow into a ghost floating above the ground. We were going to try to place the capstone on top of the barrow today, before covering it with a final layer of earth. We, and several dozen volunteers, would haul the ten tonne block of granite up the slope of earth that made up the side of the barrow, and drop it onto the upright support stones, sealing the barrow. We were leaving part of one side and the entrance clear so visitors could see how it was constructed, and compare it to the quoits that dotted the landscape hereabouts. We would do the same with some of the huts, if we ever built the damn things.

"I knew you'd be here."

I turned. Marcy was climbing the hill behind me. I hadn't heard her car approach.

"Couldn't sleep, huh?"

"No," I said. "You?"

"I was worried about you. Want to talk about it?"

"Not really."

She slipped her arm through mine.

"You'll make the students jealous," I said. Students always had a crush on Marcy. I could understand that.

She smiled sadly. "Students don't get up this early. Nor do you."

The sky overhead was a pale blue, almost white. The bracken and heather and brambles were speckled with dew. Spiders' webs bowed under the weight of drops of water.

"It's stupid," I said. "It really shouldn't have got to me. I'm over it." I shook my head. "I guess I was tired."

"Bullshit," Marcy said. She grabbed my arm so I had to turn to face her or I would have jerked my arm away. "You're not over it, Cam, and you've never been over it. You've never talked about it. You've just bottled it up as though that'll make it go away. Well, it won't." She took a breath and glared into my eyes. "Shit, why do you think Alice left you? You never even talked to her."

I recoiled. Marcy never held back, but she'd never thrown that at me before. My face reddened, and I started to turn away.

"Cameron..." she said. She tugged my arm. I closed my eyes and breathed deeply. "I'm sorry," she said. "Just ... just talk to someone, Cameron. If you can't talk to me or Frank, talk to a doctor."

"I don't need to talk," I said. My throat was so tight it hurt to speak.

She pulled me round and to her. I resisted for just a

moment, then rested my forehead on her shoulder. Tears were cold on my cheeks. "I don't know what to do," I whispered into her rough hair.

"Talk," she said. I shook my head against her shirt. Talking would only hurt more. Better to bury the hurt, like ashes in a barrow.

Eventually she pushed me away and wiped my eyes with a corner of her scarf.

"I'm sorry," I said. "I'm okay."

Marcy gave me a sad grin. I knew she didn't believe me. Hell, even I didn't believe me.

Someone shouted, "Hey," from down the hill. We turned to see Frank.

"I thought I'd find you two canoodling up here," he said.

The mist must have been killing the sounds of cars. There could have been a convoy down there.

"It's a morning for early mornings," I said.

"It's not an early morning," Frank said. "It's a late night. I spent the night in the trailer studying the bones." He looked at me. "I figured you'd want to know."

"And?" My voice caught on the word and I had to repeat it. "And?"

"It's pretty hard to know without getting them into a lab, and even then…"

"Guess," I said.

Frank shot a glance at Marcy, then shrugged. "A young boy, probably between seven and twelve or so. It's difficult to tell until we know exactly when the bones are from. People's development rates have changed over time. I would guess they're late Neolithic, but that really is a guess until I get the carbon dating results."

"What killed him?"

Frank grimaced. "It could have been anything..."

My heart hammered. My mouth was as dry as sand.

"The head?" I croaked.

"Yes, it could have been the head wound. Maybe a blow from a weapon, or an animal, or maybe just an accident. We'll never know." He shrugged again. "I'm sorry."

"It's okay." I turned away. My chest was tight and I couldn't get enough air. "It's okay."

THE CAPSTONE GOT STUCK HALFWAY UP THE SLOPE OF THE barrow when the rollers sank into the soft earth. Bennett suggested using a crane, but apart from the fact that we didn't have one, that would rather have destroyed the point of the exercise.

I stood with Marcy and Frank on top of the barrow, just above the gaping burial chamber, and we scratched our chins, three bruise-eyed, tired archaeologists whose theories had just collapsed.

"Bigger rollers," Frank said.

"Tougher volunteers," Marcy said.

"Planks," I said.

We didn't have a clue.

THE FROST IS HARD ON THE GROUND. THE COLD BITES INTO MY skin. It is dark, but the moon is bright. I am standing in the shadows of a hut. It is round, with stone walls sealed with dried mud, or perhaps dung. The thatching protrudes almost to the ground, and the roof is steep. The door is a thick fur. From here, the dwelling appears to be sunk into the ground. It looks like Marcy's design for the Neolithic huts, apart from the roof.

Where the Hell am I? It reminds me of my dream, but it seems too real for a dream.

Nearby, I see three other huts. Between them is a low stockade. I can see three or four goats huddled together, breathing clouds of hot breath into the air. I smell smoke and goat dung and something else I'd rather not think about.

The door of one of the huts pulls open. A man steps out, then pauses and looks around. He is dressed in a heavy, hooded fur cloak. I guess he is about five four tall, but heavily built. He has a long black beard and long straggly hair. I can't see his eyes.

He grunts, then turns and walks from the huts by a path that leads up the hill. I follow him. He doesn't seem to notice.

The path curves around the side of the hill as it goes up, passing through a stand of trees. I think I can identify oak and lime, and maybe hawthorn.

Something howls. My mind says wolf, but how can it be? Wolves have been extinct in Britain for hundreds of years.

I emerge from the trees. The man is fifty yards ahead of me, but I see him clearly. He is near the brow of the hill.

There is a barrow there, a dark silhouette against the moonlight.

The man reaches the barrow and circles it. Then he climbs to the top and peers around. His shoulders slump. He descends and sits before the barrow, crouched over. Within minutes a small fire springs up. His face is made gaunt by its flickering light.

I think that maybe he can't see me. I can't be here, so he can't see me. I start up the trail again.

The stones are hard and cold beneath my feet. My joints ache.

I reach the barrow and the sitting man. He is staring into his fire. I step past him.

"He is gone," the man says. I jump, then turn to him. He has a deep, accented voice. If he is Neolithic, as he seems to be, he can't be speaking English, but that is how I hear it.

"Who?" I ask, softly. Maybe he isn't talking to me. Am I here, or is this a dream? If so, whose? Mine or his?

"The boy. My son. He is gone. I fear he is dead." He looks up at me. "The boy has no fear."

Sadness rolls over me so suddenly that I have to close my eyes and clamp my jaw. He *is* dead, I want to say. Nine years old, I want to say, and hit by a car. It didn't even stop.

"Can a boy survive seven days out here?" the man asks. "I have searched everywhere. I cannot find him." His eyes are staring straight into mine when I open them. They are a deeper blue than I have ever seen. His voice turns soft, so that I have to strain to listen. "He had only three scars. Now he is gone. I cannot find him. I cannot bury his ashes. He cannot travel to the *tchetchla*." I don't recognise the word. "Help me," he says.

I stand. On the other side of the hill, I see a wooded valley. It looks very familiar. If it had no trees, and a small stream, and a road, and a couple of trailers...

I leave the man behind and descend into the valley. It is hard to place myself, but I think that there is where Bennett's trailer would be, there in the trees.

A film of ice splinters beneath my feet. The ground sinks, and peat-dark water wells up. Not far away are the tracks of a large animal. Something bigger than me, with claws.

And there, just ahead, where the mud is deep and only a couple of dead white tree trunks stretch from the water, there is where the trench will be. I feel sick.

"You look bloody awful," Marcy said.

My head hurt. I was sure a migraine was coming on. "Bad night."

"We're going to try the capstone again, tomorrow," Frank said, looking pleased with himself. "We're going for larger rollers."

"Round huts," I croaked.

"What?"

"I think we should have round huts, like Marcy said, and steeper roofs."

"Traitor," Frank whispered to me, then glared at the smirking Marcy. "Go suck on your trowel."

"What's on the agenda today?" I asked. Pulses of pain were making my vision swim.

"You're going home," Marcy said. "Me and Frank have been talking. We're going to gang up on Bennett and make him give you a day or two off, and we're making an appointment for you to talk to your doctor."

"Don't..." I said, then took a breath and started again. "Don't tell me what to do." Pain thudded through my head and I grabbed at my eyes instinctively. "I'm coping," I whispered.

Frank and Marcy exchanged glances.

"No," Marcy said. You're not," She had her fists on her hips, and her lips had turned white. "I've been watching you this last week. If you go on, you're going to have a breakdown. You're going to talk to someone, if we have to drag you there by brute force. I'm not joking."

I looked her in the eyes, through the pain. No, she wasn't joking. Something crumpled in me. I nodded carefully. "Okay," I said. "I'll talk to someone." And I would.

I PARKED THE CAR BESIDE BENNETT'S TRAILER. THE LUMINOUS hands of the clock showed 3:15. It was a clear night, with a thin layer of mist floating just above the valley floor. I pulled on my big coat and my gloves, and let myself out.

My nose ran immediately, and my eyes streamed. I wiped them with the back of my glove. I wished I'd worn another pair of socks and brought a hat. Too late to go back for them. Tomorrow was the anniversary of David's death.

I slipped my key into the lock of the second trailer, the one me and Marcy and Frank shared. It was slightly warmer there. I turned on the light. The desktops and surfaces were covered in drawings, photocopied articles, and bits of pottery and stone, the normal mess.

I went straight to the drawers at the far end of the trailer, and pulled open the top one. The bones were there, where I had seen Frank put them, sealed in clear plastic bags. The sight of them made me tremble. I forced myself calm. I clenched my fists until my hands stopped shaking.

Bennett would fire us for this, I had no doubt. It would be the end of my career, and God knows what would happen to Frank and Marcy and the department.

I took a deep breath. I had no choice. These were the boy's bones, I was sure, the poor lost Neolithic boy's. "I'm sorry," I muttered under my breath. What a way to repay Frank and Marcy.

I carefully emptied the bags one by one into my canvas rucksack. I heard the bones clatter together brittlely. Bile rose in my throat. I swallowed.

I turned off the light and locked the trailer behind me.

I started along the track, up the hill.

HE IS WAITING FOR ME OUTSIDE THE BARROW. A SMALL FIRE IS burning fiercely. Wolves howl out on the moor. I see trees in the valley, and on the other side of the hill, the dark shapes of the settlement huts, smoke still rising from one. I smell the goats even from here, a rich, cloying smell.

I hug my coat tight around me.

The fire is hot as I seat myself beside him.

"The boy is dead," the man says.

"Yes," I say, through tears. I see tears on the Neolithic man's own cheeks. "I loved him," I say, and when the man nods I know he knows I am talking about David. "I miss him." I think it's the first time I've been able to say this.

I pass the rucksack to him. He fumbles with the buckles, then opens them. Slowly he pulls out the dry bones, one by one, and places them on the fire. They catch quickly and burn brightly.

"I loved my boy too," he says. "Here I set him free."

Finally he removes the skull, kisses it, and hands it to me.

"Here I set him free," I say, choking on the words. *David*, I think. *Goodbye.*

I kiss the skull too, then place it on the fire.

We sit before a fire of bones, as the morning pales the sky. When the bones are entirely burnt, he scoops the still-hot ashes into a clay pot, and hands it to me. I place it in my rucksack.

In the morning I will place the pot inside the barrow, before the capstone is finally levered on.

The boy will travel to the *tchetchla*.

CAMELOT

ABOUT THE STORY

Stories come from all sorts of places, not all of them welcome. I can't remember the exact seed for the idea – Arthurian stories are hardly scarce – but this one ended up channelling my grief at the death of my younger brother. It's not easy for me to reread, even now, eleven years on.

CAMELOT

WHEN SHE FINDS ME, I'M HALF-SITTING, HALF-SLOUCHED, BUTT propped against the bonnet of my chunky old Volvo estate, shoulders hunched, flicking away madly at my fifty pence lighter, roll-up hanging from my mouth, boots still unlaced. Dignified, right? But sometimes the need takes you, and it doesn't matter where you are or what you're doing, and there's nothing you can do about it.

I need a fag, and that's that.

And, let's face it, it's not like it's going to kill me.

The bonnet is still hot under my arse, and that's something to be grateful for, because today's knife cold. The Volvo's heater broke weeks ago, and I haven't a clue how to fix it. My bones hurt.

I finally coax a flame out of the lighter. I take a drag and feel the smoke burn its way down into my lungs. Now that's what I call central heating. I'd say it's better than sex, but to be honest, it's been so long since the latter that I can't remember.

When I open my eyes, a whole coach load of Japanese tourists have drawn up and are piling out, right into my view.

It's while I'm watching them that she sidles up to me. She must have come from the other end of the car, because the first I know of it, she's taking the fag out of my fingers and lighting one of her own with the end. She returns mine with a half shrug – very Gallic – then settles beside me.

"It never is," she says.

Which is a funny fucking opening gambit, if you ask me. If it's supposed to be a come-on, it's not exactly 'do you come here often'. But, to be honest, she doesn't exactly need the lines. She's gorgeous. Hair as black as burnt wood and cascading to the small of her back, which in turn sends the eyes you know where, and once I'm there, well, I'm not looking away in a hurry.

"Isn't what?" I say, eyes still firmly where they shouldn't be.

"Camelot," she says. "It's never Camelot." She waves the cigarette at the ruins that rise on the hill above us, leaving an elegant trace of smoke in the air.

She turns to look at me for the first time, and I get the full effect of her eyes. They're almost as dark as her hair, and they near-as-fuck knock me out of my unlaced boots. I've never seen eyes like them before. My heart's hammering away like a teenager with a skin mag.

"That's what you're looking for, isn't it?" she says. "Camelot?"

"No," I say. "I'm looking for my brother."

She nods, like it explains everything.

"What happened to him?"

"He disappeared." Which is true as far as it goes. There are just a couple of details I leave out. Like, my brother was shot down over France in 1943. Like, I was twenty-two years old.

Like, I've been looking for him ever since.

Like, it's 2010 now, and I haven't aged a single day.

"Camelot," she says. "It's never Camelot."

There are things you long for. Things you need with the strength of a black hole some bastard's opened in your chest. Things you can't leave be because you'd die if you did.

I finish my roll-up with one deep suck and grind out what's left under my foot.

"I'm going to take a look."

"Fine," she says. "I'm coming."

I don't say no.

I've seen it in my dreams. The place Jack came down. I've seen weed-strewn ruins, high arches of stone, glittering glass hanging in shattered windows. I've seen fountains and a river that wells up from deep beneath the ruins to run over carved reliefs. I've seen statues and fluttering flags standing forlorn over crumbled walls. I've seen Jack lying there, his parachute crumpled behind him, his face twisted with pain, his leg bent back at an impossible angle. I've seen the cold sunlight overhead and heard the wind snatching at the stones. I'll know it the moment I see it.

This isn't it.

I didn't think it would be. After all these years, I don't expect to find that place, but I can't stop looking. It's got to be out there somewhere.

Jack fell from the sky. I can't leave him.

The Japanese tourists are all over these ruins, taking shots, laughing, talking. Steam rises from their lips, wreathing their heads like they're dragons at the fucking monsters' ball.

This is not it. I can't help but feel disappointed. You'd have thought after all this time, I'd have grown immune.

"I've got a room," she says. "Back in the village. Nothing special, but..."

I shrug. Anything's better than another night in the back of the Volvo, with ice on the inside of the windows and a crick in my neck that'll take all day to loosen.

"Sounds good."

That night, after the wine, after we've fucked, after I've stared into her eyes like into twin wells filled with ink, she shifts herself out from under me.

She gazes up at me from the darkness. "How old do you think I am?"

Trust me, there's no right answer to that. "About thirty," I say, trying to be honest.

She smiles. "Sweet boy."

"You want to know how old I am?" I say, suddenly irritated. "I'm eighty fucking nine."

Her smile widens. "You're far older than that, Sam."

As I slip into sleep, she whispers, "You're not supposed to remember. None of us are."

In the morning, she's gone, leaving only the scent of olives behind her.

I never told her my name.

A bit of that old Thomas Ford poem flits through my brain. You know the one. "I did but see her passing by, And yet I love her till I die."

I did but fuck her passing by...

Doesn't quite have the same ring to it. It's true, though. I feel like she's set my blood on fire. It's pumping through my veins with a searing pain that grows with every beat of my heart.

I'm sweating. My sheets are soaked. The hairs on my skin are standing painfully on end, and every time I brush against the cotton, it hurts like a glass cut. I'm shivering. I feel hot and cold at the same time.

Fuck. She's done something to me.

I stumble out of bed and fall, my knees crashing on the floor. The room is spinning around me. I squeeze my eyes shut and scrabble around for my clothes. I can only find one sock and my T-shirt has completely disappeared. Gritting my teeth, I dress.

I stagger to the door, crashing it open with my shoulder and almost tripping down the stairs. I hug my coat around me.

The innkeeper gabbles something at me in French. I ignore him and lurch out into the freezing morning. The light is blinding, even with my eyes almost squeezed shut.

The innkeeper follows me out, still spouting gibberish.

My car is in the lot. I reach it, wrench open the door, and

slump down in the driver's seat. My head falls forwards, smacking into the steering wheel. Distantly, I hear a blaring sound, but my head is swirling worse than ever.

The fever dream comes then, eddying up from behind my eyelids. I see fire and smoke, burning buildings and shattered walls. All around me, heavily-armoured men clash and fall. Sweat and blood and mud make everything slippery. A shape looms before me, and I swing at it. The shape goes down before I can see a face. I step over it, shield raised.

The men around me break into a run, racing towards the enormous, burning buildings ahead of us, through the captured gate, into the courtyard. The last of the defenders fall and flee. The inferno rages with a fierce joy, ripping and tearing and laughing in its hunger. The heat beats on metal. Armour and swords reflect orange and red. We're shouting in triumph, beating swords against shields.

That's when they come, walking through the fire. The old man and the young.

Our cheers die in our mouths.

The man beside me turns, screaming back to someone I can't see. "You said they were gone! You said they wouldn't be here!"

Then men are breaking, running, fleeing. I stand for a moment as the figures approach through the fire. Then I'm running too, my shield forgotten behind me.

I don't know how long I've sat there in the car. Long enough that my sweat has chilled nearly to ice. The fire that burned in me has faded, and the shivering is just because I'm freezing. The fever is gone.

I fumble out my keys and turn on the engine. There's frost on the windscreen. I should get out and scrape it off, but I don't have the strength. Instead, I start the car rolling forwards, squinting through the tiny patch of clear glass.

Futilely, I worry the little heating lever back and forth on the dashboard. Something clicks, and miraculously, a thin trickle of warm air washes over me. I want to cry.

I pull out my little notebook, still peering through the frosted windscreen, and flick through the pages. I glance down and read the next name on the list. *Château de Najac.* It's a fair drive. Not that I expect to find anything there. I've seen photos, and they are wrong. But there are only so many options left, and I can't afford to ignore any of them. Jack wouldn't have.

Jack was my little brother, but he was the one who always looked out for me. He only joined the RAF so he could keep an eye on me. So I wouldn't get myself killed doing something stupid. Then they shot him down, and he fell, and he was only twenty-one.

He was the same when we were kids. I lost track of how many times he dragged me out of ponds or caught me before I could tumble down some embankment.

Now he's lost, and the irony is, I can't die. I can't even grow old.

When he needed to be caught, I wasn't there. I was in a bar. With a couple of girls. Drunk.

They had to wait to the next day to tell me, when I was sober, but by then I'd already had the first dream of Jack lying in the ruins, and I knew he wasn't dead. He was waiting for me to save him.

Château de Najac stands on a craggy outcropping of rock over a painfully cute village. The kind of place that too-rich English bastards infest like a case of the crabs. Darling, it's so *authentic*.

I climb out of the Volvo.

This isn't the right place. I know it. It's not even close. Jack wouldn't even have been flying this far south.

A cold wind whips shreds of snow up from the valley. They scratch and melt on my bare face.

I don't remember when I last ate.

"It never is," she says, just behind me.

"Screw you," I say, somehow not surprised that she's here.

"You already did."

I glance back at her. She's showing a slight smile. She takes my breath away, just like she did yesterday. This woman is *so* beautiful.

"You can't find it like this," she says. "You can't just walk into Camelot."

My hands bunch into fists, cold fingers feeling like dead chunks of wood against my palms. "I'm not interested in fucking Camelot. I just want my brother."

"Jack," she says.

"How do you know his name?"

"It's not his real name, you know," she says. "Just like Sam's not your real name."

I shake my head, turning away.

218

In bed that night, she says again, "You're not supposed to remember."

"Remember what?" I demand.

"Who you are," she says. "What you did. They took that from us, from those cast out. We fell from grace."

I shake my head, but already sleep is claiming me, and in the morning she's gone.

The fever hits me again on the way to the car, but this time I'm half expecting it. I've got my keys in my hand, and I make it to the car without falling.

The fever dream is more real this time. More visceral. I can feel the sweat on my back and taste metal-tinged blood in my mouth. Heat from the flames beats against my armour and my exposed skin. My eyes are dry, and they sting. The armour has rubbed me raw beneath my arms and at my neck. Metal clashes around me. I block a swinging sword, and the impact judders down my arm, numbing my wrist.

When the defenders break, I scream, "No! Don't follow!" But this is a fever dream, and I am not in control. No sounds pass my lips, and I run forward with the other attackers, screaming triumph.

I feel the biting fear as the two men come striding through of the flames.

"You said they were gone! You said they wouldn't be here!" the man behind me shouts, just before we flee.

I turn and run, racing back across flagstones I fought bitterly to take only minutes before. *She* is there, standing with back pressed against the stone wall, hands folded in front of her as though she's sitting in her solar, talking to her ladies. But I see the fear in her eyes, too.

I don't have time to think. The young one, the one carrying the sword, is on us already. Men fall, cut down.

There is no way out of this courtyard. A burning beam has fallen across the gate. When it happened, I was delighted. *No reinforcements.*

I swing back to see *him* cut down another man without breaking step. There are scarcely a dozen of us left standing, fanned out before the blocked gate.

I look into that face that I once loved more than I loved my own life. But the killing rage is upon him, and there is no mercy in his eyes.

I raise my sword. At least it will be quick.

Then Jack comes stumbling from around the burning stables. He isn't wearing armour. He never joined us. I didn't tell him what we were planning to do, because I knew that if I did, he would follow me, and this was never Jack's fight.

Jack was the only one who could ever talk to *him* during one of his killing rages. Now Jack pleads, cajoles, reasons, begs, while the rest of us stand there, waiting for the end.

But slowly the killing rage fades in *his* eyes. Hardness remains, but it is the hardness of reason and justice, not of rage. I know Jack has saved me once more

Then the old one speaks. His words chill the air. Darkness gathers like thunder, oppressive, heavy, painful. A fear grips me that is so great that it stops the blood in my veins. I do not understand most of the words. They are too powerful, too potent. In my terror the only words I catch are, *Cast out, for all time.*

Then comes the fall.

I wake sweating. My hands are gripping the steering wheel so tight that they've left dents in the hard plastic. I'm shaking. Despite my thick clothes, I'm chilled through. I fumble out a roll-up. Thank God I made it last night, because right now I can hardly hold it.

When it's lit, I turn on the engine. The petrol indicator is close to empty, and so is my wallet. I reckon I've got enough for another two tanks, then I'm broke. I'll have to get a job, save up some more, before I can start looking again. Could take months. I hammer my cold fists on the steering wheel. It's been over sixty years. Jack is out there, lost, hurt. I can't bear to give up again.

I consult my notebook and my map. Then I turn the car north.

The drive takes most of the day. The frost-rimed landscape of southern France slips by, an unending sequence of towns and villages, fields, forests and mountains. Eventually, though, I catch sight of my destination, high, ruined walls against a fading sky.

It's not the place I'm looking for.

"It never is," she says.

That night, instead of making love, she sings to me. It's the saddest song I have ever heard.

"Find him," she whispers, when she's done.

In the morning, she's gone again, but there is no fever dream.

Next stop is Calais, then the ferry home. If I'm careful, I can make enough in three or four months to set out again. There are plenty more ruins in France. If they fail me, I'll try Belgium. Jack could have been blown off course. He might not have been shot down over France at all. I won't stop. Jack wouldn't have.

It's late afternoon, and the sky is fading to a wintery lilac when I catch a glimpse of something through the cold-stripped trees. It's just a flash of stone, but old instincts take over, and I slam on the brakes. In summer, I wouldn't have seen a thing.

I consult my map, but there's nothing marked.

It's probably just a tumbledown farmhouse. I'm going to be driving all night as it is. I'm tempted to keep going.

Instead, I climb out, pull on my walking boots, and crunch my way up the slope, through the trees.

I have dreamt this place so many times. The weed-strewn ruins, the high arches of stone, the glass still hanging in shattered windows. There is the fountain, empty of water now, but familiar still. Here is the small river that wells up from deep beneath the ruins to run over reliefs. I peer through the icy water and see knights carved from stone. Broken statues line the track to the courtyard. There are no flags on the walls, but my dream is of sixty-seven years ago. Things change.

I tramp towards the courtyard. Two statues stand on either side of the gate. I recognise them from my fever dream and look quickly away.

This time, I hear her footsteps before she reaches me.

Her face is flushed from the climb in the freezing air, but she is still the most beautiful woman I have ever seen. Just looking at her makes it hard to breathe. There's another car parked behind mine on the road, a low, black Ferrari.

"You've been following me," I say.

"You're a slow driver."

I shrug. "Is this it?" I say. "Is this Camelot?"

"No," she says. "But it's close. It's very close."

I make my way into the courtyard. In my dreams, Jack comes down on the far side, in the shade of the great wall. His parachute stretches across the flagstones behind him.

Here, now, the accumulated leaves of a dozen years have blown in undisturbed drifts.

When I close my eyes, I can see exactly where he should be lying.

I kneel in the rotting, frost-crisped leaves and dig through them.

The first thing I find is a buckle, still glinting despite the grime. As I move more leaves, I uncover a rotting RAF uniform, then bones. The left femur has snapped and the rest of the leg juts backwards.

My hands won't uncover any more. They tremble uselessly at my side. There's an emptiness pressing against my throat, so deep that I can't even cry or scream or shout.

I cannot die. I thought the same would be true for Jack. I thought he'd be waiting for me. I never imagined he would have died here in this cold, empty courtyard, alone and undiscovered.

Jack never failed me in all our years. I've failed him now.

The woman pushes me aside with a strength I would not have guessed. Her face is full of delight. I stare at her. She runs her hands over Jack's bones, then looks up at me, her eyes alight with joy.

I can't speak.

"We were cast out," she says. "You, me, and all the others. We fell. All of us except Jack. Jack followed you, like he always did. He wasn't banished. Don't you understand? His bones can carry us home."

I look at her with revulsion. "That's all you wanted? All of this was so that I could lead you to Jack, and you could go home?"

"To Camelot," she says. "We both could. Your brother would want you to."

The truth is, she's right. Jack would do anything for me. He wanted to make me happy and keep me safe. He *would* want me to go home.

"Who were we?" I say. "Back in Camelot, what were our real names?"

She smiles. "Follow me and find out."

I shake my head. Without Jack, there's nothing for me there. There's nothing for me anywhere.

"You'll forget," she says. "These memories will fade, like they did before. You won't have another chance."

I don't care. I *want* them to fade.

This isn't Jack. Not dead in this bleak, lost place. Not Jack. Not my brother.

I leave her there, this woman, kneeling over the bones of the British airman.

That night, I dream of Jack lying, leg broken, in the ruins. I dream of fountains and a river running over carved stone and bright glass in shattered windows. I dream of flags fluttering over high walls.

In the morning, I get into my Volvo and continue to drive north.

There are other ruins. Perhaps I was wrong about these ones.

After all, there were no flags fluttering over the walls.

The Volvo's engine is making an unhealthy noise, and the heater is broken again.

I keep driving.

CRAB APPLE

ABOUT THE STORY

It's fairly rare, in my experience, for a story to just come to you, complete, in a single flash. But Crab Apple came to me like that, fully-formed, and within a week it was finished.

Despite that, it's been my most successful story, reprinted several times, featured in The Year's Best Fantasy, and translated. You can't make a career waiting for inspiration, but in those few times it does come, you have to grab it and be grateful.

CRAB APPLE

I SAW HER FIRST THE DAY I FOUND DAD ON THE KITCHEN FLOOR.
The new girl. The wild girl.

At first I thought Dad had been drinking again. There
were beer cans scattered across the floor. But the cans were
still full, and I couldn't smell alcohol.

There was something strange about the way Dad was
lying. He was too still. His stick-thin arms and legs were
sprawled loosely across the tiles. I thought for a moment he
was dead.

He was still breathing, though, a wheezy, tight sound, as
though a plastic whistle was stuck in his throat. He didn't
wake when I shook him.

I'd begun taking first aid classes at school when Dad
started losing weight and coughing. There was no one else at
home to help. But they had never shown us how to deal with

this. I put him in the recovery position and called an ambulance.

The girl was there when I went outside to wait for the ambulance. She was squatted on our garden wall like a wild-haired monkey. She had on a dirty white T-shirt and shorts that showed scratched legs. I guessed she was about four-teen, the same age as me. Her eyes were as brown as oak and her cheeks were freckled and sunburnt. There were leaves in her tangled hair.

"What's your name?" she said. "You, what's your name?"

"Josh," I said.

"Joshua," she laughed. "Stupid name."

She winked down at me. Her grin was as wide as her face.

Then she leapt from the wall and dashed away up the hill, her wild hair streaming behind her like a comet's tail. I watched her disappear.

In the distance I heard the ambulance siren approaching.

"YOU WANT TO SEE SOMETHING?"

The wild girl leaned against the school lockers. She was wearing school uniform, without the tie, but she'd got mud on her shirt already, and her hair was the same mess.

I'd spent most the night at the hospital, by Dad's bed, waiting for him to wake up. He hadn't.

"No," I said.

"You want to know my name?"

"No."

She shoved her sunburnt face close to mine. Her brown eyes glittered. "I don't care. Stupid boy."

She laughed and spun down the corridor, arms outstretched. "Stupid, stupid, stupid, stupid, stupid," she shouted as she spun. My face turned red.

The door to the staff room burst open, and Mrs Wilson strode out, her thick skirt slapping like a whip against her legs.

"What is going on? Come back here."

The wild girl looked back.

"Screw you."

Then she ran again.

Mrs Wilson pushed back her glasses. Her lips were tight. "Little madam," she said. She glared at me as though I was to blame. "She's got the devil in her, that one. She'll be nothing but trouble, you mark my words, Josh. Nothing but trouble."

"HE'S AWAKE," THE NURSE SAID. SHE LET ME INTO DAD'S room.

He was sunk into the stiff, white sheets like a balloon with half its air let out. There was a tube running up his nose and another leading to his arm from a bag of clear liquid hooked up on a stand.

He turned his head, blinking.

"Josh." His voice was hoarse, like he'd been shouting.

"How are you doing, Dad?" I tried to stop my voice shaking. I didn't want to seem like a kid.

"Been better, been worse." He worked his lips, as though his mouth was dry. "See, the old devil's put his hand into my chest, lad. Left a bit of a gift for me."

He coughed. His thin chest shuddered. He turned and spat into a metal bowl by his bed. The spit was thick and threaded with blood. He gave me a painful grin.

"Want to hear a name for the devil they never taught you in that Sunday school, lad? Forty-a-day. Good, hey?" He laughed. It was a painful, breathless sound. "Old forty-a-day'll get you every time."

I tried to smile, but couldn't. He looked shrivelled away, eaten from the inside. His cheeks were caved in, his skin almost yellow and sagging against his bones, his eyes bloodshot and too big in his face. This wasn't my dad. It was his reflection in a dead mirror, a body from the desert.

"Want to see my X-rays?" he said.

"Okay," I said.

"End of the bed. The blue folder."

I pulled them out and held them up to the window. I could see his ribs and spine as clear white. Two large grey shapes behind the ribs must have been his lungs.

"What's this?"

I pointed at a black lump almost as large as one of Dad's fists in the bottom of the right lung.

"Apple. Swallowed an apple. Hey? Hey?" He coughed again. "I'm tired, lad. Bloody tired. You wouldn't think so after all that sleep." His eyes fluttered shut. He sighed, and his body relaxed on the bed.

I stood over him, staring down at that exhausted face. I wondered how long he'd been so tired. I hadn't noticed. Too busy rushing around. I swallowed to stop a sob. He looked twenty years older than I remembered.

For a moment his eyelids popped open again. "Don't let your mum worry, hey?" he croaked.

"No, Dad," I said.

Mum had been dead since I was five.

AUNT CHRIS CAME TO STAY, TO LOOK AFTER ME SHE SAID. SHE was waiting on the porch when I got home. She bundled Dad's beer cans into a bin bag and left it outside for the dustmen. She emptied his ashtrays and put them in the cupboard, right on the top shelf. She threw away all the old magazines and newspapers. Then she started scrubbing, as though she wanted to scrub away every trace of Dad. I went up to my room.

Something woke me in the night. The moon was heavy through the trees at the end of the garden. Somewhere in the dark, an owl hooted, a forlorn, lost sound. I wondered if that had been what had woken me. Then I heard a scratching just below the window. My heart started to thump. A bird, maybe, or even a mouse. That would be it. My hands bunched into fists around the sheets. I closed my eyes. I wasn't a kid anymore, to be frightened by my imagination.

When I opened my eyes, there was a face at the window. I nearly screamed. It was pressed up close, pale but shadowed with the moon behind it. I took a deep breath. The face moved, and I saw the mass of tangled hair.

The wild girl pulled herself up onto my windowsill, and crouched there, staring in. "Open the window," she mouthed.

Wrapping my sheet around me, I stood and hurried over.

"What do you want?"

"Open the window."

I pulled it up, letting in the cool night air. The girl hopped inside.

"Jeez, you're hard to wake."

"It's the middle of the night."

She gave me a wide grin. "You want to see something?"

"What?"

"You have to come and see."

I glanced at the clock. It was two o'clock. I'd have to be up for school in five hours.

"Good," she said, before I could answer. "I'll meet you downstairs. Get dressed." She giggled. "You look stupid with that sheet." Then she clambered back out onto the windowsill. She lowered herself so she was dangling by her hands then looked up at me with that wild face.

"You want to know my name?"

"No," I said.

"It's Emma. Do you like it?"

"It's okay."

"Good."

234

She dropped, and I heard a soft thud from the ground below. I saw her dart around the side of the house.

I thought about going back to bed, but I just had this feeling that she'd climb back up to my window if I did. I didn't even think she would care if she woke Aunt Chris. She didn't seem to care about anything.

"You should cry, you know. Or scream. Or throw something." She picked up a rock and flung it toward the rooftops below. "Like that. Let yourself go."

We were climbing Braddock Hill, which rose sharply between the scattered houses on my side of the hill and the sprawling, dirty town on the other. It was cold out, and the sky was clear.

"Why?" I said.

"Because of your dad. You can't deal with anything while you're all sewn up like a pillow. You need to escape, let all your feathers fly around the room. Then you can handle anything."

"You can handle anything, can you?" I said.

She jumped in the air, twirling as she did so. "Anything." She laughed. It was a feral sound, like a fox barking in the darkness.

We topped the hill and began to descend. The ground flattened to the left. Emma led me that way, into the trees. I hung back for a moment. It was dark in there. I wasn't so sure this was a good idea anymore. Emma looked back.

"Scared, Josh? You a stupid, scared little boy?"

"No," I said, and followed her in.

There had been an orchard here once, but it had been long abandoned. Hawthorn and ash had sprung up between the apple trees, and tangles of brambles rose in hillocks between the trunks. Right in the centre, larger than any of the other trees, stood a spreading crab apple tree. Nothing grew beneath its branches save a layer of thick moss.

Emma stopped beneath it.

"It's a tree," I said. "Big deal."

She leaned back against the bark. "Come closer." She crooked a finger and stared up at me through her eyelashes. Her sweater was tight against her chest. She winked. My heart trembled. My pulse fluttered loudly in my ears. My lips were dry.

She pushed herself away again with a squawk of laughter.

"Just wait," she said, "and watch."

"What?"

"There." She pointed to halfway up the trunk of the massive tree. For a moment I couldn't see what she was pointing at. Then I saw it. The bark of the tree was pulsing, as though there was a slow heart beneath it, or a giant insect trapped in syrup.

The pulses grew. The branches shuddered.

Slowly, something pulled itself from the tree. The bark stretched like toffee, clinging to the creature that was emerging, and then finally snapping back. I thought of a butterfly emerging from its cocoon, but this was no butterfly.

It was shaped almost like a man, but it wasn't a man. It was wrong. Its fingers were as long as my forearm. From its head and its elbows and its knees grew twisted twigs. Its skin was as rutted as bark, but as silver as the moon. Its teeth, when it spread its wide mouth open, were as sharp as pins. Its eyes were bright yellow. I saw claws curling from its fingers and toes. It clung to the tree, and then slowly turned, so that its head was pointing downwards, and began to descend.

It moved with the reaching slowness of a stick insect. It would take forever to reach the ground, I thought, but even as I thought that, it moved in a rush I could hardly follow, and it was standing beneath the crab apple tree, not a dozen steps away from us. My breath turned to tar in my throat.

The creature was male, I could see that now. He wore no clothes. Moonlight gathered around him like cold mist. He was tall, towering above me. I wanted to reach out and touch him. He was beautiful. He was the way I thought an angel should look, glorious, alien, and terrible.

I was cold. My legs shook. The hairs on my arms and neck stood painfully on end. I thought he would drown me with his radiant, ugly beauty. I was dark and insignificant before him. He sucked at my thoughts, leaving my head empty. I was inadequate, pathetic, scared.

Through a dry mouth I said, "Who ... who are you?"

He was right in front of me. He reached a long, twisted hand towards me, brushed sharp fingers that could slice skin across my face. Suddenly, all I wanted to do was run.

"Crab," he said. "They call me Crab."

He stepped back, and Emma was beside him, grinning her wild grin at me.

"Isn't he beautiful?"

His cruel hand smoothed over her hair, her face, her neck, her shoulders. I backed away. She leaned against him, a little scrap of wildness against his terrible form.

I turned and ran. Behind me, I heard her voice cry out, "Josh. Come back." But I didn't. I just kept on running.

Dad was asleep when I visited during the next two days.

"You mustn't disturb him," the nurse said. "He needs all the strength he can get."

So I sat beside him, holding his hand, gazing at his wasted body and his face that was so tired it looked bruised.

We used to play football in the park. If I scored a goal he would throw me over his shoulder like a fireman and go whooping down the pitch and dump me through the other goal. I reckoned I could pick him up with one hand now he looked so frail. His breathing was a thin wheeze, in and out, in and out, each breath creasing his face. Once I broke down and sobbed on his chest, but he just kept wheezing in, wheezing out. His skin was as dry as a winter leaf.

On the third day, he was awake, propped up on his pillows. He smiled at me when I came in.

"Been waiting up for you, lad," he said. "Well past my bedtime." He gasped a chuckle. The effort exhausted him.

His eyelids fluttered almost shut, but he forced them open again. "Don't let me fall asleep."

"How are you feeling, dad?"

"Been better, been worse."

I sat beside him. "Brought you some cards." I set them out on the table.

"Nice," he said. "Lad, I got my biopsy results today."

"What's a biopsy?"

He screwed up his old face. "They stuck this tube up my nose, all the way down into my lungs and scooped out a bit of that apple I swallowed." He coughed. "Tested it." He reached out to me with a frail hand and laid it over mine. His fingers curled around mine. "No surprise," he said, looking at me. "It's cancer."

My hand tightened, and he winced.

"Sorry," I said, but I croaked so much it hardly came out.

"They're going to operate," Dad said. "Take out that whole side of the lung. Probably do some other stuff too. Chemotherapy or radiation therapy. We haven't decided yet."

I couldn't move. My whole body was shaking.

"I'm sorry," he said. And as he did, I started to cry, big, painful sobs that shook the chair and his bed.

He waited until I'd finished, and then pulled my hand closer. "Listen, lad, I've been wanting to say this. The drink, see, it took away the pain. Just thought I was getting old. Didn't want to think it was this. So I got drunk and tried to ignore it. I'm sorry."

His breath had become gasps. He was sweating from his

forehead. His eyes were bloodshot and tinted yellow with exhaustion.

"Go to sleep, Dad," I said, and he did.

I HADN'T SEEN EMMA AT SCHOOL DURING THOSE THREE DAYS, but the day after, she was there, leaning against the lockers again, grinning at me.

"Where you going?" she said.

Her hair was more of a mess than ever. It was full of leaves. I shuddered when I thought about where they might have come from. That tree. That creature in it. I had tried to tell myself it was a nightmare, but I knew it wasn't. My shoes had been muddy when I'd got back, and there had been dried leaves on my bedroom floor, near the window.

"First aid class," I said. But I didn't move, just stood there and stared at her.

"Skip it," she said.

I shrugged. "Okay." There didn't seem much point in it anymore. Not unless they could teach me a cure for cancer. I had no time for bandages and mouth-to-mouth.

It was lunchtime. The corridors were heaving, but no one was taking any notice of us. I grabbed Emma's arm as we let ourselves be swept along towards the lunch hall.

"What is he?" I whispered. "Crab. What is he?"

"He's a Dane," she said.

"What, like from Denmark?"

She rolled her eyes, and her mouth turned down. She

almost hissed in my face. "No, not like from Denmark. Stupid, ugly, stupid boy. No. The Danes, like in the Fates, the People of Peace, the Fane, the Pharisees." She lowered her voice. "The Fay."

"You mean fai—"

She yanked my arm. "Don't say it! It's bad luck to say that name." She hunched her thin shoulders. "Bad luck."

"That's ridiculous," I said, but my skin wanted to shiver.

"Oh yeah," she said. "So what is he then?"

I shook my head.

"He likes you," she said. "He wants you."

I squinted at her. "What does that mean?"

She bit her lip. For an instant I thought she looked scared. "I don't know," she said. Then she stared defiantly at me again. "I don't care."

We came out into the dining room. Mr Miller and Mrs Wilson were on duty. Mrs Wilson glared at us. I turned away, but Emma stuck out her tongue. Mrs Wilson went stiff, and her neck reddened.

"Why did you do that?" I whispered.

Emma shrugged. "Why not? Did you see the look she gave us? She can't stand me."

"Let's get something to eat," I said.

Emma touched my hand. I glanced at her. She looked nervous. There was a line of sweat above her lip, and her hand was trembling. She licked her lip. "I brought you something to eat."

She held out her hand. "It's an apple," she said.

It was tiny and too green. I took it from her hand.

"It's okay," she said. "It tastes fine. Eat it."

She didn't meet my eyes.

Slowly, watching her all the time, I brought it up to my mouth.

Someone put a hand on my arm. "Don't eat that."

I looked up. Mr Miller was standing in front of me.

"That's not a real apple," he said. "It's a crab apple. It's a nasty, bitter, sour thing."

I looked at Emma. She just stared at her shoes.

"Why did you give him that, Emma?" Mr Miller said softly.

"Because she's an evil little cow," Mrs Wilson said from behind us.

Emma's head jerked up. "You're the evil cow," she shouted at Mrs Wilson. "You're the evil, fat, ugly, stupid cow. You."

Emma shoved past us, out into the middle of the hall. Her body was shaking like a branch in a storm. Her arms windmilled madly around her, sending plates and trays cascading onto the floor. All the while she kept up an inhuman shriek. In the middle of it all, her eyes fixed on mine, and I could have sworn that they were no longer wood-brown, but yellow. Burning yellow.

I found her later in the schoolyard, back pressed up against the concrete wall of the science block. She was staring up at the thick woods that cloaked Braddock Hill. She had been crying.

"I'm sorry," she said. "I'm so sorry. I didn't mean to do any of that. It's just…it's just…"

"Just what?" I said.

She turned on me, her eyes narrowed to slits. "Nothing. It's nothing. Dull, stupid, ugly boy. Go away, go away." She leapt to her feet and ran.

~

"Mrs Tully from school says you've got a new friend," Dad said. "What's her name?"

"Emma."

"What's she like, hey?" He winked.

"Wild," I said, sighing.

"Wild, hey?" He laughed his breathless laugh.

~

Sunday afternoon, and dying summer had decided to cast up one final, wonderful hot day. The air was still and clean, the sky a ferocious blue.

Emma was waiting at the garden gate. She wore jeans and a light, long-sleeved T-shirt.

"Want to walk?" she said.

"Not to the orchard," I said.

"No." She shivered as though a spider was crawling up her back. "Not to the orchard."

We climbed the path that led around the other side of Braddock hill. The Somerset levels were laid out before us, lush green and gently rumpled. Hundreds of irregularly sized fields, divided by head-high hawthorn and blackthorn hedges studded with ash, oak, and hazel, stretched to the rise

243

of the Mendip hills in the distance. Sunlight glittered from the streams and drainage ditches, like trails of mercury laid on green felt. Grey stone farmhouses were dotted here and there. Once, every one of them would have had an orchard. Not any more.

We walked close, almost touching, arms brushing once or twice.

"Is your dad going to die?" Emma said.

My throat turned to miserable stone. "Maybe. I guess."

"Oh."

She stared into my eyes. Hers were wide and that deep, swallowing brown. "I don't think I'll die," she said. I could hardly hear her voice. "But...but I think it might be worse."

I touched her shoulder.

"I want to help you," I said. "If I can."

She shook her head. "You can't," she whispered. "He's inside me."

"I could try. If you told me how."

I thought she might cry.

"Let's get out the sun. It's too bright." She pointed to a stand of trees.

We sat in the shade, our backs against a tall oak, sharing the Pepsi and Mars Bar she'd brought with her. I could hear insects buzzing, but they left us alone. The air was so clear it might not even have been there.

I glanced over at Emma. She was staring far out over the levels, watching something I couldn't see. Her face was peaceful, relaxed. She had a twig sticking out her hair. I reached up and pulled it to get it out. It snapped off. Her head jerked forward and she screamed. Sap welled up in the broken twig, and a single drop of blood.

She turned on me, jumping to her feet. Her brown eyes had turned yellow. Her face was twisted. I scrambled to my feet too. I grabbed her arm and pulled up the sleeve. The skin below was wrinkled, hard, and silvery. I felt sweat under my collar, on my hands.

"You're becoming like him, like Crab," I shouted. "Aren't you? Aren't you?"

She swung for me. Fingernails like claws scraped along my arm. I jumped back.

"Keep away from me, Josh. Keep away."

She turned and was gone, into the trees.

I DIDN'T SEE HER AGAIN UNTIL THE END OF THE MONTH. DAD came home for a couple of weeks. His operation wasn't scheduled for three months, and the hospital said he was strong enough to be discharged. He didn't look it. His skin was pallid and unhealthy. I could see his veins through it. He couldn't walk more than about four steps without panting.

Aunt Chris cut her way through the jungle that was the back garden, uprooting weeds, cutting back plants, while Dad sat and glowered from the window.

Thursday evening at the end of Dad's second week home, and he had to go back in for tests. Aunt Chris went with him. I sat at home, by the phone, waiting for one of them to call. At ten, the phone went. It was Aunt Chris.

"Listen, Joshua," she said. "We're staying here overnight." I heard her voice tremble. "They ... they say the cancer has begun to metastasise. It's begun to spread. They're going to operate tomorrow at two."

"I want to come in," I said.

"Tomorrow," she said. "He's got to sleep now."

I stood and went to the window and stared out across the moonlit garden.

It took me several minutes to notice the shape at the end of the garden, because it didn't move, but then I saw it for what it was. A person, standing rigid, half-hidden by shadows.

I went to the door, and opened it, stepped out.

Her head snapped around. It was Emma. I'd known it would be.

"Stay away from me, Josh," she hissed, then turned and ran.

This time I wasn't going to let her get away. I followed her. She ran fast, keeping to the shadows at the side of the road, but I knew where she was going. To the orchard. To Crab. I dashed after her.

I was out of breath by the time I reached the orchard. My lungs were raw and my throat painful. I saw her standing beneath the crab apple tree, staring up.

She turned, and in the moonlight I saw her clearly. Her fingers were too long. Twisted sticks poked from her head and elbows and knees. Her skin was silver and creased like the bark of a tree. Her eyes were burning yellow, bright in the darkness. Her teeth were pointed and sharp.

"Josh…"

Above her, the bark of the tree began to pulse and bulge.

I ran towards her. She hissed, and her razor-sharp claws darted at my throat. I threw myself back, and she followed. There was nothing of Emma in those eyes.

She swung again, and I ducked, feeling the claws slice through my hair. I punched. My fist caught her jaw. She stumbled back.

She blinked. For a moment her eyes were brown again. I saw panic and fear in them.

"Let me help you," I shouted.

Crab had freed one of his twisted limbs from the bark of the tree. His head was turning to peer down at us.

"Get it out of me, Josh," Emma whispered, her voice cracking. "Get him out of me."

She started to cough, great choking coughs that shook her whole body. Then her eyes turned yellow again.

Before she could move, I darted behind her and grabbed her, my arms circling her body. Above us, Crab freed his last limb and began to descend.

Emma's claws raked my arms. Blood trickled over my skin. I bunched one hand into a fist, crossed the other over it. Emma was struggling, lashing her twisted body to and fro, screaming. But still she was coughing, and still I held her tight.

A thud, and Crab landed in front of us. He rose, his radiance growing. For a moment I felt weak, scared, pathetic. His magnificence was like a tonne of sand, pushing down on me, burying me. My arms weakened, and I almost let go. But then I remembered Emma's frightened brown eyes, and I knew I wouldn't let him take her.

Ignoring the pain and fear and weakness, I pushed my fist below her ribs, the way they'd shown us in first aid class, and jerked it upwards in time with her cough.

Her body convulsed and she choked, gasped. Something flew from her mouth. We collapsed forward together.

Lying on the moss, still damp from her saliva, was a small green crab apple.

I looked up. Crab was standing there above us. But he no longer looked fearsome or terrible. He looked lonely. He looked like an old, old branch of a tree that had broken off and fallen. His yellow eyes gazed down at us. Then he turned, and climbed back into his crab apple tree.

"I'll be honest with you," the doctor said, looking down at me over his little glasses. "Your dad's got a twenty percent chance, at most. We've got to get the whole cancer out in one go."

Emma and I sat side by side. We had just seen Dad's trolley being pushed into the operating theatre. They had wheeled him away like they'd wheeled Mum away when I'd been five. She had never come back.

The doctor gave us a nod and then disappeared through the door.

My throat was hard. My teeth were clamped tight shut. I had to close my eyes to stop tears coming.

"Twenty percent," I whispered. "That's no chance at all. He's going to die."

I felt Emma reach for me and take my hand. She pushed something solid and round into it. I opened my eyes. It was the crab apple, whole, undamaged, out of her. She was smiling a wild, free smile. I smiled back, and clasped her hand.

We sat, the crab apple held pressed between our palms, and waited for the doctors to come back out.

THE SEA BEYOND THULE

ABOUT THE STORY

The Sea Beyond Thule *is part of a very loosely linked series of short stories (all of which stand alone as individual stories, too). There are two other stories,* The Land of Reeds *and* The Western Front, *that are also part of this series, both of which you can read in this short story collection, as well as a couple that I never quite got to the stage of being ready for publication. Maybe one day.*

THE SEA BEYOND THULE

Dicaearchus has always claimed that the Kasiterides Islands lie to the west of Gaul. Dicaearchus is a fool. Let him sail to the west if he wishes, if he ever moves his fat arse from the library in Athens. No, the Kasiterides Islands are due north of Gaul. We left them behind two days ago, with a fair warm wind behind us.

I have calculated that the coastline of the main body of the islands is 40,000 *stades* long. You would not think it a quarter of that from Dicaearchus's map. He was ever careless in his work. I burned his map and let the ashes flip free in the wind.

The natives call the Kasiterides Islands *Pretannia*. We stopped on the southern-most shore to lay on the cargo of tin my sponsor hopes will make him rich, but then we turned north once again. Sometimes, as we passed up *Pretannia's* western shore, a ghost wind blew from the land. The ship's master swung her wide then. He would not make landfall, even though we ran short of bread. He feared *Pretannia's* savages. I told him that the Phoenicians trade up and down these coasts. If the Phoenicians do not fear the savages, why should we? But the fool refused to listen to me.

When we return, I vow to walk in the interior of these mysterious islands. Let Dicaearchus grovel at Aristotle's feet. *I* will show them who should have been Aristotle's student when I return with my discoveries.

The sun stays long in the sky as we sail further north. Sometimes, in the ever-shorter night, I wonder if the sun accuses me with its presence. But no, I tell myself. It was ever the fault of Dicaearchus, not I. I bear no guilt.

Three days north of *Pretannia*, the fog and cold close around us, swallowing the sun in a wet veil.

"We must turn back," the captain says, his beard jutting like a finger at me.

"No," I say. I turn my back on him and stare out over the rail to the ghostly shapes the fog forms.

"The sailors fear," the captain says.

I do not look back. "Sailors always fear."

The *Pretani* savages told me there was a land still further to the north where the natives brew a drink from grain and honey, live in houses of logs and mud, and thresh their grain in barns instead of the open fields. If such a strange land exists, I, Pytheas, must be the one to discover it. Dicaearchus has discovered nothing.

In the thick fog, we sail more slowly. The wind has fallen, and the captain fears to raise all the sails. But there is a current in this sea that carries us on to the north that no civilised man has ever seen.

On the morning of the fifth day, I am awoken by shouts from the sailors. I hurry up from my cabin, thinking they have seen land, but their babble is of sea monsters. Frowning, I peer into the fog.

Huge beasts move through the water. From time to time, spouts of water erupt like geysers from their bodies. The sailors shriek and pray, but they are superstitious fools, and eventually the beasts slip behind.

We sight land on the sixth day. Grey cliffs loom from the fog. White surf breaks on stony beaches. I am chilled to the bone by this never-ending fog. The near-constant sun is but a leached outline of its normal self. Part of me fears that. Part of me fears that I am to blame, that the sun dies. But it is just the fog that hides the sun.

For a day we sail along the coast, until we spy low, long houses beyond a beach. A boat carries us to the shore. The water that splashes from the oars is icy cold. This is a miserable land.

I set up my *gnomon* on a flat rock to measure our position, but the sun is too dull to cast a shadow.

The captain leads us up the beach towards the longhouses. The fog hangs on the grass and the crops beyond the village. The ground is wet and runs with the effluent of animals.

The savages in the village must have seen us approaching, for when we arrive at the largest log house, a line of men are arrayed before us. They are big, hairy men, wrapped in stinking hides. They carry bronze weapons openly, but they are obviously farmers, not warriors. One calls out to us in his savage tongue.

The captain looks at me. I shrug. Does he expect me to speak such savage tongues? Still, the *Pretani* understood my gestures and my offers readily enough. These will do the same. I wave over the sailors with their trinkets for gifts.

I am about to offer the gifts to the savages when a woman pushes through the men. She is wrapped in the same hides as the men, and her face is obscured. I do not recognise her until she speaks.

"Pytheas," she says. Then she spits into the mud.

Danae. My dearest wish. My darkest nightmare. My only regret.

She turns from me and walks past the savages. She grunts something at them, and they part to let me by. For a moment, I am too shocked by her presence here to move, but then I hurry after her.

"Why are you here?" I call. "How are you here?"

"Do you think you are the only one who can travel, Pytheas? Did you think you had *discovered* this land?"

"I..."

"The Phoenicians know *Prettania* and the *Pretani* know *Thule*. It was not difficult."

"*Thule*?" I say, stupidly.

"This land. The natives name it *Thule*."

We enter the long house. It is dank and dark and smells of smoke. The windows are closed by shutters against the fog.

"But why are you here?" I say. "I thought you would be with Dicaearchus." His name is dust on my tongue.

Danae turns to me. Motes of gold float in her dark eyes like fragments of the sun. I drop my gaze.

"Tell me first why *you* are here, Pytheas. Tell me quick, because I have little patience for you. Do you come to make good the wrong you did?"

I feel heat in my cheeks for the first time in months. "I? I did nothing. If anything was done, Dicaearchus was to blame, not me."

Danae takes a fast step towards me. The gold in her eyes flares. "You stripped the soul of a god from the sun. The sun is dying."

For a second, I cannot breathe.

"We did not know," I whisper.

"You did not care."

Again, I drop my eyes.

"The solstice comes in a week," Danae says. "Tomorrow I begin my journey north. Think on what you did and think whether you would make it right."

I FIRST MET DANAE IN ATHENS THREE YEARS AGO. I WAS FORTY-nine, an old man, and Danae was but twenty-two. Yet I was a renowned navigator, mathematician, and astronomer, and she but served in her father's taverna. It was right that she should notice me and I her.

I showed her how to calculate the distance north with a

gnomon and how to navigate by the stars. Her hair was as black as the night in which my stars floated. I determined to win her.

I bought her jade from Egypt and bronze jewellery from Massallia. She rewarded me with kisses and a promise in her pure dark eyes.

All was fine until the day of the festival of Helios when Dicaearchus came with his friends into Danae's taverna. He was thirty years younger than I, Aristotle's new favourite, golden haired and as tall as a god. I saw Danae's eyes follow him as he crossed the room. He laughed at me when he saw me there.

"Old man," he called. "I have heard tales in the dockside inns that you call yourself a *mathematician*."

Jeers spilled from his companions.

"I have calculated the circumference of the Earth," I said.

"Child's play," he sneered. "I did that in my cradle."

"Then what have you done?" I was half drunk and red-faced.

"It is not what I have done," the arrogant oaf said, "although you could not understand half of it. It is what I will achieve."

Danae brought a flask of wine over to the Dicaearchus's table and poured for him and his friends.

"I hear you are the old man's woman," Dicaearchus said to her. "You are wasted on him."

"I belong to no man," Danae said, and it was as though a bone was thrust through my heart.

"Then perhaps I will make you mine," Dicaearchus said.

She stepped away from him, laughing. "You would have to do great things to win me."

He tipped back his head. "I intend to."

I stood. "Anything you can do, I can surpass."

That flash youth turned to me, and there was malice in his eyes. "Then I challenge you, old man." He glanced around. "Today is the festival of Helios, the festival of the sun. Let that be our challenge. You say you are a mathematician and an astronomer. We will use our skills, you and I, and we will study the sun. We will measure and learn all there is, and by this time next year we will see who has reasoned the most. He who wins will take the girl. He who loses will leave Athens and never return."

"Done," I said, with force.

By the time I thought to look, Danae was gone from the room.

Over the next year, I studied and I calculated and I made note. Never had I worked so hard. I was a man obsessed. Reluctantly, Helios gave up his secrets to me. I knew him. I stripped him bare and wrote down every syllable of his name.

But Dicaearchus did more. And on the next festival of Helios, I left Athens forever and returned to Massallia.

By late afternoon, the fog lifts and I am able to take my measurements. I calculate the position of this land and write it in my book. No man has discovered this land before. I will map it. All the civilised world will marvel at what I have found on this voyage.

The sun leaves the sky for no more than a couple of hours each night, and it dips but low beneath the horizon. If we travel north, I wonder, will we see where it rests at night? It would be fine to map that place. Perhaps I will accompany Danae when she journeys north.

DANAE COMES TO ME THE NEXT DAY. I DO NOT KNOW THE HOUR, but the sun has been in the sky for several hours. I have not slept yet in this land. The never-ending sunlight troubles my old body.

"I will come with you," I say.

I turned from her once, when Dicaearchus won her. I will not leave her again.

"Good," she says. "We will take your ship. The journey over land would be hard."

I assent.

The savages who have hosted her bring a strange boat down to the shore for her. It is long and thin and made of hides stretched over a frame of light wood. When I ask her what it is for, she merely says, "You will see."

We load her boat onto the ship. The captain complains, but I have long learned to ignore him.

We follow the coast west then north, drawing ever further towards the night-time sun.

Sometimes I try to talk to Danae about the old days in

Athens, but she does not smile and she does not laugh. Only when I mention Dicaearchus does she react.

"You fool," she says. "Did you think I would take up with that arrogant child? He was as bad as you. Did you think I was a prize to be tussled over like wrestlers in the games?"

After three days of sailing, we leave the coast of *Thule* behind us. The sea is cold and the air colder still. Danae stands at the bow and stares forward, towards the sun.

One day further, and the sea begins to change. The progress of our ship slows, as though something tugs against us. The sailors fashion charms for their gods and prostrate themselves on the deck.

I order a bucket lowered over the side. When it comes back up, the water has congealed. It is cold to the touch and has the consistency of a sea lung.

For a few more hours, our ship struggles on, but then the captain comes to me.

"We can sail no further," he says. "The very sea resists us." He looks away. "We reach the end of the world."

I have studied this new medium in the last hours. The captain may be right. This is not water nor land nor air, but as an amalgam of all three. Not many *stades* north of here, the sun sleeps at night. There, the sky must join the Earth. I believe this medium must hold the earth in the heavens. We are not far from the end of the world.

Danae turns from the bow and joins us.

"The people of *Thule* say that you cannot walk or sail on this," she says. "You can take me no further. Put my boat onto the water. It is light enough to pass over the thickened sea."

I have not wanted to ask the question on our journey, but now I must. I do not wish to lose Danae again.

"What are you doing?" I say. "Where are you going?"

When she looks at me, again I see the shards of sunlight trapped in her dark eyes.

"When you took the soul of Helios from the sun with your reasoning and your measurements, it began to die, for if the sun has no soul, it is just a fire that burns out. If it dies, the whole world will fall into darkness. Both you and Dicaearchus knew this, but you chose to ignore it. I cannot.

"On the solstice, when the sun just touches the world to the north of here, I will give myself to the sun. I am not a god, and I cannot return to the sun what you took from it, but I can stop its death." She takes my hand, as she did so many times in Athens before Dicaearchus came between us. "Come with me, Pytheas." She smiles. "Together, we might brighten the sun."

I tug free. "Dicaearchus should do this," I say. "It was his fault, not mine." I step back. She does not know what she asks of me. My life is too valuable to be cast away. "I have my work to complete. My exploration. I must draw my map. Humanity needs my knowledge."

She spits on the deck at my feet. I jump back.

"You and Dicaearchus are the same," she says. "You always were. You can see no further than your own pride."

"It's not true," I protest. "He was the one with pride, not I. My work..."

But she answers no more.

I watch her lower her boat into the strange sea and slowly paddle away north, towards the low sun.

Together we might brighten the sun, she said.

We might.

But by the time I believe it, Danae is far away, and she does not see me reach out my hand nor hear my cry, and the ship can sail no further.

THE LAND OF REEDS

ABOUT THE STORY

I don't know when I first became fascinated with Egyptian history and mythology. I first visited Egypt when I was eight years old and my family and I were in the process of moving back to England from Zambia. Egypt was a brief stopover, along with a longer stop in Kenya, where my mother had worked as a nurse. We weren't in Egypt long, but we certainly had time to visit the pyramids at Cairo and the Valley of the Kings at Luxor.

I went back again when I was in my twenties, but by that time I was already a fan. I always found it more interesting and absorbing than Greek, Roman, or Norse mythology. As well as The Land of Reeds *and another short story that was never good enough to publish, Egypt was an enormous influence on my first two children's novels, SECRETS OF THE DRAGON TOMB and THE EMPEROR OF MARS.*

This story is set in the time of Ptolemy IV, about 120 years after Alexander the Great claimed the throne of Egypt.

THE LAND OF REEDS

THE DEAD, HE HAD DISCOVERED, HAD MOUTHS AND COULD speak, but they could not be heard.

Or, they could not be heard by the living: the dead talked among themselves with voices of sand and dust. Amenemhet did not wish to talk to the dead. A man who has been murdered wishes to speak to those still living, to lay testament before them, to give warning.

The dead, in their crowded voices, said that *Re* no longer travelled through the underworld each night. They said that his face was now no more than a ball of fire in the sky. There were no more demons in the underworld, no *Apep* the serpent, no *Amemet* the great devourer, no gates, no judges, no scales. There was no Land of Reeds.

The dead said *Amun-Re* died on the day the Macedonian usurper sat upon the throne of the two lands and proclaimed himself Pharaoh, for Alexander was no true son of *Re*, no true son of *Osiris,* and so no god.

Perhaps, Amenemhet thought, they were right. All his life, he had studied the map that showed the path through the underworld and learned the words of the *Chapter of Renewing the Gates in the House of Osiris which is in Sekhet-Aanru*. After his murder, Amenemhet had watched through the eyes of his *ka* as the *sem* priest prepared his body and performed the sacrifices and as the *kher-het* priest read the prayers and instructions. All had been in order, and Amenemhet had felt his *ka* slip free.

But when night came, his *ka* had not entered *duat*. It had remained in the desert sand, and Amenemhet had become aware of the press of the dead around him and the whispers of their dry voices like the desert wind. "*Re* no longer travels the underworld at night," they whispered. "His face is but a ball of fire..."

HE LEFT THE TOMBS AND THE DEAD BEHIND HIM AND WALKED down into the town. The narrow streets were busy with the living. Amenemhet passed easily through them, his *ka* as insubstantial on their skins as his words were on their ears. Other *ka*s of the dead also moved through the streets. They stared at him with drawn, grey eyes. Amenemhet stepped around the dead, sometimes stepping through the white-washed, mud-brick walls of the houses that lined the tight streets to do so.

Once, in the market, he shouted furiously at the living: "*Rep-a* Djau has murdered me. He slipped a blade into my throat and left me to bleed to death." But the living kept on their way, chattering and laughing. Amenemhet spat emptily onto the ground.

"They can't hear you, you know."

Amenemhet looked around. The *ka* of a child was standing behind him. She could not have been more than eight years old when she died. She scarcely came up to Amenemhet's waist.

"I know," he said. "Go away."

Her *ka* held ghosts of colours. Specks of precious gold swam in her eyes. Most of the *ka*s he had seen had been grey.

"We could help each other," she said, scampering after him as he strode through the crowd. "I was poor and young. I never saw the maps of the underworld. I never learnt the words to speak at the gates."

"Go away," Amenemhet said. "Those things are as dead as *Amun-Re*. The Land of Reeds is no more. And what could you offer me?"

Amenemhet's house was on the southern edge of the town, a mile from the rich flow of the Nile, set among the estates of the wealthy. Amenemhet had been *hety-a* of the town, and all had been pleased to pay him court and to seek his wisdom. Now those same people saw him not and heard him not. The only one who paid him court was the *ka* of the wretched urchin who dogged his heels like a loose bandage.

"Something," the child said. "I have been dead for a long

time. I know the world of the dead among the living. I know things."

"Go away," Amenemhet repeated.

A golden chariot stood outside the gate of his house. The sight of it plunged Amenemhet's *ka* into coldness. *Rep-a* Djau was here. With a roar of rage that did not even stir the dust in the air, Amenemhet plunged through the outer wall.

The murderer was not in the square court, but the door in the north portico stood open, and Amenemhet heard voices from within.

Amenemhet stepped through. *Rep-a* Djau stood in the centre of the reception room, clad like a pharaoh in his green and gold gown and his bead necklaces. Baketamen, Amenemhet's wife, sat on an earthenware bench before *Rep-a* Djau. The two girls, Meryt and Kawit, and his little son, Hori, who was scarcely off his mother's breast, stood behind Baketamen. Baketamen had obviously been crying, but she had dried her eyes and looked up at *Rep-a* Djau.

"I have always been a good friend of your husband," Djau was saying. "He trusted me. Anything I can do for you, I will."

"Liar," Amenemhet screamed. "He always envied me you. It wasn't enough that he was richer than I, that he had the ear of the *Tjaty* of the two lands. He wanted you. He killed me. Don't listen to him."

Baketamen smiled. "You are kind, *Rep-a*. We will remember your kindness."

Djau bowed. "You may always call on me."

Then the murderer turned, and strode out of the house.

When Amenemhet finally thought to look, the *ka* of the troublesome child had gone.

THE SERVANTS DID NOT COME THE NEXT DAY. WHEN Amenemhet's *ka* searched through the house, he found his wife sweeping the sand from the floor. With every stroke of the brush, a tear fell from her face into the sand to be lost in the water she had sprinkled there. His children, even little Hori, were building a fire from dried dung. When he had been alive, they had burned only wood in this house.

"There is a new *haty-a* now," a voice said. "You are dead. Your place is not here. The taxes you once received now go to another."

The *ka* of the child stood beside him.

"Go away," Amenemhet said. "Why do you bother me with things I know?"

THE FIRST CREDITOR CAME AT DAWN ON THE THIRD DAY. He was a grain trader from Thebes. Amenemhet had met the man only once. The man had stuck to *Rep-a* Djau's shoulder like a shadow to a wall. Amenemhet had disliked the man and refused to do business with him. That had angered *Rep-a* Djau.

"It grieves me to trouble you at such a sad time, *Nebet Per*," the trader said to Baketamen, "but your husband owed

271

me money. The debt is long overdue. I would wait longer, but my farmers need payment."

Outraged, Amenemhet swept through the man. "I have done no business with you. You lie."

"You are mistaken," Baketamen said. "I keep the household accounts. I have no record of any debts unpaid. My husband told me of no contract with you."

The trader bowed his head and passed a rolled papyrus to her. She flattened it. Amenemhet peered past her. The bill of sale was clear. His seal had been pressed firmly onto the papyrus.

Hesitantly, Baketamen said, "It is a large sum."

"You see my dilemma, *Nebet Per*."

"I made no such contract," Amenemhet shouted. "The bill is false. *Rep-a* Djau must have stolen my seal when he murdered me."

Baketamen rolled the papyrus and returned it to the trader. "You will be paid."

The trader bowed deeper.

"How?" Amenemhet said, but none answered.

THEY CAME LIKE THE FLOW OF THE NILE, THE CREDITORS, EACH with his papyrus. With every payment, Baketamen's face became more drawn, her figure more bent. Her eyes grew desperate. She did not sleep.

At last, near the end of the second week, when the latest

in the flow of creditors had gone, Baketamen dropped to her knees on a floor mat.

"Amenemhet," she wailed. "How could you?"

"But I didn't," he said.

She did not hear him.

"WE MUST SELL THE HOUSE," BAKETAMEN TOLD HER CHILDREN. "That is the only way we can pay your father's debts. This is a good house. It will bring us enough."

"Where will we live?" Kawit asked, through tears.

"We will find a small place in the town. It will just be one room, but it will shelter us."

"We should go to *Rep-a* Djau," Meryt said. "He would give us rooms in his palace. He is kind."

Baketamen shook her head. "Your father would not like that. We still have our pride."

"Who cares about father?" Meryt shouted, little Meryt with the wide brown eyes and the thick black hair, his jewel. "This is all his fault. I hate him. I wish *Rep-a* Djau was our father."

She turned and ran from the room, passing through Amenemhet's stricken *ka*.

Amenemhet's anger lifted him like a feather in the wind from the north. Yet it seemed a distant anger, an anger drained of colour. His *ka* drifted through the town, across the rich fields, to the desert beyond and the tombs. For a while, he

273

forgot his family and slipped only among the *ka*s by the tombs. They did not revolt him as they once had. He found comfort in their endless, repeated words of despair. *Re no longer travels the underworld at night. His face is but a ball of fire in the sky*

Time passed, a scarce-noticed breeze.

One day, a golden chariot drew up before Amenemhet's tomb. A tall man in green and gold alighted. Disquiet grew in Amenemhet.

The tall man hitched up his robe and urinated onto Amenemhet's shrine, befouling the offerings left there.

Amenemhet howled. *Rep-a* Djau. Fury revived him, and his memories tore back. He chased the speeding chariot towards the town, throwing curses at the *rep-a*'s back.

Once in the town, he slowed. The streets here were narrow. The *rep-a*'s chariot could not move swiftly.

Amenemhet surveyed the crowds of the living. How bright they were. He became transfixed, and soon the chariot was gone.

Wailing from one of the low buildings reached Amenemhet. He passed through the wall.

He did not recognise his family at first. These people were strangers to him. They were dirty, bent, sun-darkened, and poorly dressed. Yet when Baketamen looked up, Amenemhet knew her.

Beside her, Meryt and little Hori stood over their prostrate sister. Kawit moaned and twisted on the dirt floor. Her skin was oily with sweat. She seemed very close to Amenemhet, as though her *ka* wished to slip from her body and begin the journey to the Land of Reeds.

Baketamen brought a rag from a bucket and squeezed water over Kawit's hot skin. The girl moaned in response.

"Mother," Meryt said. "Kawit is dying. She will not last another day if we cannot bring a doctor."

"We have no money for a doctor," Baketamen said. "It is all gone."

"*Rep-a* Djau has money," Meryt said. "He has his own doctor. He would help us. You know that."

Baketamen bent her head. Then she straightened. "You are right. We have waited too long. Help me with your sister. We will go to the *rep-a*."

AMENEMHET FOLLOWED HIS FAMILY TO THE *REP-A*'S PALACE. A guard let them through the massive external wall, while another hurried off to fetch servants. Beyond the wall was a garden. Date palms, pomegranate trees, sycamores, and acacias lined the winding paths. The roof of a pagoda jutted from the shrubbery to the left. Blossoming vines trailed over it. Around the edge of the gardens, Amenemhet saw kitchens, workshops, stables, cattle sheds, and a wide granary.

"I never could offer you this," he said, unheard. "Yet you loved me."

Servants arrived to carry Kawit on a litter. Baketamen and the other children followed a scribe through the gardens. They passed a large rectangular pond from which grew lotus plants, papyrus reeds, and water lilies. Amenemhet saw the thick brown bodies of fish slide through the water.

The enormous house stood on a plinth at the end of the garden. A colonnaded flight of stairs led up to a vestibule. There *Rep-a* Djau stood, his smile as wide as the river. Amen-emhet saw the *rep-a* take Baketamen's arm. Then a silent wind took his *ka* and bore it away.

Time passed. Dust settled on his eyes. His *ka* grew gaunt and listless. He found himself drifting through the streets, dragged again and again to the crowds at the tombs. He forgot his name and his purpose.

"You're becoming like the rest of them," a small voice observed. "You are fading. Your *ka* will forget what it knew, and all you will be able to do is repeat the same words all the other *ka*s repeat."

"Go away," he said. But there was no force to his words.

The *ka* of the child continued remorselessly. "You will forget the map of the underworld. You will forget the path to the Land of Reeds. You will forget the words to speak at the gates."

"Go away. *Re* no longer travels the underworld at night. His face is but a ball of fire in the sky. There are no demons anymore in the underworld, no *Apep*, no *Amemet*, no gates, no judges, no scales. There is no Land of Reeds."

"Listen to yourself. You just repeat the words. Maybe *Amun-Re* is dead. Maybe *Re* no longer travels the underworld.

That does not mean there is no Land of Reeds. You know the map, yet you will not follow the path."

"There is no path," he said.

"If you help me, I will help you," the dead child said.

Amenemhet's *ka* drifted, caught by a dead wind.

Time passed.

Something was pulling at him. Amenemhet realised he was at the tombs. *Kas* pressed tight around him. He could hear words coming from his mouth. "—are no demons anymore in the underworld, no *Apep*, no *Amemet*—" He cut off the words.

The *ka* of the child stared up at him sadly. "Your colours are almost gone. You are near to forgetting."

"Then let me," Amenemhet whispered.

"Your daughter is well. She has recovered from the fever. Your family now live in the house of your murderer. He speaks of marriage to your wife. Perhaps soon your son will number among the dead. Your murderer resents that your blood flows in your son's veins. Accidents are easy. I know."

Already the words wanted to bubble from Amenemhet's lips. *Re no longer travels the underworld at night. His face is but a ball of fire in the sky* Instead, he said, "Help me."

"Come, then," the *ka* of the child said. "I will take you to one who can speak with the dead."

THE CHILD LED HIM DOWN TOWARDS THE RIVER, WHERE THE poorest lived. Sometimes, in the inundation, these rough houses were swept away by the river. When living, Amenemhet had not come this way. The narrow streets stank of human waste.

The hut the child took him to had partially collapsed in an inundation. One wall was gone. The roof dipped towards the floor. Amenemhet dipped so he could see within.

"Come," the child said. "To the living, she is deaf and blind."

Amenemhet stepped into the dark.

"I see you, oh dead," a voice said. "I smell your dust, and I hear your pale breath."

Amenemhet bent towards the sound. A crone sat huddled among rags.

"Who are you?" he said.

"No one you would know, oh grand *hety-a*." She cackled. "So grand to come so low."

"I was murdered," Amenemhet said. "*Rep-a* Djau slid a blade into my throat and left me to bleed to death. You must tell everyone. They must know the truth."

The crone rocked back and cackled again. "Who will listen to the words of an old woman against the word of the *rep-a*? They would throw stones at me."

Amenemhet fell to his knees. "I was always a loyal servant of Ptolemy Philopator. Once, he touched my hand."

"Go," she said. "The *ka*s of the dead have no place with the living. Go to the Land of Reeds or go to fade. I do not care which. You know the map of the underworld, and the child is a true child of *Re*. Between you, you can reopen the path once more."

"I do not know where the path begins," Amenemhet said.

"It begins where it has always begun," the crone said. "It begins where life meets death, where they combine, and where life fails."

Amenemhet stood. "I will not go while the *rep-a* lives. Justice must be done."

"Then fade," the crone said, "but bother my rest no more."

THE TOWN WAS FILLED WITH CELEBRATION. CURIOUS, Amenemhet followed the crowds.

Rep-a Djau's house was surrounded by flags. Amenemhet heard music within. He passed through the wall. The child followed behind.

His wife stood on the top of the steps leading to the *rep-a*'s house. Beside her, *Rep-a* Djau stood, garbed in a wedding robe.

"He has married her," Amenemhet said. He swept forward, his *ka* buoyed by rage. He pummelled his fists through *Rep-a* Djau. They had no effect.

He felt the dead wind try to lift him back towards the tombs.

The *rep-a* lent towards Baketamen. "Tonight," he said, "you are mine."

Amenemhet saw his wife shiver and a tear lay its trail down her cheek.

He drew back. His *ka* grew cold.

The *ka* of the child gazed at him, her face sad.

Amenemhet looked up at *Rep-a* Djau. "I know where the path begins," he said.

THE DEAD WERE EASY TO LEAD. THEIR *KAS* HAD BECOME GREY. They had lost their will. They could only repeat words. Amenemhet became his own dead wind. He passed through them, drove them, tugged them. And he taught them new words to repeat.

Slowly, the *ka*s began to drift from the tombs.

A cold wind passed through the town, and even the living moved aside.

It reached the walls of *Rep-a* Djau's palace and passed through them. The guests grew silent.

At the high table, *Rep-a* Djau stood, his forehead lining, his mouth growing tight.

The cold wind reached him. The dead reached him.

"Follow," Amenemhet said. Behind him, the dead whispered their new words.

Amenemhet flowed up into *Rep-a* Djau's heart. There the *ka* of the dead met *Rep-a* Djau's living *ka*.

Grey dust fell from Amenemhet's *ka* and drifted down onto the *rep-a*'s heart. Amenemhet's colours grew. Ahead of him, he saw the path.

The *ka* of the child came next. *Rep-a* Djau clutched his chest as the cold touched his heart.

Then the river of the dead swept through him.

Amenemhet saw the grey dust fall from their *ka*s. As each of them passed through Djau, they spoke the words Amenemhet had taught them: "I am *Rep-a* Djau. I am a murderer and a liar. The gods judge me. I have murdered *hety-a* Amenemhet."

Rep-a Djau's lips twitched. Sweat sprang from his pale face.

Still the dead came. Still they spoke the words.

Rep-a Djau stiffened. His head tipped back and the words poured from him in a scream: "I am *Rep-a* Djau. I am a murderer and a liar. The gods judge me. I have murdered *hety-a* Amenemhet."

Then he fell.

The last *ka* to pass onto the path was the *ka* of *Rep-a* Djau.

Amenemhet took the hand of the child who had helped him. The map that showed the way was clear before him. The words to speak at the gates sat on his tongue.

"Come," he said. "Together we will find the Land of Reeds."

THE WESTERN FRONT

ABOUT THE STORY

The Western Front *took a ridiculous amount of research (and I'm sure I still got some things wrong). I was working at the University of Leeds at the time and had access to their library. I spent many lunch breaks with maps of battlefields spread out in front of me, working out the advances of various forces at various times, as well as reading through letters, journals, and newspapers of the men who fought on the Western Front. It's fascinating stuff, and fascinating stuff is a dangerous place for any writer. But I hope I resisted the temptation to include most of it in this story.*

THE WESTERN FRONT

My Dear Helen,

I still have the rose you gave me when we parted. It is pressed between the pages of my diary so that I will see it every day when I start to write. It is easy in this war to forget that which matters; with your rose, I shall never fail to remember it.

Finally, I have learned the details of my posting. You will appreciate that I cannot reveal them in a letter. I can tell you, however, that I am full of confidence.

I travelled north by train with Captain Dawson. The weather in France was glorious, almost like England at its summer best. I daydreamed of you and little Steven in our garden. It is at moments like these that I know that what we are fighting for is true and right, and that we will prevail.

The weather changed as we approached our destination. Low, grey clouds and a damp drizzle replaced the sun. We disembarked at the railhead. The fields of wheat were ripe here, but unharvested. The hedgerows were overgrown. This is a land abandoned by civilisation.

Several hundred men had travelled up with us on the train, packed tightly into open wagons, along with several artillery pieces. Captain Dawson and I watched the artillery being unloaded then hitched to mules and dragged away. I am told that we have a significant advantage in guns. You see, my sweet, your fears were unfounded. We cannot fail.

Finally, a flustered and apologetic runner arrived to guide us to General Gough's forward command post, where we received our disbursements. We are still far from the front. Gough gave us sherry and cigars, and we played cards late into the night with one of his aides (not for money, you will be pleased to hear; we have retained some civilised traits, even here).

Tomorrow I will be taken to meet my platoon at the front. My own platoon! Oh, Helen, I am so proud. This is what I trained for. I will win this war for you. Jerry's army is ready to break; Haig is sure of it, and he will put everything into our push. I will be home with you soon.

Give my love to little Steven, and tell him what a brave and glorious man his daddy has become.

With all my affection and love.

Richard

15th July, 1917

DIARY OF LIEUTENANT RICHARD STARK, 16TH JULY, 1917

Gough's maps are astounding. We have mapped every single one of Jerry's trenches and fortifications in painstaking detail. Every brigade's push is clearly marked and objectives set, hour-by-hour. My unit is part of the 21st Division, 2nd Corp, under Brigadier-General Goodman. Gough had nothing but praise for the man's courage and honour. When the offensive begins, my unit will help secure the Gheluvelt plateau.

Gough has a relief model of the terrain. Jerry holds the high ground and uses it to observe our movements, although our taking of the Messine ridge has given us a foothold of our own. Within seven-and-a-half hours of the beginning of the assault, my platoon will have established itself within Polygon Wood, and the push on the whole Passchendaele Ridge will begin. Then Jerry will break.

After the meeting, we took another train to Ypres. The city is a ruin, the ground around it pocked with old craters. A guide met me there, and I said my farewells to Captain Dawson. I do not know if I will see him again. This war has taken so many, and even with Haig's best plans, we will lose more here.

Beyond the Menin Gate, the terrain began to change. The land was more broken. Where once trees stood, shattered stumps poked jaggedly into the dirty sky. The earth was over-grown with weeds, and it had not been cultivated for some time. Here and there, craters were ripped from the soil, and in the bottom of some of them, black water glistened.

We passed our rear defences and took a duckboard path towards the front line. It took us near on an hour to reach the trenches. No doubt my lack of surefootedness on the treacherous duckboard paths slowed us.

Only two hundred yards separate our front line from Jerry's forward zone, if I recall Gough's maps correctly. I did not risk a look. I followed my guide, head down.

About a hundred or a hundred and fifty yards to our right, our forward line cuts into the shattered tangle of Sanctuary Wood. I am glad not to be stationed there. I would not wish to advance through that zone.

My 'men' are a sorry-looking bunch. I do not know the last time any of them saw a razor or boot polish. Their uniforms are dirty and worn, and I would have struggled to tell them from Germans under the muck. They did not rise when I entered this section of the trench. They glanced up, and then returned to their activities. It is no wonder we have made little progress on this front. The men lack discipline.

Half-a-dozen sat playing cards around an upturned crate. Others lounged about, reading or talking. Another stood, peering over the edge of the trench with a periscope.

A shot rang out. Like a fool, I ducked.

The man at the periscope turned with a grin and held up a finger. Cheers arose from my men.

"Their engineers are out," my guide explained. "Probably laying wire."

A moment later, a figure slipped over the edge into the trench, shouldering his rifle.

"That sent Jerry back to his hole," the soldier with the periscope said.

"For now," the newly-arrived man said. He fumbled in his pockets, pulled out a cigarette, and lit it.

Frowning, I stepped forward. "Soldier."

He blinked, as though he had only just noticed me. "Who are you?" he said. There was an arrogance to the way he spoke that I disliked immediately.

The men call him Bird, I have discovered. I can see why. His eyes are small, black. His nose is sharp and long.

"I am your commanding officer," I said. "Now put out your cigarette."

"Is that right?" Bird sauntered over and blew a cloud of smoke in my face. "Well, let me tell you something. We've had a dozen lieutenants here in the last six months. Lieutenant Donald lasted longest. Hard as old oak, he was, with eyes in the back of his head. Come up from the ranks, see? He managed a month before Jerry put a lump of lead through his throat. Took a day to die, he did. Never screamed once." Bird scratched behind his ear. "Mind you, it's hard to scream with most of your throat gone." Someone sniggered behind me. Bird continued, "The others, Jerry's guns took four of them. Two more tried to nut shells, and one didn't get his mask on quickly enough when the gas rolled in. Nasty one, that." He shook his head.

"And the rest?" I asked.

Bird smiled. "They got careless. Tripped backwards, all four of them, one after another. Fell onto knives." He stepped past me, and as he did so, he whispered, "Welcome to Wipers, Lieutenant. Try not to get anyone killed before you cop it."

I heard laughs around me.

There is a cancer at the heart of this unit. Its name is Bird. I will cut it out.

DIARY OF LIEUTENANT RICHARD STARK, 18TH JULY, 1917

We can't keep the water out of the damned trench. I've had the men pumping, but they work lethargically, and when I turn my back they stop. And the water just seeps back in. Everything is damp, my boots, my clothes, my skin. Everything stinks of mildew and rot.

The bombardment of Jerry's front line began not long after my arrival, and it has increased hourly. I cannot sleep. The explosions shudder through the earth. The detonations punch the air. Two nights without sleep. My head aches. My eyes are filled with needles. Sometimes I find myself just standing there, having forgotten what I was doing. I long for the order to attack.

When the bombardment began, I overheard the men talking.

"Might as well send Jerry a letter to say we're coming," Bird said. "When it gets heavy, he'll just pull back from the front line and pound us as we advance."

"Keep your opinions to yourself," I snapped. "You are no general."

Bird just looked at me, his gaze unwavering, and I am ashamed to admit that I looked away first.

It has gone on long enough. I will confront Bird.

The cloud-cloaked dusk has faded. The shells fall and shiver through my exhausted bones.

There are rats in the trenches. I can hear them in the dark.

I will confront Bird now.

DIARY OF LIEUTENANT RICHARD STARK, 19TH JULY, 1917

Bird was not there when I went to confront him last night.

"He's out on patrol," one of the men said.

"I gave no orders," I said.

"Bird don't need no orders," the man replied.

I waited, as though I were the corporal and he the lieutenant. Eventually, close on dawn, Bird slithered, like the reptile he is, back into the trench.

I stood. "Where have you been?" I demanded.

He made a show of looking around. "Just stretching me legs."

"I could have you shot for desertion," I shouted.

Those horrid little bird eyes stilled on me. "Do you know what we're here for, Lieutenant?"

I blinked.

"We're here to kill the Hun," he said. "That's all. Forget your nanny's tales of honour and glory. Those was just lies to keep you from crying in the dark. Well, guess what? Those lies don't work in this dark, and it just keeps getting darker. The only truth is the killing. That's what I do. I kill the Hun." He stepped up close. "I won't have no wet-behind-the-ears boy with a few stripes on his jacket getting in my way." He lit up a cigarette. It glowed red in the darkness. His face showed strange shadows from that glow. "Understand that, Lieutenant, and you might make it for a couple of weeks." He chuckled, a nasty wet cough of a laugh. "After all, it'll all be over by then, right?"

My Dear Helen,

It has been raining for a week. God, how I miss those English summer days. I have not seen the sun once on these Ypres fields. I swear it grows darker each day.

Not long now, my love. The push will come soon. Jerry will break. I will be home to you before Christmas. Imagine that! We'll have presents and a roaring fire and everything will be dry.

The shelling never stops. Our guns pound away night and day. It is impossible to sleep for more than five minutes at a time. I fear it may drive me mad. I am almost driven to use strong language, but I would never do so to you.

Do not fear for me, Helen. I am just tired, and you know that makes me bad-tempered.

All will be well. We will win. We must.

If only I could see the sun again. If only I could sleep.

My love to you and Steven.

Richard.

23rd July, 1917

. . .

DIARY OF LIEUTENANT RICHARD STARK, 23 JULY, 1917

Bird came up behind me when I was writing my letter to Helen. He moved silently, even in the liquid mud that covers the bottom of the trench. I didn't hear him until he spoke.

"They'll break?" he said. "Is that what Haig told you?"

"Yes. How dare you read my letter?" I glowered at him through the rapidly falling dark.

"That's what Haig told us on the Somme. Ready to break, he said. Just one push." He shook his head. Then he turned, and without asking permission, climbed out of the trench and disappeared towards no-man's land.

DIARY OF LIEUTENANT RICHARD STARK, 25 JULY, 1917

I think I have lost Helen's rose. When I opened the diary, it was not there. It must have fallen into that horrible, liquid mud and sunk. I might have shed some tears for it. I could not tell. The raindrops draw permanent tears on my cheeks.

Bird came sliding into the trench near dawn, as he always does. I rose as he did, but he ignored me and strode straight towards the other men.

"You two," he gestured. "Come with me. We're going back out."

"What's up?" one of the men asked.

"Jerry's abandoned his front line," Bird said. "We're going to find out where he's dropped back to." He shook his head. "I don't like it. It'll give him too much clear ground to hammer us."

The men grabbed their rifles and followed Bird out. None of them glanced at me. I might not even have existed.

I do not know the names of my men. I don't know how that happened.

Perhaps I should send a message to Command about Jerry leaving his trenches. But my men should not be out there. They have no authorisation.

I don't know what to do. I don't know what to do.

I will go back to my dugout. Maybe I will sleep.

DIARY OF LIEUTENANT RICHARD STARK, 26 JULY, 1917

Bird. His name is a curse that hammers through my head with every hammer blow of those damned shells. If it wasn't for him, my men would obey me. I should go up to him, put my pistol to his head, and blow out his stupid brains.

God, give me sleep. Please.

There was a dogfight over Jerry's lines today. I pulled out my map and stared at it, trying to work out where they were fighting. The marks on the map made no sense to me. I couldn't even tell where we are. The dogfight went on most of the day. I think we won. It hasn't made any difference to the bombardment.

We began to drop gas on Jerry yesterday. I peered through the periscope and watched the gas settle over the broken woods and Jerry's trenches. All along his line, I heard spoons clattering against plates and empty shell cases.

Bird and his men – my men! – were out all day. God

forgive me, but I found myself praying that the gas or a shell had found them.

When they returned, Bird seemed different, troubled, quiet. Perhaps the bombardment is getting to him, too. He did not speak to me. Instead, I saw him whispering to my men. They are planning something. Bird will not meet my eyes. He looks away when I look at him. Has he seen something in my eyes? Maybe madness dances there.

I will not turn my back on these men.

Bird left just before dawn, taking two different men with him. They have not yet returned.

DIARY OF LIEUTENANT RICHARD STARK, 28 JULY, 1917

A shell burst in our trench today. I was in my dugout, so I didn't see it, but I felt the concussion through the earth. When I got to the trench, a crater had been ripped through earth walls. Three of my men were dead. I did not know their names.

Each day, before light, Bird takes different men from my platoon, and they slip out of the trench. They do not return until after nightfall. I sit here in the never-ending rain, under ever-grey skies, listening to the nerve-fraying thump of shells, and wait for the men to return. I have tried to question them, but they do not answer me. I held my pistol to one man's face. He just turned away. I could have pulled the trigger. I almost did. My fingers shake all the time.

Yesterday, two of the men did not return.

Where do they go?

My Dear Helen,

All is well. Do not fear for me. You are too prone to worrying.

I know the sun must be up there, behind those clouds. It must.

I think my feet are rotting in this damp.

God help me, but these damned shells are driving me insane. Thump. Thump. Thump. It never stops. I want to scream. I cannot take another fucking, God-damned minute of it.

I have received word to prepare my men. My men. God, I want to cry.

The push cannot come too soon. Even Jerry's bullets would be better than this.

You know I love you. All will be well. I am sure. You must believe me. I am not without hope.

Give my love to our son. I find I have forgotten his name for now, but it will come to me soon. I am just tired.

Richard.

29th July, 1917

Diary of Lieutenant Richard Stark, 31 July, 1917

It is night. Maybe 1 a.m. In any case, it is past midnight. I am out here, far from the safety of the trench. We are huddled in a shell hole, in the midst of the tangle of smashed trees that is Glencourse Wood. It is cold. The rain falls.

I had fallen asleep. I know I must have, despite the pounding of shells, because I was suddenly awake. I was sitting at the table in my dugout. I had fallen asleep over the map of our section of the front, trying to make some sense of the blurring lines and symbols. I could not have been asleep long, because it was not yet dawn.

Silence woke me. Not silence of the guns – they never end – but the smaller silence of absent voices. I have grown used to the men's voices in the night. Not now.

I jumped from my seat, grabbed my gas mask, shoved this diary into the pocket of my coat, pulled my pistol, and headed out into the trench.

My men were there, lined up at the front of the trench, and one-by-one, they were going quietly over the top in the dark and drenching rain.

"Stop!" I shouted, pointing my pistol. The men froze. That may have been the first of my commands that my men have obeyed, and the last.

"Where are you going?" I demanded.

The men exchanged glances.

Bird's head appeared over the lip of the trench. "What, do you think we're deserting, Lieutenant?"

"Well," I said, awkwardly.

Bird's voice was wet with sarcasm. "If we was deserting, don't you think we might be heading in the other direction?"

With an effort, I reasserted myself. "Where the Hell do you go every night? Are you traitors? Are you telling the Hun our plans?"

Bird considered for a moment. Then he said, "If you want

to see, you'd best follow. We ain't hanging about, though. If you don't keep up, we'll leave you."

With that, he disappeared. The men resumed their climb out of the trench. My pistol felt like a toy in my hand. After a second, I holstered it and followed my men over the top, into the night.

I cannot adequately describe that journey. No man's land was a hell. Rain poured down. Mud sucked at our boots. The shell holes had overlapped to form black lakes.

Within minutes, I no longer knew where I was nor where we were heading.

Up ahead, a heavy machine gun stuttered. I threw myself to the ground. Bullets smacked the mud.

"They ain't seen us," Bird's whispered voice came back.

We crawled forward. My hand pressed on a face jutting from the mud. I turned away and forced myself not to vomit.

A shell ruptured the earth nearby. Mud hammered over me. I bit my tongue to stop myself screaming. I rubbed the mud from my face.

When I could see again, I realised my men were no longer in sight. Panic took me. "Wait," I whispered. "Wait."

No one answered.

I was alone in no man's land. All around, shells thumped and shook the ground.

I stumbled to my feet and ran. The machine gun stuttered again to my left. I turned towards the sound.

A shell hole opened in front of me. I tumbled, fell, hit black water. I struggled. The mud below sucked at me and pulled me down. Water soaked through to my waist. This time I did scream.

A hand grabbed my hair and tugged my head back.

Bird's face glowered down at me from the edge of the shell hole, not two feet away. "Shut up that noise, or I'll put a bullet through your head myself."

Golden specks seemed to swim in his black eyes.

With a gulp, I clamped my mouth shut. Still, I felt myself sinking.

"Good enough," he said. He pulled me agonisingly by my hair from the mire.

The men were waiting not a dozen yards away, pressed flat in the mud and ragged weeds. Without a word, Bird led them into the rain and dark, and I followed.

The ground sloped up. We crawled over an abandoned German trench. *Two hundred yards,* I thought. That was all we had come. Two hundred yards.

Beyond the trench, the wasteland continued. Cold rain and mud soaked through my clothes.

At some point, we crossed a road. It was cracked and cratered. In the darkness, a German soldier rose in front of us. Bird's bayonet slid in and up, and the man slumped without a sound.

We reached a broken mass of trees. Wire had been strung like a chaotic spider's web through the stripped trunks and scattered branches. Bird led us up, without pause, through this mess.

A shell sent splinters spinning through the air. Several

embedded themselves in my cheek. I slipped and fell onto jagged wood. I dragged myself up, sobbing silently.

"God, let us turn back," I muttered beneath my breath. "Please."

There was a man hanging on the wire, scarecrow-loose and sagging. I recognised his face as we passed. He'd been one of my men.

"Jape's been on the wire for two days," the man in front of me whispered. "Still smiling, though."

We left the body behind. All around us, the bombardment continued. Flashes lit up the blackness, blinding us. The earth shook. Shrapnel tore through the darkness. Rain fell.

Cylinders thudded into the woods.

"Gas," Bird called, and moments later I heard the hiss. I fumbled my mask on, just before the grey cloud rolled over us.

We crawled through the shattered woods and wire and gas. Shells fell. Machine guns chattered. One of my men reared up before me, fell. I crawled over him, feeling his warm blood on my hands.

"I don't know your name," I whispered to him. "I don't know it."

He didn't answer.

I could no longer think. I just followed.

In time, the gas cleared, and we pulled off our masks.

Helen, how did I get into this?

I heard words spoken ahead. Then Bird and the other

men dropped down from sight into a deep shell hole hidden by broken trees. I followed.

There were other men there. I recognised their uniforms. Germans. I whipped out my pistol.

"I knew it," I shouted. "You're traitors. All of you are damned traitors." My finger tightened on the trigger.

Bird moved faster than I could follow. His right fist buried itself in my stomach as his left hand knocked my pistol from my hand. I staggered and doubled over, gasping for breath.

"You don't understand," Bird whispered. "You don't understand anything at all. This ain't about sides no more. It ain't about killing. It's more important."

"What?" I choked out.

"It's nearly dawn," he said. "You'll see."

I waited, never taking my eyes from these men. How long, I wondered, had this been going on? How long had my men been meeting the Hun in this wilderness between our lines? There was a cancer, I had been right. But the cancer was more than indiscipline. It was treason. But treason to what purpose?

Light grew in the rain-washed sky. Thick clouds hung heavy and dark and low. I shivered in the pre-dawn chill, in my sodden clothes.

"It's almost time," someone muttered, and as he spoke, the sun rose behind the clouds.

A single ray of sunlight cut through clouds and rain like a sword. I followed its path with my eyes.

The sunlight stabbed down straight to a spot on the edge of the shell hole. In that spot, a single rose bloomed.

A sigh passed around the men in the hole.

"See," Bird whispered.

"This is what you go to see?" I asked. "Sunshine falling on a rose?"

I wanted to cry. I had forgotten what sunshine looked like, in the dark and rain.

"No," Bird said. "The sunshine ain't falling on the rose. Look closer."

I scrambled over and peered close. It took a moment for my perception to shift, but when it did, I could do no more than blink.

Bird was right. The sunshine did not fall on the rose. The sunshine came from the rose, instead, and pierced the clouds, shining up to the sun.

"It feeds the sun," Bird said, close over my shoulder. "If the rose should be destroyed, the sun will never shine on Ypres fields again. We don't come to see the rose. We come to defend it. Soon the push will come." His lips brushed my ear. "The rose will not fall."

I sat there with my men and their German counterparts, and watched the rose as the day crept on, the heavy rain fell, and the sunlight from the rose crept up, across the sky, and down towards the horizon.

The sun has set. Night draws on. We wait.

The bombardment has increased tenfold. The shells are a constant rumble. In the darkness, blinding flashes of star shells sear away the black. My fingers are cold. The pages of this diary are damp. My pistol lies close by my hand.

With dawn, the rose sends its single beam of sunlight through the massed clouds and pouring rain.

The bone-shaking rumble of shells draws closer.

"Here it comes," Bird shouts. "Heads down."

DIARY OF LIEUTENANT RICHARD STARK, 1 AUGUST, 1917

I had thought crossing no man's land was bad. I had thought my days in the trenches were bad. I was wrong.

At walking pace, the bombardment crept up the slope towards us. Above and around us, in the tangle of Glencourse Wood, German emplacements opened up. The German heavy guns sheltering behind the Gheluvelt plateau sent their own barrage in response.

A thermite shell burst in the woods to my left. Heat rolled over the shell hole, turning rain to steam. Someone screamed and lurched across the hole.

The bombardment reached us. Concussions shook the ground. Mud, splintered wood, shrapnel, and fire filled the air. The earth bucked beneath me like a kick. Shockwaves battered the breath from my lungs. My eyes streamed stinging tears.

I think I must have been screaming, but I couldn't be sure; the noise had deafened me. I could still feel the monstrous sound pounding through my body.

A star shell burst above, turning the thick dawn white.

My muscles and bones had turned to liquid. I lay, face pressed into the mud, hands over my head, in the bottom of the deep hole. Earth and fragmented metal pattered onto my back.

Someone booted me in the side. I pulled my face up. My vision was seared from the star shell. I could still feel the shells thumping. I blinked to focus. Bird was bending over me. "Get up," he mouthed. "Get up."

Men were rising in the shell hole, checking their guns. I scrambled up. Sunlight was still streaming from the rose. I gulped back a sob. Three men were not moving. A shard of shrapnel jutted from the bloody back of one man's skull.

"Take positions," Bird shouted, although I only saw his lips move. "They're coming."

He turned and clumped back down the hole. He grabbed me by the collar and pulled my face near. "Shoot anyone who comes near. Anyone. Understand?"

I nodded, and Bird shoved me towards the edge. I scrabbled up, not looking at the bodies.

The shells were still falling. I could see gouts of earth erupting not a hundred yards away. New holes had been gouged in the woods all about.

There was no movement. I narrowed my eyes. The infantry should have followed the progressing bombardment, sheltered by its deadly screen. Yet they were nowhere to be seen.

One by one, the German machine guns began again. My pistol was cold and heavy in my hand.

Men streamed from the forward dugouts, ant-small in the distance. The guns found them and took them. Bodies jerked and danced and were flung aside. More came. Earth sprayed. Shells shook and smashed the ground.

A squad emerged from the edge of Sanctuary Wood. Bullets cut through them.

More men came, pouring from the dugouts. For every three who came, two fell before they had covered a hundred yards. Others threw themselves flat and wormed forward through the mud and rain and falling metal.

A dozen men, led by a captain brandishing a pistol, rushed a German emplacement. Only the captain reached it. I saw him leap into the emplacement, his pistol firing. Moments later, the machine gun fell silent. *That should have been me,* I thought. *I should have led my men like that.* The captain did not emerge.

Slowly, the advance crept forward. Men slipped into water-filled holes and were gone from sight. Bullets violated flesh and smashed bone. Shells ripped bodies to rags. With every step, a hundred lives were lost, like bright night stars engulfed by a cloud.

Still the advance came on, in rushes and starts. I wept tears of loss, and blinding hate for Gough and Haig and all the fools who sent men into this scythe.

Figures came up through the woods. I saw bullets smack home, men thrown onto wire. Rain lashed my face. Dark clouds hung low.

"Not this way," I whispered. "Don't come this way."

Around me, men raised their guns. I steadied my trembling hands.

Hell broke around us. A shell erupted to the side, tossing

men like paper. British soldiers rushed towards us. I fired, and others fired with me. Men fell.

The return fire came. The man next to me jerked and rolled away. I ignored him, kept firing.

Wave after wave came. I could not think, could not pause. When men drew near, I shot them, coldly, mercilessly.

I think I put a bullet through Captain Dawson. He was running at the head of his company. He turned towards our hole, and I fired. He went down.

For uncounted hours, we fought, hours that became days that became centuries that became aeons. *The rose*, I thought, as my dead fingers pushed more bullets into my pistol. *The rose must not fall.*

A splinter of shrapnel cut through my left arm. Blood flowed with the rain over my face from a wound I hadn't felt.

A Tommy hurled himself towards our hole. He had lost his rifle. His face was blank with terror. I shot him through the throat.

A German machine gun found our hole. The bullets tore through my companions and smacked the mud around me, before a brave squad of Tommies rushed it and silenced it.

At some point, Jerry counter-attacked, and we reversed our positions and killed the Hun.

A shattering barrage of shells crashed around us. The concussions tossed me like a rag in a stormy sea. Something smacked me on the back of my head, and I lost sight.

When consciousness returned, the firing had stopped. I could no longer feel the rumble and chatter in my bones, nor the heat on my skin. I arose, shaking. Smoke drifted across the shell hole and the mud and the broken stumps of trees.

Over. It was over.

I turned. Bird was behind me. He lay, curled, in the mud on the side of the shell hole. Shrapnel studded his back and legs. His thick blood had mixed with the black mud. I stepped towards him.

He moved, rolling over onto his pierced back. His eyes were golden. They blinked once, then became glass. He did not move again.

Where he had been curled, a single beam of sunlight cut up through the rain and clouds from the rose.

The rose had survived. The sun would shine again.

I picked up Bird's rifle, checked and loaded it, and sat beside his body, waiting, waiting.

The push may come again.

I will not let the rose fall.

DRAGONFLY SUMMER

ABOUT THE STORY

Back in ... 2007, I think, I went to the wedding of one of my best friends from university. We hadn't seen each other for a long time, but at university we had shared houses for several years. In fact, I hadn't seen any of my university friends for over a decade. Things happen, we go in different directions, to different parts of the country and different countries, and time passes.

But this wedding was a chance to catch up, and it was ... weird. People were both different and the same, and it left me feeling a little melancholy and nostalgic for those final summer days of university. In some ways, the predominant feeling was sadness, not for days gone but for paths not taken and dreams set aside or replaced.

Dragonfly Summer *was my attempt to put that into words. I should emphasise, of course, that none of the people in the story are based on anyone I knew, nor are any of the specific events. I think we all parted on good terms, unlike the people in this story...*

DRAGONFLY SUMMER

HOWIE TRACKS ME DOWN OVER THE INTERNET.

Man, I hadn't even thought about the guy in maybe fifteen years. I guess I wanted to forget him. Last time I saw him he was standing over me, fists clenched, face twisted in fury. He knocked me flying, even though he was scarcely half my size. Can't say I blame him.

When his email turns up in my inbox, I almost spam it, but then my mind holds up one of those little red flags, and I pause, cursor hovering over *Spam*.

Howard Hawkins. Double-H.

Fuck.

~

I PULL MY CAR INTO THE CAR PARK IN THE MIDDLE OF THE afternoon. It's a Saturday, a couple of weeks later. There's only one other car there, a battered blue Volvo with its back bumper hanging half off. There's no one in it, but it isn't a Howie car. Howie would have something low and black and fast. Maybe it would be dented and a little old, but it would be hot. Nothing about this car says Howie. So I sit there, staring out over the estuary to the wading birds on the silver-streaked mud, enjoying the peace, waiting.

When I forgot Howie, I forgot this place too. I reckon if I just drove past, I wouldn't recognise it.

They've paved the lane, flattening out the narrow, potholed track and replacing it with sleek asphalt. They've put in this whole damned car park, complete with information board and little padlocked iron donation box. Progress. It makes the whole place feel tired rather than fresh. Or perhaps that's just me. I'm not nineteen anymore, and everything seems old.

I'd brought a map, but in the end, despite it being twenty years since I was here, I hadn't needed it. Yeah, I'd forgotten it, but Howie's email had brought it surging back like a tidal bore.

I put the steering wheel lock on – you can't be too careful, even out here – then lever myself out the driver's seat. We aren't due to meet for almost half an hour. Might as well take a look around. See the old sights.

School books sprawl over the back seat of the Volvo. Dozens of them. Definitely not Howie. Howie would be – what? My brain suddenly can't come up with what Howie might do for a job. The whole idea of Howie working nine-to-five just doesn't fit in the space in my head that Howie occupies.

The pub's still there, but it isn't The Saracen's Head anymore. It's something called a Hungry Horse, whatever the fuck that is, complete with a new glass-walled extension containing colourful plastic structures and screaming kids. The peeling paint, cracked brickwork, and smoke-stained windows have been facelifted away. I walk past it, onto the towpath between the canal and the estuary.

Half a mile seems longer than it used to. I've been meaning to get down the gym more often, but this last year, things have been too busy, and anyway, there always seems to be something else to do. At my age, everyone gets a few extra pounds, don't they? A couple of beers at lunchtime and a couple after work every day. They soon add up, even if you don't eat that much. But what can you do? It goes with the job, just like the fags. My fingers are itching for one again. I pull the box (crushed) out of my back pocket and work one free. I let the wreath of stained smoke slip into the warm air.

At first I think I've remembered it wrong. Around the bend, past the first of the concrete boats dragged up onto the bank to act as makeshift breakwaters. I was sure I would find the windmill there. Isn't that what we've come to see, after all? The scene of most of our triumphs and a fair few of our disasters? That damned windmill.

But it's not there. There's just a strip of grass, stretching to the bushes and heaped wild roses on the edge of the mud beach. And standing there, a small, middle-aged woman.

Her black hair is cut short and peppered with grey. She

wears a thin, too-old jacket. Smoke rises like an emaciated, pale finger from her cigarette. Some people smoke with style and some smoke comfortably. I'm one of the latter. This woman is the former, in spades. I take a step forward.

"Sophie?"

She glances back. Her face is narrower than I remember, like it's been drawn back by a pinching hand, and slightly yellower.

"Howie contacted you too?" I ask, then realise it's a stupid question. Of course he has.

"All of us," she said.

"Fuck."

"It's gone," she says.

I step up beside her.

"Look," she says, pointing with her chin at the grass. "You can't even see where it used to be."

She's right. The grass is unmarked. I feel a hollow bubble press against the inside of my ribs then burst. The vacuum it leaves is shockingly painful. I force myself to ignore it.

"Twenty years," I say. "Things change."

She shakes her head.

Even back then, the windmill was old. Its sails were rotting ribs, stripped of the canvas that once drove them. In the wind, it sometimes creaked like an old man. There were cracks in the walls, and the dust and bird shit were thick on the wooden floors. But it still looked like it would last forever. Everything looks like that when you're just a kid.

"Do you remember?" Sophie says. "Up there on the top floor, in the old straw? We fucked like rabbits."

"Sophie!" I'm obscurely shocked that this forty-year-old woman would say fuck. Back then, she wouldn't have dreamed of it. Back then, I probably said it every other word, and she was the one constantly shocked.

"It's true," she says. "I'd only slept with a couple of other guys before you, but you didn't let that slow you down. You fucked my brains out anyway."

"You told me I was your first," I say. Shit. Now I sound like an offended teenager.

She shrugs again. "It's a good line. Doesn't really work after you pass thirty, though."

I look around, desperately looking for something more normal to say. Seeing that cynicism in Sophie is like looking into an all-too-clear mirror and not liking what you see.

"So," I say. "Got any kids?"

"I've got thirty different kids every hour, six hours a day," she says. "You want me to take some of them home?"

Something clicks in my mind. The Volvo. "You're a teacher?"

"Yeah. Gold star."

"How about husband? Boyfriend?"

"Men are bastards."

"Right."

She blows out a cloud of smoke, then drops her cigarette and grinds it out under her heel. "Fancy a drink?"

"For old time's sake?" I say, not able to stop the grin spreading on my face.

"No. It's just a drink."

I glance at my watch. "What about meeting Howard?"

315

"Fuck Howard," she says.

~

I'M HALFWAY DOWN MY SECOND PINT OF GUINNESS WHEN
Howie finally finds us. I don't know what I'm expecting, but
it's not this. Balding, frown lines, small, university-lecturer
glasses. This isn't die-young Howie. This isn't the wild kid
who almost got me killed half-a-dozen times. I just stare at
him, unable to say anything.

Howie doesn't have the same problem. "Where were you?
I said the car park."

"Hi, Howie," I say. "Good to see you too."

Trailing in behind Howie, a slight look of distaste
squeezing her mouth, comes Trish. Of all of us, she is the
only one who seems not to have changed. Yeah, I can tell
she's nearly forty, but she hasn't *changed*, not past a few wrinkles at her eyes and skin that looks tired.

The wildness in Howie's eyes subsides slightly.

"What? Yeah. Hi." He shakes his head.

I squint at Howie and Trish standing there above our
table, then I let out an incredulous laugh. "You married her,
didn't you? Even after she and I–"

"Why don't you shut the fuck up?" Sophie drawls.

Probably just in time too. Howie had a mean punch back
then, and he looks like he's about ready to swing at me again.

I drain the end of my Guinness, feeling the black liquid
slide thickly down.

"I'm going to get a drink," Howie mutters.

"Mine's a whiskey," I say. "Double."

That's what we always had here, back when.

"Don't you think you've had enough?" Trish says, eyeing the glasses in front of me.

I snort. "I've hardly started." God knows, it was a bad idea agreeing to meet. But I was curious. I relax back in my chair and let my eyelids droop closed.

I remember lying there in the old windmill, Sophie half-draped over me, naked, while dragonflies darted through the air above us like little shards of rainbow. There were hundreds of dragonflies that summer, a whole damned Biblical plague of them. Sophie had some kind of whacked out theory about the dragonflies, didn't she? I don't remember what it was. I'm not sure I ever knew. I was more interested in Sophie's body than her ideas. That and getting Trish out of Howie's bed and into mine. I feel a grin spreading on my face.

Howie smacks my drink down in front of me.

"Something funny, Paul?"

I straighten. "Nah."

I pick up the glass. A single. Tight-fisted bastard. I toss it down while he and Trish draw up seats.

"So what's this about?" I say.

"Old times," Howie mutters.

"The windmill's gone, you know," I say.

"We know," Trish says. "We came down here a couple of weeks back."

Right before Howie contacted me.

"That's what it's about?"

Trish shakes her head.

"Then what? You're not going to pretend either of you wanted to see me again."

"I've been having dreams," Howie says, not looking up. "Bad dreams."

"So see a psychiatrist," Sophie says, lighting up another cigarette.

"Don't be a bitch, Sophie," Trish says.

This isn't working out the way it's supposed to. These people were my friends – my best friends, for those three summer months. When you meet up with old friends, it's supposed to be all hugs and laughs and reminiscences and the occasional awkward silence. Not venom that could paralyse a cobra.

"Dreams about what?" I say.

"Us. This."

I shake my head. "Howard, it was a long time ago. We've moved on. All of us." I look around at them. None of them answer.

Haven't we? I certainly haven't been dwelling on the bust-up for twenty years. I don't even really remember it. So Howie caught me in bed with Trish twenty years ago? So, big deal. We were young.

We sit in silence for a minute or two. I turn my empty glass in my fingers, wondering if I should get another. A pleasant numbness is sinking into my legs. If I wasn't driving, I'd be at it like a shot. As it is, I've probably drunk far too much to drive on already.

A bar maid – can you still be a bar *maid* at seventy? – makes her way over and starts clearing the empties.

"You from around here?" I ask her, tired of sitting in this silence.

"All my life, love," she says. She gives me a look like she thinks I'm flirting with her. I ignore it. Satudays aren't my flirting-with-pensioners days.

"That old windmill?" I ask. "What happened to it? When did they pull it down?"

She frowns. "Windmill?"

"You know. Down the towpath. Maybe half a mile. Right on the edge of the estuary."

She shakes her head. "Not around here, love. Never was. You must be thinking about somewhere else." Now she thinks I'm drunk.

"There really was," I say, feeling my neck turning slightly red.

She gives the table a perfunctory wipe, spreading around more dirt than she wipes off. "Not here."

I watch her toddle off. "Daft old bat," I mutter. I wish I'd got that other drink.

"She's right, Paul," Trish says. "When we came down here and found it gone, we asked around. No one had ever heard of it. We even checked out the old maps and borough plans. There's never been a windmill around here."

"I fucking know there was," I say, my voice rising too high. If this is some kind of game, I'm not finding it funny.

We went to the windmill a couple of dozen times that summer, all four of us, or just me and Sophie (and me and

Trish, that one glorious time, just before the end). I can almost smell the dust and crumbling brickwork, hear the creaking sails, see the dragonflies.

I subside. The other three are looking at me, not saying a thing.

I blow out a heavy breath, pick up my glass, realise it's empty and replace it.

"*What?*" I say.

"WHAT EXACTLY *DO* YOU REMEMBER ABOUT THAT SUMMER?" Trish asks me.

I feel that stupid, drunk, juvenile grin start on my face again, and I force it away. That isn't what she's asking about. Which is more the pity, because she still looks pretty hot, even after all these years.

After another drink, we left the pub and now we're walking along the tow path towards the windmill. It feels like old times. Except that now there is no windmill, and there never has been. So where the Hell does that leave those old times?

What do I remember? I remember Howie running along the edge of the beach, long hair and leather jacket flapping wildly in the wind. Sophie in one of her skimpy little outfits, legs drawn up, showing pretty much everything. Trish standing watching the rest of us, all class and style and care-fully-designed distance, a sardonic grin never far from her perfect lips. Piles of empty beer cans. Laughter. Smoke rising from our fire against the purple evening sky.

"The windmill," I say. "I remember every last inch of it. Every crack and corner. I remember the way the sails creaked and groaned. I remember which of the steps up to the top storey were rotten. I remember the old millstone with that split across one side. I remember that damned grinding pattern cut into it." The others are nodding, and I can tell they're seeing it too. "I remember those half-rotten sacks in one corner, and the almost-gone paint, and the view out over the estuary from the top." I look at the rest of them. "So does someone want to tell me how the Hell it was never there?"

"Anything else?" Howie says.

"Yeah," I say. "The dragonflies. I always thought they'd be brittle if I touched them. They looked brittle. They looked like flakes of glass. But one landed on me once and it felt soft." I shake my head. "I never figured out where so many of them could have come from."

"The estuary," Sophie say. "They came up with the tide."

She's staring ahead, not really looking at anything.

"That doesn't make any sense," I say.

She shrugs, blows out smoke.

We were all at the end of our second year at university that summer. I was taking physics – something I've managed to avoid since, thank God – and I should have been revising, but summer had arrived gloriously early, so I was lying out by the lake sunbathing instead. I'd met Howie a couple of times before at Rock Soc events, so when he came wandering out with two gorgeous girls, I didn't hesitate to go over and say hi.

"We should go somewhere," Trish said, that life-kissed afternoon.

"Where?" I said.

"Anywhere."

So we did, and that was how we found the windmill. That same night, Sophie took me to bed, and the next three months were the best of my life, and then it ended as suddenly as a thunderclap.

"Tell me about the dreams," I say.

Howie hunches his shoulders uncomfortably. The air is descending into evening chill. We've tried to build a fire – old times, old times. It hasn't really worked, and there's no windmill to retreat into. But the sky is that familiar purple, and no one has suggested leaving.

"Go on, sweetheart," Trish says, surprisingly gently. "It's why we're here."

Howie nods, but he doesn't look at me or Sophie. Maybe we aren't exactly what he was expecting either.

"We're here," Howie says. "Not now, but back then. Right near the beginning when we'd only just all got together." He glances at me, then away. "Back when we were two couples, you know? We're sitting on the beach in the late sunlight. There's beers and a bottle of cheap wine. We're talking about something. I don't know what. Something. And behind us I can feel the windmill, looming over us like some black storm."

He stops, and sits in silence.

"That's it?" I say.

He shrugs. "Yeah."

"Fuck it, Howie. You dragged us out here for that?"

He shrugs again.

"Jeez."

Howie drops his head, and in that motion, I recognise the old Howie for the first time today, recognise him as clearly as if it was yesterday.

And I know he's lying.

"How long have you been having these dreams?" I ask.

"Years," he says. "On and off. Sometimes more often, sometimes less."

"And now?"

"More. Much more."

He removes his little glasses and squeezes his knuckles into his eyes.

"I'm not sleeping much. Not well." He lifts his head again. "Am I the only one? Doesn't anyone else dream about ... about all that?"

The silence is broken only by the cry of a bird swooping low over the estuary, its silhouette sharp against the silver mud, and the dispirited crackle of our failing fire. Then Sophie flicks away the glowing butt of her cigarette, pulls another from its packet, and lights it with a match. She breaths in deeply.

"I do," she says.

I blink at her.

"You?"

"Yeah. Why not?" Smoke drifts from her nostrils, up past her eyes. "It's like Howie said. We're on the beach, just about where we're sitting now, and I can feel the windmill behind us. So I get up and walk towards it. The last of the evening light is catching on the top sails. I walk up to the windmill, and it seems to be leaning over me, as though it's a giant face peering down at me. I reach the steps and start up them, and just as I get to the door, I find myself wondering: Where have all the dragonflies gone? And then I wake."

She's telling more than Howie, but I can't shake the feeling that Sophie isn't letting on completely either.

The rest of them look at me.

I shake my head. "Not me. No dreams here."

"Trish?" Sophie said.

"No. Sorry."

"Why the Hell is it just us?" Howie demands.

A look flashes between him and Sophie, and my eyes narrow. What did that mean?

No one says anything. The last flame flickering in our fire dies, leaving a weak collection of dulling embers.

"We should go," Trish says.

"Where?" I say.

"Back to the pub. It's late."

We kick dirt over the almost-dead fire and pick up our beer cans.

Behind me, I think I hear a tired creak, like the sails of the windmill, but when I turn, there's nothing.

~

HOWIE HAS BOOKED US ALL ROOMS IN A BED AND BREAKFAST not more than a mile away. Hasn't bothered to ask, of course, just assumed. But, folks, I'm so hammered by then, I couldn't have got my keys in the ignition let alone driven. We have dinner in the pub – fake Thai food, all chillies and not much else in the way of flavours, washed down with more beer than was strictly necessary – then Howie drives us to the B&B. Trish and Howie head off to their room as soon as we got in, leaving me and Sophie alone in the corridor.

"You're a teacher now, right?" I say, even though she told me so earlier. I'm slurring my words and noticing it.

"Yeah."

I pause. "I work in finance." *In finance*. That's not a job. It's a fucking abstract. The phrase has never sounded so empty to me.

Sophie agrees. "Fuck, Paul," she says. "You used to have dreams."

That hurts. If you've never had someone take a look at your life and then kick it away like a kid with a sandcastle then you don't know how much.

"Thanks," I say.

She fumbles in her shoulder bag for another cigarette.

"You smoke too much," I say.

"Fuck off," she mumbles around the cigarette.

The corridor is dim, the wallpaper is seventies-patterned and textured, worn thin by a thousand brushing shoulders. The wall is hung with the kind of prints of horses you only see in cheap little guesthouses like this one. The whole thing depresses me.

I indicate the door to my room with a nod of my head.

"Do you want to…?"

"Fuck, no."

She must see the spasm of pain on my face, because she lays a hand briefly on my arm.

"I've learnt one thing in these twenty years," she says. "You can't go back. Ever. There are gates you walk through, and they close behind you. You can't storm them, you can't break through. You just have to keep going forward, wherever it leads you."

Then she unlocks her room and leaves me standing in the corridor. The last of us. Again.

My room has a view out over the estuary. When I can't sleep, I stand there and watch the dark river slip by beneath the bright moonlight.

You can never go back.

I never wanted to. Until now, and all the doors are shut behind me.

The river slips by. It never turns back. Until the tide rolls in.

THE BEGINNING AND THE END. ONE AT THE START OF THAT summer, the other at its finish. The days could have been swapped around with little change. Bright blue skies. A furnace of a sun. The canal choked with reeds and rushes. Birdsong in the trees and bushes. Sophie slipping her hand into mine.

No. That last bit only happened on the first day we were all together, not the last. That was a difference.

She slipped her hand into mine, and I was so startled I almost stumbled. Startled and heart-stoppingly delighted. Dragonflies hovered in and out of the rushes and reeds in the canal and over the towpath. I gave Sophie an astonished look. She winked at me and kick-started my heart again. I remember I found walking difficult that afternoon.

Howie looped his arm over Trish's shoulders (that didn't happen on the last day either – all those signs of the coming storm, and not one of us stupid kids realised).

We were all laughing at some crap joke when we came around the corner and saw the windmill for the first time, bulking incongruously from an expanse of grass between the canal and the estuary.

I had a good time at University. Okay, the lectures were mind-numbing, and the labs seemed to stretch on forever. But that was only the days – the mornings, mostly – and the rest of the time was mine. There were some bad moments, too, of course – some storming hangovers; being dumped at a party with half my friends watching – but it was a good time on balance.

On that first day with Sophie, Trish, and Howie, it

seemed to take a step up. The sun seemed brighter, the colours more vivid, the sounds sharper and clearer. As though we'd opened a door in the clouded glass that had always separated us from the truth of the world.

Later, on that last day, when it all turned to ash, it was as though we stepped back out that door and shut it behind us.

I think Sophie must have seen the windmill first, because I heard her shout, "It's perfect," and then we all saw it, looming above us.

Pulling me along by the hand, Sophie raced towards it. Moments later, I heard Trish and Howie come chasing after. We all clattered up the steps, burst into the windmill, and stopped. The space was still, eerie. Light filtered in strands through cracks in the brickwork and between shutters. The windmill seemed to hold the ghost of an indrawn breath. A word struck me at that moment: potential. Not potential as in the mundane sense of this-could-be-renovated-into-some-yuppie-apartment-full-of-chrome-and-spotlights potential, but potential as in the physics I was half-heartedly studying. This place seemed to exist at a higher state of energy. An electrical potential difference drives a current around a circuit. This place seemed poised to drive ... something through us. Enliven and quicken us. Power us.

"Yow!" Howie screamed, and a faint echo bounced back.

We laughed, and tumbled together into the potential.

I SLEEP EVENTUALLY. MOST NIGHTS I DON'T SLEEP WELL, AND tonight is no exception. I don't dream about the windmill, even though I'm half expecting to. Instead, I dream of the slow river flowing on through the estuary to the sea. It's not a restful dream, and sometime in the night I awake to find tears streaming down my cheeks. I'm sobbing.

I left my soul in 1987. I left my heart and my love and my dreams, and I want them back. I want them back.

My tears taste of salt and whiskey.

NORMALLY, I SLEEP BADLY – HANGOVER SLEEP – BUT I'M HARD to wake in the morning. I have two alarms, one by my bed and the other across the room, staggered by a couple of minutes. Most days it's enough. When it's not, I skip breakfast. This morning, it's different. I'm awake and up by six, pacing my bedroom. It's cramped and claustrophobic, even when I throw the window open and let the cold dawn air in, but breakfast isn't until seven, and there's nowhere else to go. I wonder what I'm doing here. These people aren't the people I knew when I was at University, and remembering what they were – what I was – leaves me empty. There was potential, then, and now it's gone. The people we were are gone. Sophie was right. You can't walk back through those gates.

Suddenly it's too much. I don't want to see Howie or Trish or Sophie anymore. I don't want to stare back at the past and see a future that should have been but never was. I thump out of the room, downstairs, and out the front door. My car is still parked where I left it the day before, but that's only a mile or so away. I start to walk. I'm light-headed from lack of breakfast and dehydrated from drinking too much.

I intend to get straight into the car and head off, never look back, never see any of them again. I even slide myself in behind the steering wheel and fumble the key into the ignition. But then I sit there, staring out at the morning-painted river and silvery mud banks. We came here once in the early morning, Sophie and me. We snuck out of dorms while it was still dark, and Sophie drove. We bumped the car over the potholes then pulled it off the track, against the brambles. In the dawn, the windmill was a silhouette against a pastel-blue sky. We hung around, smoked a bit, then tumbled, naked and chilly, under the old sacking. The dragonflies were already there.

Trish and Howie turned up before we were dressed. Howie looked away while we crawled out, laughing, and pulled out clothes on, but Trish kept looking, watching me get dressed, with that sardonic curl to her lip. That was the first time I reckoned I might have a real chance with her. I don't think Sophie noticed.

I decide to take one last look all on my own, before I leave all this behind forever. Maybe I'm hoping the windmill will be there.

It isn't. There's no sign it ever was. The grass is unmarked. There are no dragonflies.

I walk out to the edge of the mud banks and wait. I'm not sure what for.

"You're a bastard."

The sudden voice makes me turn. Howie is standing there behind me, his thin shoulders pulled up tight.

"Yeah," I say.

"It was your fault it went wrong," he says. "You and your fucking dick. So why the fuck aren't you the one haunted by it?"

I shrug. "Guess it never bothered me. Anyway," I glance at him, "she was a beast in bed. Why–"

I don't get time to finish. Howie might be scrawny, but he's still got that punch. He lashes out and catches me square on the jaw. I fall to the ground.

"She was my first girlfriend," he shouts. "My only girlfriend. I loved her."

My jaw hurts, and I'm lying in the mud.

"You've still got her," I say.

He kicks me, hard, flipping me over.

"It's not the same. It's never been the same."

He kicks me again. I feel something crack.

"I'm sorry," I say. I don't know where it comes from.

He pauses, foot drawn back, staring down incredulously at me.

"I'm sorry," I repeat, and I mean it. I'm sorry for all of it.

Howie drops down beside me, sitting cross-legged in the wet mud, not seeming to notice it.

"I'm not going home with her," he says, quietly.

I force myself up onto an elbow. My rib grates agonisingly.

"Shit, man," I say. "I'm sorry."

THAT FIRST DAY, WE DROVE OUT HERE FAST IN HOWIE'S battered old car. Howie had a new Whitesnake album. He played it over and over in the cassette deck and drove way too fast. He already knew all the words, and he belted them out, even though he couldn't sing a note. I was breathless with laughter.

The last day that we all came up together (just a few days before the very last time any of us were here), we drove in silence. It wasn't our worst day, but it was close. In truth it had been coming for a week. Trish and Howie were hardly talking. I was getting bored with Sophie. We drank a few cans, but no one said much, and we left before it was fully dark.

Two or three days later, I came out of my last exam – I'd failed it, I knew that; I'd known before I even went in – and Trish was standing there, opposite the exam hall, leaning on the wooden railing. Smoke drifted from a long cigarette. She levered herself off the railing, that sardonic, faintly-amused expression still settled on her face.

To be honest, the idea of getting Trish out of Howie's bed and into mine had palled in the last week. Maybe even then I knew it was over. Maybe that was why I walked up to her anyway and took her face in my hands. I kissed her hard, tasting the tobacco on her lips and tongue, breathing it in from her hair.

"The windmill," I said.

She writhed briefly against me, then stepped back with a laugh. "The windmill. Always the windmill."

And that's where Howie and Sophie found us, four hours later.

~

THE SOUND OF A FOOTFALL BEHIND US MAKES ME LOOK BACK. Sophie and Trish are standing there together.

"The windmill," Trish says. "Always the fucking windmill."

And there's not much more to say. There is no windmill. There never was. Call it hallucination or magic or collective delusion. It doesn't matter. We are all that there ever was. Our present defines our past as much as our past ever defines our present. If there was a windmill, once, a potential, then now there never was. It's over.

We stand together, for a while, all four of us, as though nothing has changed, looking out over the estuary. The tide has turned and is coming in. Water eddies into the channels cut in the mud. It swirls against the river flowing out. A small tidal bore, no more than a couple of inches of water, makes its way up the estuary and is gone. A single dragonfly darts by.

Slowly we trail away. First Sophie and Trish together, then Howie on his own, not looking up from the ground, his thin shoulders hunched, until I'm left standing there on my own.

It's almost a pain inside me, the regret. We could have done it. We could have done anything. But we didn't.

The air is full of dragonflies now. They've come in with the tide.

I turn and walk away, heading back towards my car.

Behind me, I hear the windmill creak. I smell the dust and old sacking and rotting wood. But I don't look around. We had our chance, and we blew it.

There's no going back.

THAT NIGHT I DREAM OF THE WINDMILL.

We're sitting on the thin strip of sand between the grass and the mud banks that lead down to the water. There's a small fire, more glowing coals than burning wood, and thin smoke rising into the still air. There are some empty cans on the ground, and an empty bottle. Howie is telling some wild, ridiculous story, and the rest of us are laughing. The air is thick and sticky, but, unusually, there are no dragonflies. The tide is on its way in, but there are no dragonflies.

I hear the creak of the windmill, and feel it lowering over us like a great, black storm. I turn, and there it is, as clear and real as it ever was. I walk towards it, climb up the steps, and then I wonder, Where are all the dragonflies?

I pull open the door.

My feet crunch on something. It sounds like very thin glass. I look down. The floor is covered in dead dragonflies. Under my shoes, they are brittle.

I press on. I walk around the cracked millstone to the wooden steps that lead, ladder-like, up to top level. I climb.

Up here, the dragonflies are thicker on the floor. They're almost ankle-deep. I kick through them, like through autumn leaves.

I see us lying there in the corner, Trish and me. Naked. Young.

"Was that all?" I want to scream. "Was that all that killed it?" A bit of stupid, physical, meaningless sex. It wasn't even that good.

I surge forward, angry, ready to pull us apart. To kick some sense into us, to tell us it wasn't worth it. To change the inevitable. But it's too late. The door is opening downstairs. Howie and Sophie are on their way up.

READ MORE!

If you enjoyed this collection, why not read some more of my work?

THE MENNIK THORN NOVELS

Mennik (Nik) Thorn is a freelance mage, happy to scrape a living breaking simple curses and hunting ghosts, and trying to keep out of the way of the city's high mages. But trouble finds Nik like flies find shit, and sometimes all that stands between his city and disaster is one second-rate mage.

Book 1: Shadow of a Dead God

Book 2: Nectar for the God

"I loved every moment of this book. In terms of sheer entertainment value, its certainly one of the best I've read this year and it's been a while since I've had such fun with a book." – Rowena Andrews, *Beneath a Thousand Skies*

"The Mennik Thorn series is the start of something great." – Novel Notions

"Fast-paced, quick-witted, deftly plotted and as well-thought-out as it is well-written. Highly recommended, and I'm already looking forward to the next one." – Juliet E. McKenna, Author of *The Tales of Einarinn*, *The Aldabreshin Compass*, and *The Green Man's Heir*.

THE CASEBOOK OF HARRIET GEORGE

Mystery, murder, and adventure on Mars...

Mars in 1815 is a world of wonders, from the hanging ballrooms of Tharsis City to the air forests of Patagonian Mars, and from the depths of the Valles Marineris to the Great Wall of Cyclopia, beyond which dinosaurs still roam.

Join Harriet George and her hapless brother-in-law, Bertrand, as they solve mysteries and try to save their family from ruin.

Volume 1: The Dinosaur Hunters.

Volume 2: A Spy in the Deep.

AUTHOR'S NOTE

PLEASE REVIEW THIS BOOK!

Reviews help authors more than you probably imagine, and for independent authors, they are everything. It would mean an awful lot to me if you could leave a brief review – a sentence or two is perfect! – on Amazon.

I love finding out what readers thought of my books – good or bad – and I make sure I read all the reviews.

KEEP IN TOUCH

Subscribe to my newsletter to get a free short story in the world of SHADOW OF A DEAD GOD and NECTAR FOR THE GOD, and to be the first to find out about future books: patricksamphire.com/newsletter/

You can find out about all my other books and stories at my website: patricksamphire.com

You can often find me on Twitter
(twitter.com/patricksamphire) as well as on my Facebook
page (facebook.com/patricksamphireauthor/).

ABOUT THE AUTHOR

Patrick Samphire started writing when he was fourteen years old and thought it would be a good way of getting out of English lessons. It didn't work, but he kept on writing anyway.

He has lived in Zambia, Guyana, Austria, and England. He has been charged at by a buffalo and, once, when he sat on a camel, he cried. He was only a kid. Don't make this weird.

Patrick has worked as a teacher, an editor and publisher of physics journals, a marketing minion, and a pen pusher (real job!). Now, when he's not writing, he designs websites and book covers. He has a PhD in theoretical physics and never uses it, so that was a good use of four years.

Patrick now lives in Wales, U.K. with his wife, the awesome writer Stephanie Burgis, their two sons, and their cat, Pebbles. Right now, in Wales, it is almost certainly raining.

He has published almost twenty short stories and novellas in magazines and anthologies, including *Realms of Fantasy*, *Interzone*, *Strange Horizons*, and *The Year's Best Fantasy*, as well as two novels for children, SECRETS OF

THE DRAGON TOMB and THE EMPEROR OF MARS. His first full-length novels for adults are the fantasy mystery stories SHADOW OF A DEAD GOD and NECTAR FOR THE GOD.

facebook.com/patricksamphireauthor
twitter.com/patricksamphire
instagram.com/patricksamphire

Lightning Source UK Ltd.
Milton Keynes UK
UKHW041816120223
416649UK00023B/745/J